DANCING IN THE JUNGLE

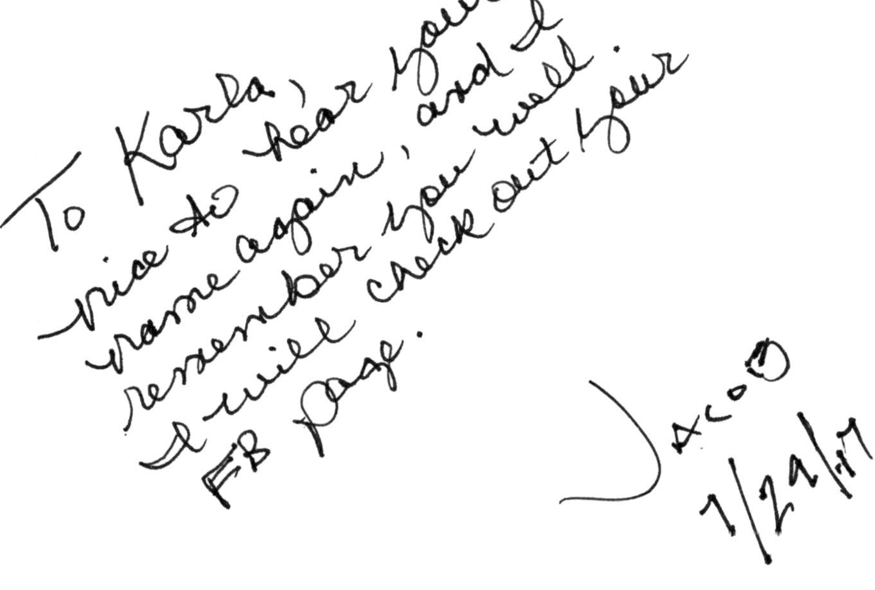

Jacob Gottfredson

ISBN: 1508576629
ISBN 13: 9781508576624

Dancing in the Jungle

To my wife who saved me from myself.

PROLOGUE

Is each step that one takes in life not the movements of a dance, simply the choreography set by his parents, family, acquaintances, education, experience? And wherein lies the truth? Is life in the Southeast Asia jungle or the jungle of the city not simply made up of the steps we take whether willed, driven, or coerced, moving as though in a dance?

Grown older, one sees the end of one's life and wonders if parts of it were not just a construct. Do we delude ourselves? In the back of our minds are hidden assumptions, biases, and prejudices that determine how we perceive reality.

Where do the snippets of reality in Anderson's life become truth and where to they become fiction? Wherein lies the game as he fights to stay alive and save his love? It is left to the reader to decide as each dances through their own jungle.

De Oppresso Liber.

J.L.G.

The stream of Time, irresistible, ever moving, carries off and bears away all things that come to birth and plunges them into utter darkness, both deeds of no account and deeds which are mighty and worthy of commemoration; as the playwright [Sophocles] says, it "brings to light that which was unseen and shrouds from us that which was manifest." Nevertheless, the science of History is a great bulwark against the stream of Time; in a way it checks this irresistible flood, it holds in a tight grasp whatever it can seize floating on the surface and will not allow it to slip away into the depths of Oblivion.

*Anna Comnena, The Alexiad of Anna Comnena **(1083-1153)***

CHAPTER ONE

Alex felt the tiny muscles in his forehead spasm. It was an annoying twitch that had plagued him off and on for the past several hours. The beginnings of fitful premonitions continued to spark and work their way to his conscious mind, pointing to an unknown danger that gnawed at him. Something was wrong; he could feel it, like the prey senses the predator. He nervously flicked the end of the small piece of plastic film he always carried in his left hand, a visible symptom of his paranoid personality. A bead of sweat rolled suddenly from a dark, thick eyebrow into his eye, and he flinched as the salt burned momentarily. He rubbed it with the knuckles of his right hand, blinked, and then looked again at the jungle wall in front of him. Something felt ... wrong.

He was aware of a movement to his right in the dimly lit bamboo hut. A momentary flutter in his stomach subsided as he watched the small, yellow dog approach and sit beside the table.

"Careful, Bitch. Dogs end up in the pot around here," he warned softly. Alex wondered again about the breed. It reminded him of an Australian Dingo or a Basenji mix. The dog waited patiently for scraps to fall from the edge of the table, considering the floor her domain. Her ears would perk and her head tilt as she glanced quickly with alert brown eyes at the floor with each movement the man made.

He pulled on the cigarette, exhaled slowly, and watched the blue-white smoke curl toward the ceiling and then disappear quickly as the slight draft from the small window caught and hurled it into nothingness. Beneath the window lay his bed: long poles of tan, grease and sweat stained, split bamboo matting rested on the floor of the same material. On the table, inches from him, stood a small oil lamp fashioned from an evaporated milk tin. His bronze skin glistened from sweat and soil as he swirled the warm Nescafe in the metal cup and watched the tiny flame grow dim.

The ramshackle hut had precious little space, barely enough for the bed and the table. The pungent smell of rats and rotting vegetation rose from the jungle floor and permeated the air inside the hut. Thin bamboo walls invited the soft morning light to filter through and cast slivers of bright, gray shafts across the room like sunrays bursting through the clouds.

At least he was still alive to dream of more, much more, enough to sustain him until it was over, he thought as he looked toward the door.

The slim, muscular man got up from the table, took four steps, bent down, and then stepped through the small doorway of the hut and looked overhead. He watched the failing reds turn to pink and pale yellows, signaling the end of morning, glorious dawn of a new day in North Vietnam. In hell. Once again his eyes surveyed the wall of vegetation several hundred yards to the west with that same relentless feeling of apprehension.

He felt a slight gust of wind gently nudge at his left shoulder and worry the brown stock of hair from his ear. The mild morning breeze moved the yellow grass in the field between the hut and the forest, its soft undulations bending southward like waves upon a lake, beckoning him to ride the crests, searching for a remembered home. He looked over his left shoulder at the small bamboo huts fifty yards away and then started to walk slowly in their direction. Bitch followed lazily, her head hung low, swaying slightly from side to side, so close that she flirted with the danger of the man's heel striking her lower jaw. Both were gaunt from the meager ration of rice and vegetables and an occasional bit of fish. And both relied on their youth for the strength and resilience to go on.

Alex wondered if a man knows when the end is near. He searched for his identity with each step, his eyes on the forest. Alex Brenner. Alex Brenner, he repeated rhythmically. American.

Hidden within the shadowed foliage to the west, the cross hairs of a scoped rifle quartered Alex Brenner's head, following his movement with relentless, smooth precision. The right index finger of a skilled rifleman began to delicately, inexorably apply pressure against the trigger.

Without discourse, without choice, the lives of these two men, victim and executioner, had come to the mount of the inescapable and the ridiculous, to the horror and corruption of war.

CHAPTER TWO

The Major turned to Colonel Langlinais.

"Jim, not only have I found the right man, but he's already one of ours."

The Colonel's eyes found the worried Major's form in the smoky room.

"Oh, and who is that?"

"A guy named Anderson."

"Have I met him?"

"Donno. Maybe at the Opera Hotel. He's one of a five man team working Laotian and Hmong commandos across the border, stationed in Nakomphanom. So I s'pose ya have. Anyway, you'll get another chance tonight. That's the team comin' in."

Colonel Langlinais and Major McCauley had been an inseparable pair since Korea. It was said that they had led the last charge of the war on a Chinese encampment the day after the cease fire and Langlinais had won the Medal of Honor for it. The young officers had spirited themselves to fame and glory in that afternoon. As a team they functioned like the shark and the remora. Colonel Langlinais was the sacrosanct politician. Tall, dark, and handsome, he had inherited the gift of southern hospitality and charm. His roots were Acadian: a Cajun son who had worked hard at displacing the Coonass misnomer. Abbeville residents in the know had hailed their warrior during the few times he had returned to his hometown and held court at Black's Oyster Bar over the past thirty years. While everyone loved him for his jovial cordiality, he was a hard taskmaster to anyone who served under him.

But it was the pugnacious Major McCauley who supplied the North-South symbiosis that held the relationship together. His mind was as agile as his carriage was military, a Bostonian whose Irish brogue was as ingrained as the Colonel's Creole. Anyone who witnessed the Major both in and out of the presence of the Colonel would think he was schizophrenic: dutiful at the Colonel's side, his brilliance was overshadowed by his opinionated, explosive, and profane behavior otherwise; often harsh and confrontational, his sanctimonious attitude had put him in too many pine boxes over the years to be anything but the Colonel's boy.

Now, working the CIA angle, they had reached the apex of self-indulgent power. In a world of clandestine maneuvering, they danced and pranced and showed their stuff to the round eyes who ventured forth from the world to peer into the eye of the demon.

The Opera Hotel in Bangkok, Thailand was their stage, their meat market, where they put on display the warriors whose lives they controlled. They talked for endless hours of their exploits, of war games, of vicarious adventure in the guerrilla-controlled jungle, and of the war in Vietnam to the east.

No one particularly disliked this back slapping pair; no one took them seriously either. Career army can turn even the most Ivy League among their ranks into redneck, good-ole boys. As harmless as they liked to appear, they were always interesting.

Cozy and luxurious in the penthouse suites of the grand hotel, the guests waited anxiously for the Colonel's "boys" to appear out of the night. The team was always brought in under cover of darkness to the roof above the penthouse. The whop, whop, whop of the chopper's prop brought fright, adrenaline, and the thrill of being part of the energy and madness of war, and of the mysterious men inside. What, exactly, will exit from the mechanical dragonfly's belly tonight?

The ladies in their gowns waited impatiently for the first sounds of the men. The hush of the team's carefully padded gear belied the sound of quiet power, the sound of death, the sound of the most evil in human behavior.

As the team members entered the carefully construed environment, astonishment fell over the spectators. Only dreams, only nightmares could construct such scenes of this other world. Ratiocination was chaos as the painted faces stared back with sullen and stiff indifference. The smell of the jungle and of sweating bodies and of excrement filled the room. The animal that was called homo sapien was among them, flexing its murderous jaws and exposing black teeth trained to rip through the bloody flesh of its foes. The affluent, seeking the bizarre, had come face to face with what they had unwittingly exposed of themselves, stitching the skin of their materialistic needs and the soul of their own intent to these ghastly implementers. Sitting at home in the States, their lives quite unchanged, they had not, could not have known what was now beginning to soak into their pores.

The unison of breathy gasps pleased the Colonel as he broke the resulting silence of the moment with his loud, raucous voice.

"Well here they are: my boys. What do you think of them? Just returned from a mission and don't look too much the worse for wear."

The ladies and their fare stood silent, caught up in the sensuality and danger apparent in their midst. The team carried subdued black weapons of the sort that whispered high tech carnage. Black jungle fatigues, painted faces, and collections of outrageous experimental equipment strung from every limb spoke of excitement, of stealth, and of control.

Angela, one of the Colonel's guests, dared not move. How was it that she found herself in a situation that so overpowered her sensitivities? She could not move, though she wanted to. She wanted to run, or to wake up. Coldness gripped her thighs and weakened her knees as she fought the sensation to faint. The walls, the floors dripped with the thick, viscous scent of the unknown, oozing through her soul with every movement of the brutish reality of these warriors.

Then, through the millennia of silence, came the firm but friendly voice of the team leader.

"Hello. How are you all tonight? Please excuse our rather frightful appearance. Believe me, we're friendlies. Let me introduce the team. On my left is Lieutenant Robert Endis: intelligence. Next to him is Master Sergeant Leo Sconds. And over here, on the far end, is Staff Sergeant John Masten: communications and demolitions. Next to him is Joe Two Dogs: light weapons and communications. Finally, this young man is Staff Sergeant Anderson: our medical and light weapons expert. My name is Mike Scorza, Captain, US Army Special Forces."

A nervous, forced giggle erupted from the spectators, belying their remaining anxiety. Finally, the terrible edge dulled, the crowd started to murmur with excitement and wonder. One of the ladies, bespeckled and decked out in recently purchased Asian jewelry, waddled forward, stuffing an hors d'oeuvre into her mouth that she had snatched from the table behind her. She breathed heavily, her mouth an open, moving red gash that cut through a pasty face as it continued to chew on the remaining morsel.

"Mr. Maston ... John, is it? Well, John, tell us, where have you been?"

"It's Mike. I'm sure you'll understand if I decline your question. I really apologize, but we can't afford to compromise our marching orders." His tone was friendly and gracious.

"Oh, yes. But it's so interesting. Have you been out all night? Doing what, if I'm allowed to ask?" Her nose twisted and her nostrils flared, obviously proud of her bravado.

"Well, Ma'am, mostly walking and getting tired to tell you the truth. In fact, I've worked up quite a thirst."

"Hell man, come on over here. What's your poison? Come on you boys and soak up some suds. Whiskey," he lifted the bottle, "we've got everything," the Colonel bellowed.

The crowd of opposites, strange in their procession, moved toward the hors d'oeuvres. The young woman held back, timid, until she stood apart as the crowd slowly made their way to the food and drink. Anderson watched her and did not move. It was his first time in the barrel, and he, like all the rest, dreaded it. Coming to be stared at, to see a little part of the world again, was not something they relished. And Damn, to see a round eye.

My god ... she's beautiful. If she looks at me I'll lose it.

Anderson's five feet, eleven inch frame topped out at an even one hundred seventy five pounds on a best day after he had first touched down in country, but three months of diarrhea, sweat, and exertion had left him a gaunt one fifty. His mind's eye saw himself as having reasonable looks, short brown hair, and an OK body. The truth was that he had been blessed with exceptional athleticism, a capable mind, and the cautious instincts of a hunter.

He caught his breath and tried to muster up his own brand of bravado. But it only left him thinking how much less frightening was their recent firefight than this drop into a world he had left behind. The girl was as beautiful and as desirable as the lost love he had tried to rid from his memory for many years. He was only saved by the bearing he had been so carefully trained to assume. And though his thighs burned with the sudden rush of forgotten emotion, he managed to emit the indifference he felt most secure with.

"Hi there. You look like you're a long way from home." Anderson ventured, feeling stupid for pointing out the obvious.

Angela stood, looking easily poised, watching the crowd mingle near the table that had been prepared for them. She was accustomed to such ceremony. Parties and social events had filled much of her life, and she had grown used to their cadence, their requirements of polite, if not always truthful, looks of interest and pleasure. But she had not been prepared for this. She stood cold, timid, unsure, though her straight back never wavered. Through her mild shock the voice next to her finally collided with her consciousness. She turned her head suddenly.

"Hi," she said hesitantly. "I'm sorry for staring. I must look dumb."

"No. It's OK. We do look pretty weird. I can't blame you for being shocked. To tell you the truth, the whole damn thing shocks me too."

His voice astonished her. His manner was not nearly so strange and threatening as his appearance. In fact, somewhere under all of the modern warrior facade his soft voice and intonation seem to belie the existence of a plain, everyday American.

"Anderson," the Colonel called, "can I see you for a second?"

Anderson excused himself and walked to greet the Colonel, glancing back at the girl as he went, as if to convince himself that what he was leaving behind truly existed.

"Yes sir."

"Do you have plans to stay at the Opera tonight?"

"Yes sir."

"I have rooms at the end of the hall. I would like to see you there at 0200 hours."

"Yes sir." The vague image of a broken record and its monotonous stumbling flitted across his mind.

"Thank you, Sergeant. You can get back to the young lady then."

"Yes sir." Anderson said, knowing a salute was not appropriate in light of the "Good Ole Boy" atmosphere the Colonel had created.

He turned and walked back to the girl, wondering as he went what the hell that was all about.

"Sorry about that," Anderson apologized.

"No problem."

"Where are you from?"

"Well, I'm originally from Denver. I'm living in Los Angeles now. My father has a small business that boomed in the early sixties. We moved there with dad's business to be, 'closer to the action', as he puts it." The soft, breathy tones of her voice moved like silken threads vibrating across a tambour, sending sudden shrills of rapid spasms through the muscles of his lower abdomen.

"How did you come to be here?"

You must taste delicious. You look delicious. You even sound delicious.

"Oh, dad knows Colonel Langlinais and the Major. He invited us over to vacation and see what was going on. Dad and mom couldn't though. I asked Colonel Langlinais if it were safe for me to come alone. He said it was safer than living in Los Angeles. I just graduated from UCLA in May and wanted to know a little more about the war. And, well, I wanted to get away."

"You just got here then?"

God, her lips are works of art. No doubt about it: if they touched me, I could never close my eyes again. Quit thinking you fool; she expects a conversation, not lust.

"Yes."

"Have you seen the sights of Bangkok yet?"

Her neck. Her shoulders. So smooth. Perfect. Think of something else you fool or you'll soon embarrass yourself.

"No, actually I haven't."

"I'm not liking this shindig much. I've got a room. Would you like to take a tour of the city after I change into something a little more conventional?"

"Oh, God yes. I wouldn't mind getting out of these clothes either."

"What, an hour?"

"That's cool."

Cool?

Anderson found the team leader, Mike Scorza, buried in conversation about the war effort.

"Mike, got a minute?"

"Yeah, what is it?"

"Can you make my excuses? I'd like to get the hell out of here."

"Sure stud." Scorza eyed the beautiful young woman.

"Hey man, just a friendly face from the world. Same age, same background, see the sights, you know," He said with a tight but revealing grin.

Bullshit. I'm going to pass out in a minute from lack of blood to my brain, and he knows it.

"Better wait until the Colonel finishes his speech though. We wouldn't want to upset him." Mike said with a grin.

CHAPTER THREE

It wasn't long before Langlinais got started. He stood stiffly in the middle of the room, his hard, burned face and gray hair complementing his aristocratic features.

"Ladies and gentlemen," the Colonel began, "I know you are all curious. But before I get into that, let me say that I hope you are enjoying your stay and that your shopping has been both enjoyable and inexpensive. Please relax and don't leave me with any of that food. Hear?

"Now then, to the business at hand. Most of you, I dare say all of you, have come to Thailand to see one of the many officers in country and spend a couple of weeks with a husband or loved one. As you have no doubt been told, it is quite safe here. Once a month we try to offer a little of ourselves to a few of you. I believe it is important that we connect with friends back home, that you leave with a realization that we are doing our jobs, and that we share a common moment together.

"Let me begin by giving you a bit of history of our presence here. You have, by now, found out that these men are Army Special

Forces, Green Berets more commonly. They were part of the 46th Special Forces Company activated April 15, 1966 at Fort Bragg, North Carolina as Company "D" 1st Special Forces Group, 1st Special Forces.

"The Unit departed Fort Bragg, North Carolina on October 15, 1966. They initially established a Special Forces Operational Base at Camp Pawai, Lop Buri, here in Thailand. They also established three major camps: Nam Pung Dam in northeast Thailand, Nong Takoo, southwest of Korat, and Ban Kachong in southernmost Kra Isthmus.

"In deploying to these locations, Special Forces Operational Detachment B-430 conducted the longest parachute infiltration to date utilizing C-123 aircraft.

"The 46th Special Forces Company initially conducted counterinsurgency training for the Royal Thai Army, Marines, and Police Forces, to assist these forces in their combat operations against Communist terrorists in the northeast and southern portions of Thailand.

"The unit was re-designated the 46th Special Forces Company on April 15, 1967.

"You will note the distinctive black and silver crest in the center of the flash. This was approved for Special Forces by the Department of the Army on July 8, 1960. Each element incorporated in the shield was derived from the World War II Special Service Forces. Emblazoned on the shield forming the crest is the Special Forces motto 'De Oppresso Liber' meaning: 'To Free The Oppressed'. The crossed arrows represent the use of two crossed arrows as collar insignias by the First Special Service Force, which, together with the fighting knife, symbolizes the Special Forces role in unconventional warfare.

"The distinguished insignia, flash, of the 46th Special Forces Company has a yellow border trim and a black background on which is superimposed diagonally the national colors of the kingdom of Thailand, signifying the unit's activation for duty in Thailand.

"The team that I have arranged to greet you tonight has just returned from a training mission. Please ask them all the questions you want about it. Be bold. They don't bite; they just look like they do.

Training my ass.

"Now ladies and gentlemen, please, return to your favorite libations and hors d'oeuvres."

Anderson was amazed by the Colonel's canned speech. Although it was true enough for the most part, it had not a damn thing to do with Langlinais nor even his teams, at least not now. The men had all been conscripted from the 46th and were no longer part of anything anyone knew about - not even the hush, hush SOG CCN reconnaissance teams that worked in from the east. In fact, as far as he could tell, the Colonel's teams didn't officially exist in the military's logs. But it sure was one hell of a smoke screen and seemed to satisfy the guests. Question was: how could he entertain civilians with the realities of men who didn't exist?

Anderson hurried down the back staircase reserved for the Colonel's men. His room was second on the left. He took the key Langlinais had given him and opened the door. Boots, fatigues, and socks flew. Anderson relaxed in the luxury of the hot water and felt the soap cut into the grime. The shower nozzle hammered clear liquid droplets over his tired body and rejuvenated the young life within. He allowed himself the briefest of pauses to rest, watching the rivulets of water roll down his chest, tracing tributaries along his stomach, and then cascading off the end of his penis as from a stone cherub. He carried almost no body fat. The dehydration of illness and constant exertion in the humid atmosphere had laid bare his muscled body, leaving him cut with fine definition. His dark, brown hair was kept short. "Utils" he called it. If it didn't have utils, he had no use for it. Long hair had no utility, nor did jewelry, nor did emotional ties. But now ...

He was ready in twenty minutes. Now he wished he had not hurried. Nothing to do but sit and wait. He couldn't go to her room early; it would be rude. What the hell would he say to her? He knew he would look stupid in his silence and searched his chaotic brain in desperation for something sane to latch onto, to appear interesting, humorous, worthy.

Shit. A round eye and a beautiful one at that.

It was all crazy. How in hell's name could this be happening? From the jungle, from painted face and garish garb, from rifle and determined acts of survival to this: a round eye in ballroom taffeta.

He paced the floor until the appointed hour and then tore open the door to his room. He was nearly in a trot when he realized that he was sweating, nervous, and uncomfortable. He came to a stop, took several deep breaths, and then continued on at a slow and deliberate pace. His clothes were already wet from nervous anticipation, the sultry, humid air, and his anxious, awkward efforts to shave, brush, comb, and dress. The clothes stuck to his shoulders and made his shirt look more like a collar splint than normal attire.

He remembered when he first landed in Thailand. The doors of the plane opened and presented an invisible wall of heat, overwhelming heat without relief. It was the hottest place that he had ever encountered. Even in the shade his body and clothes would be saturated with a wetness that extracted weight from his body. That coupled with three months of dysentery had robbed him of thirty five pounds. Only time would equilibrate this madness with his body.

And the snakes! The venomous little bastards were everywhere. Banded kraits, kraits, vipers, little Asian cobras, huge king cobras. One of the indigs told him that if he were bitten in the hand by a banded Krait, the only means of survival was to immediately sever your arm at the elbow.

Shit, he thought once again, *firefights and snakes had to be less nerve racking.*

His knock brought silence at first, then her melodic, feminine voice called out to him, a voice like the one from within his loneliest nights that made his life both worth living and miserable.

"Anderson, is that you?"

"Yes."

"Come in. I'm almost ready."

Anderson opened the door to her room. If it had been occupied by a burly, drunken, ex-prize fighter, the effect on Anderson would have been the same. Just the fact that he thought she occupied it made the room soft, mysterious, and female. He could smell her where there was no scent. He could sense the softness in the room where there was nothing more than partially finished construction in the middle of Southeast Asia. His mind saw what it wanted to see. He was captivated by the idea of being back in the world where no such world existed. He could feel the chrysalis opening, the cold detachment that kept him alive was being threatened.

"Hi there." Her youthful enthusiasm illuminated the room as she entered the main sitting area.

"Ready?" Anderson asked.

"What are we waiting for?" She caught his hand and was out the door and down the hall, off to explore one of the most exotic cities in the world.

CHAPTER FOUR

Colonel Langlinais sat, sullen, studying the paperwork in front of him as Anderson approached the small, teakwood desk.

"Staff Sergeant Anderson reporting, sir."

"Have a seat, young man."

Anderson felt awkward sitting down. His civilian clothes didn't make him feel any more comfortable. Sitting down, chatting with officers of this one's caliber was not something he did every day. At last the Colonel spun around in his chair and looked him over, a long moment of awkward silence.

"I understand you're some sort of a marksman," he finally said.

"I don't ... Who told you that, sir? I mean ..."

"We've been doing some research. Seems you're somehow connected with a group of accuracy purists. Supposed to be able to hit with small arms fire with some kind of phenomenal precision. Is that true?"

"Well, I guess that's true, sir." Anderson managed a bit of obsequiousness.

"Tell me about it, Sergeant."

"Nothing much to tell. It's an association. Just a bunch of guys who love precision accuracy. It really has to do with building rifles and loading ammo with known accuracy techniques and then tuning the ammo to the rifle. The game is to guide several rounds through the conditions in front of you and into one hole. Some of us use what we know on hunting rifles as well."

"How come you didn't politic for assignment to a sniper unit? You are also the team's light weapons specialist aren't you?"

"Too many other things going on. Besides, the rifles the Army supplies aren't up to much. The Army issues factory made ammo and rifles. It's only chance if it's tuned to the harmonics of the barrel. Minute of angle is sometimes possible, but in my book that's a pretty sorry rifle. Not that it matters. We are under orders to carry foreign gear. That's even sorrier."

What the hell are you up to, Colonel?

"I understand you grew up in a small town in the mountains. Sort of a loner. You must have spent a lot of time hunting on your own?"

"Yes sir. What's ..."

"We need you, son."

"Yes sir."

Langlinais studied the young man in front of him. Did he have what it took? How would Anderson deal with what he was about to tell him? He saw an average man in his late twenties, nothing striking, plain. But the eyes, there was something about the eyes that was different: intense, determined, hard.

"I don't know how else to put this, Sergeant." He paused. "One of our own ... we've got to take out one of our own men."

Anderson's blood turned to ice. The Colonel didn't have to be any more direct than he already was. He was about to order Anderson to waste a fellow American. Fear, shock, and a great desire to flee congealed into an indigestible mass under his ribs, sending a peculiar pain though his body that exited in the slightest of shudders from his shoulders.

"What time is it?" Langlinais asked.

"0215 hours, sir."

"Look Sergeant, we've got a problem. Seems one of yours, a Staff Sergeant Alex Brenner, tried to skip out on Air America and got his ass caught. Worse, he turned. Worse yet, he's teaching everything to North Vietnam Army Regulars that SF taught him at the Warfare Center, and he's doing it right under the noses of American prisoners."

"Excuse me, sir, did you say Alex Brenner? That's got to be a mistake. Anyway, I'm short time. My zero's coming up. Isn't there someone else?"

"I'm afraid not. We've looked."

"I don't mean to be disrespectful, sir, but why don't you just level the place? Why not take them by force?"

"If nobody's told you that our whole operation out there is absolutely clandestine, I'm telling you now. In fact, consider this your final debriefing. You are not to state anything to anyone about your activities across the North Vietnam border or in Laos. The Army spent a fortune picking you, Sergeant. One of the criteria was that you are a closed mouthed son-of-a-bitch. Now you get a chance to prove it. Besides, there are American prisoners.

"Look, I understand that you're about to muster out. I also know that this is a hell of a lot to ask. I think I can offer some things that will soften the deal. How would you like to spend ten days State side first?"

"No sir."

"Why the hell not?"

"It took time to get used to this shit. Send me back to the world now, and I'll return with my convictions in the palm of my hand. I'd lose my edge, sir. No way."

"Whatever you say, Staff Sergeant. If that's it, then come here. We've got work to do."

The Colonel pulled maps and a file folder from a manila envelope and spread them on the floor of the penthouse suite of the Opera Hotel in Bangkok, Thailand. Anderson saw what transpired in those early morning hours as incredulous. Stories of cloak and dagger shit had enticed him to enlist and ask for Special Forces, but now that it was happening he realized he had never really believed any of it. Spook and hero were only words, romance, the movie set. Yet here it was right in front of him, created by personality, by a man who was drawn to it himself and who had the ability to create it if he chose to do so. He was lost in thought. The rustle of papers tugged at his consciousness, forcing him back to the despicable reality in which he now found himself caught, the victim of some social malfunction.

Langlinais pointed to a clearing on the aerial map just across the Laotian border. Approximately 200 klicks north of the demilitarized zone lay a small encampment of bamboo huts. Stuck in the North Vietnam jungle like a tiny island lost in the sea, the clearing was not more than 1000 yards wide, a hole amidst the topographic contours, as though polarized against the disinterested phantasms of black snakes writhing across the lime green surface of the linen.

The Colonel had one hell of an intelligence network. An incredible amount of data accompanied the maps. The area of concern had been enlarged to reveal exhaustive detail, and the yardage from every conceivable point at the edge of the jungle had been inscribed to almost every point of interest within the encampment.

Anderson wanted no part of it. Interdiction against the enemy was one thing, but wasting a fellow American was the kind of bullshit he was not into.

It was nearly dawn when the Colonel finally decided to end their studies.

"Have you got it, Staff Sergeant?"

"Yes sir. I'm familiar with the area." Anderson replied.

"Can you put together the right equipment?"

"Well, I suppose I can find some half-assed stuff in country, sir."

"What do you need?"

"A sub-quarter inch rifle that I can trust, sir."

"So what does it take to get one?" The Colonel pondered over what Anderson was talking about.

"Sir, there aren't ten men in the world that can smith a rifle like the one I need, and they're all State side."

"You have a sub?"

"Yes sir, Sten. But I don't much care for it. The side mounted magazine gets in the way," said Anderson.

"What's your preference?"

"Sir, a Danish Madsen M53. When I went through small arms training, it was the best I tried, although a bit heavy."

"You know where to get one, Sergeant?"

"Yes Sir. I saw one in the C Team's armory," said Anderson.

"I'll call them at eight this morning. You can pick it up before you leave."

The Colonel turned and walked to the small bar that had been installed in the room to suit his needs. He drew himself a scotch, neat, and laid it on top of the teakwood. He glared at the tumbler, watching as the condensation grew heavy, forming rivulets that found their way to the bottom of the expensive glass and deposited a ring of water on the beautifully polished wood. He was lost deep in thought. Anderson waited. The Colonel turned, finally, and placed his palms on the smooth lacquered furniture behind the bar. It was heavy, and the Colonel struggled pulling it away from the wall. Anderson could see the gunmetal gray edge of a safe stored behind the cabinetry. Langlinais bent to one knee as he rolled the dial back and forth, forced the handle, and swung open the heavy door. He brought his hand out of the safe full of bills.

"At last count there were nineteen thousand dollars in there. It's yours. I think you're going to need it."

Anderson thought he was dreaming. First he lands on top of the finest hotel in Bangkok, Thailand after a commando raid into North Vietnam and then meets and spends time with a beautiful round eye. If that isn't improbable enough, in the early morning hours he is ordered to take out an American soldier, an acquaintance. He hoped there were no more surprises after this: an American Colonel handing him nineteen thousand dollars, just like that. All he could do was stare, and wait.

"It's yours. Go on, take it."

"I don't get it, sir. What is this for?"

I'm getting screwed here aren't I, sir. I'm not sure how, but I'm getting screwed.

"To put the operation together. Remember kid, no outsiders. This one must be guarded closely. You can imagine the repercussions among the civilian population if they got wind of this. They wouldn't understand. Even Westmoreland would throw a fit. And not a word to your team. Hear?"

Anderson didn't understand either. Where the hell did Langlinais get all the money he kept passing around? Anderson knew that the Colonel had given Scorza seven thousand dollars for the team to start the commando operation, but it was more bonus than anything else, and he knew that the money had kept coming, always in a brown paper bag. Scorza kept the money under wraps; although two other members of the team said they had gotten a share.

It didn't make any sense. The Army supplied what they needed for the most part. Even so, the money kept coming. It was rumored that the money came from the CIA and was meant for setting up intelligence networks among the indigenous personnel. Anderson didn't know. It sounded more like speculation than fact, but it sure as hell came from somewhere. He looked at the bills, green and off-white and new, protruding from his fist. A traitor's thirty pieces of silver? He had never seen so much cash. His stomach churned as he realized his dilemma: if the Colonel's honor had crumbled over the years, he sure as hell didn't want to hear about it from some Staff Sergeant; if it were some part of a larger scheme the "powers that be" were investing in, who the hell was he to tell them how to run the war? He said nothing.

"Let me sweeten the pot. You go on home. Build your rifle and any other equipment you need. Just remember, no U.S. marks. Nothing can be traced to us. Take it easy. I'll start the paperwork so you can muster out a couple days early."

Anderson's instincts told him to buy in quickly if he wanted to see home at all. Something wasn't adding up. Colonel's don't offer shit to grunts, let alone fortunes, early outs, and R & R State side just because they think you're a nice guy who ought to get a break. What made him think Anderson would return? Why did there seem to be time to take vacations, strolling around the world building fancy rifles? Didn't add up.

"Yes sir. I've got something to finish up here, and I'll be on my way. I can leave day after tomorrow."

"OK son. I'll cut the orders, and I'll let Scorza know. Fourteen days, you get your ass back here ready to go to work."

"Yes sir." Anderson turned and walked to the door. As he grasped the handle, Langlinais' baritone broke the silence.

"Sergeant. Two more things: no one can see you, and you cannot be captured. If you are, we will deny everything. We're not even supposed to be on the trail. Understand?"

> *Translates: I'll take the glory, wine, and dine the women, and you take the fall. Right, Cochise. I'll give you the money back, Colonel, if you'll tell me the truth.*

Anderson glanced back at the Colonel and nodded. His eyes trailed down to the floor in front of the khaki clad officer. The file folder lay closed where it had been tossed among the symmetric designs of a tapestry throw rug. It read: Operation Deja Vu.

CHAPTER FIVE

He was exhausted. The mission, the party, the girl, the Colonel, the hours without sleep had taken it out of him. He couldn't think straight anymore. All he wanted was sleep, clean sheets, the air conditioning in the Opera Hotel, and his own room, safe, dark, away. He opened the door, turned on the light, and looked around. The bed. No way, not yet. He blocked the air and lay down on the floor.

Operation Deja Vu. What in the hell is that supposed to mean? He tried to hold on to his thoughts: vaporous entities that seemed to drift away from him like the discrete shapes of cottonwood seeds softly riding the wind under the white, veined puffs of a winter parachute. Neon lights blinked red through the window with a relentless rhythm, reminding him of the winged tube inside which he found himself so often captured, waiting, waiting for the time. He, the captive audience by his own doing, waiting for the green light and the door and the jump into the night and the parachute's soft tug. The girl, the father, the Colonel. Jesus, he was just a grunt, a pool hustler, a predator in the forest. Taffeta, hair spray, perfume, conversation, money. He might survive in either world but not in both. It angered him that he could not control his surroundings because he neither understood them nor was ever made privy to them. The dark pulled in around him at last.

A soft, constant pounding woke Anderson. At first he thought about the incessant blinking light from across the street, but then realized it was not his sense of sight that was being disturbed, but his hearing. The door, someone was knocking on the door, not loud, but insistent.

"Yeah, who is it?" he asked sleepily.

"Angela. Are you awake?"

"Give me a second. Wait, I'll unlock the door. Count to ten and then come on in. I need to, well, just count."

Anderson grabbed what clothes he could find and headed hastily for the bathroom, bumping into walls as he fled. He heard her come into the room as he threw water in his face. What to do first?

"What's going on?" Anderson had not expected her. He was pleasantly surprised.

"Nothing really. I've been thinking about you, that's all. I wondered how you had slept. You left so suddenly last night."

"Oh, no big deal. The Colonel. I don't know, just Army stuff mostly."

Anderson started to shave, thought better of it, and turned on the shower. He hoped it would end the conversation, or at least the present subject matter. He scrubbed quickly, fearing that if he took too long she would leave.

"Still there?" Anderson yelled out as he turned the valve off.

"Yes."

He toweled his hair and his body with vigor, hurried, slipped into pants, and made an effort to comb his short hair. He still was not sure she would stay. He saw her in his mind's eye: concentrating on her surroundings, anxious, nervous, like an animal, ready, and then in flight. He remembered his baseball coaches' screams as he, for the umpteenth time, tried to throw the ball to first before he had caught it. Catch the ball first this time he admonished himself. He burst through the door, towel still in hand, to ensure that he caught her in time, quelled her fear, stroked her, settled her desire to flee.

A different vision stopped him short. This girl was not about to flee; she was here to stay. Anderson stopped in midstream; the sight of her startled him after his mental conjuring. The topcoat she had obviously worn was on the floor, touching her feet as if to warm and protect them. She wore only pink, sheer material slightly open in the front; the edges cascaded between and below her breasts. The pale light of morning played through the blinds, touching her form with alternating strips of dark shadow and crimson. His senses sprang to life, rising to exhilarating heights; it had been a long time. A moment of madding silence sounded loud and long in his brain. He felt the human male in him, in his loins, drawn to the form, to his other part. He existed in this moment like no other.

He stepped forward, steadied himself. He could see her dark eyes watching him as through a blind, bathed in a pale red veil. The same horizontal strip of light played across her nipples, and again the width of her waist. He looked again at her eyes, mesmerizing in their hypnotic gaze. She slowly arched an eyebrow as he moved closer. For an instant he was horrified. Had he done something wrong? The expression seemed to enhance the mood or to explode it. He wasn't sure.

"I ... I ..."

She didn't respond.

He moved closer. He felt at once both foolish and natural. Her tanned skin was smooth, stretched over a muscular body modeled to luxuriant perfection. He moved closer. Her eyes followed his every move like an animal waiting, expecting, ready, in control but excited, wild, and eager. She was woman watching man, knowing, waiting, ready, watching.

He touched her face. Was she real? What he felt under his fingertips might have come from his dreams. A slight movement of smooth, soft lips called to him without emitting sound. He drifted, flew, soared, held on. Her breath was warm, alive, on his mouth. She did not move. He slid the pink material over her shoulders and let it fall. His fingers traced the contours of her arms, and then moved slowly over the round hardness of her breasts, her sides, the curves that made her woman. He stood back and let the pants he wore fall also. He looked at her and she at him. Their naked forms, the blinking light filtering in, Asia ... past, future, time, all in this moment, it all came to this moment. There were no names and no complications. There was man and woman, one. It was the only thing that truly mattered. All else was filled in by man waiting for woman, and by waiting for the product of themselves, and by waiting for death. This was life's most important moment, not the war, not the social mutterings, not the busy labor of man's gatherings.

He savored the Epicurean essence of her form. He moved forward slowly; his eyes bathed her supple, lithe body, golden, rosetted in the light and shadow like a leopard waiting to spring. She watched him move past her, around her, until he was behind her, and she could no longer see him. He stood there, seconds, looking at her, lovely and beautiful and waiting. His fingers followed the line of her dark hair that fell like blackened, waxed silk to her shoulders. His tongue tasted her neck. Angela's eyes closed, and her head fell back onto his shoulder. His touch sent magical, electric shocks through her body as he knelt to her beauty, gliding down, lower, over her smooth curves and long slim legs with his fingers and lips that cradled and caressed her need.

Anderson stood and felt her body turn explosively to him. Angela's lips found his, devouring him. Her fingers found his hair and drew him closer to her and down as her hips moved of their own volition ... to him. She felt the heat of desire, passion, want for him. She had expected, wanted, tenderness, but now her body moved on its own. Something stirred inside her. It was not her mind. It was not her heart. It was her being, her most basic self. She guided him to her, powered by instinct. She was the leopard. She knelt to him, tracing her fingers over his muscular body, her soft lips against his torso. She knelt to the male, tracing him delicately with her fingers, then with her tongue, devouring him with the wet, warm sensations that drives the human libido to heights of chaotic pleasure. The drive that cannot be stopped overcame his being as she lifted her body up around his. Her body screamed for him, for the need of him, for want of him. He supported her weight as she lowered herself carefully, and, with perfection, opened her body to him. His youth parted her, penetrating deeply, smoothly, carefully into the pink, soft, hot depths of her body and her passion. The warmth there was pleasure-pain, the wetness lubricating, and he felt again the tingle of a thousand tiny needles converge on the skin of his thighs, working their way deeply into the muscle.

Lord, if I've got to die, give me just one more hour.

She moved slowly above him, her lips on his. Her head pulled away, her eyes fixed to his. He saw in her his yearning for life and love. He moved slowly to her rhythm, letting her guide him. She knew his desire, and she gave to him; she gave to the war and to this young warrior.

Her firm nipples moved slowly down his chest, creating tiny muscle spasms along their path and sending chills of pleasure through his torso to his spine. Anderson's back arched as if agonized by electric shock. The weight of her body on his heightened his sensation as she arched her back, bringing her pelvis closer, harder against his. Then, involuntarily, muscles convulsed and flooded their young bodies with the exquisite pain that sends life to hunt and to struggle for its essence.

She lowered her head to his shoulder; her hair covered his face. The warm perspiration on her neck, the smell of her hair, a wafting of the contentment for which he longed, controlled Anderson and his ever present struggle to protect his vulnerability, to maintain his edge.

They dropped to the bed, still holding on to the adventure of their indulgence in what they were. There was no other meaning in the darkness of life, no greater mystery in the terror of the jungle, no more they wished for. If but for moments, they were truly the only thing that man and woman were meant to be.

They were both shocked by their passion. They began to laugh. They knew the intensity of it had to be dampened, muffled, or they would soon be left embarrassed by it.

Anderson felt born again as he and Angela explored Bangkok's mysteries, her temples, her food, and Bill Baedeker's Cellar Bar. Angela took to Bill at first glance. The college football star entertained her with the goings on of a struggling entrepreneur in Southeast Asia. Bill's Siamese wife paid homage and played social servant, indulging them with heaping plates of exquisite, fried, battered frog legs. Iced Scotch washed them down with a typical ethered, smooth dichotomy of temperature and taste. Anderson felt that life was good with this woman by his side. Even so, it was tainted by frequent thoughts of the Colonel and his orders. Bill's conversation pulled him back.

"Los Angeles? That's where I was born and raised. Wild city! So what kind of business is he in?" Bill asked, placing his wide, thick hands on the bar and leaning toward her. Angela could see the broad, heavy muscle bunch up above his shoulders until his neck seemed to disappear. Hair, darker than the shadows of his eyes below the single light, shimmered as the bulb vibrated slowly from the traffic on Salom street.

"Oh, he's got more than one, I guess. Something to do with separating Platinum from refinery waste products. Then he has something going on in Southeast Asia. I don't know; he has various products manufactured over here and shipped back home. He doesn't sell them exactly. He is more of a distributor. I guess I don't know what my father does, really. Whatever it is, it suits me. If he didn't know Colonel Langlinais and some of his men, I wouldn't be here." She glanced at Anderson.

"And some of his men? What does that mean?" Anderson was surprised.

"Well, he knows the Major. He visited the house a couple of times. Kind of a strange person though if you ask me."

Anderson and Bill laughed. The Major was strange all right, living on past exploits and braggin' rights, following the Colonel like a puppy dog and jumping to fetch his Gentleman Jack for him before Bill's wife could bring it round. But Anderson wondered at the coincidence. Small world where everyone seemed to know everyone else half way around the damned thing. Oh well, what the hell. Who knows what the idle rich do when they're bored? Get in tight with the military for no apparent reason, he guessed.

"So how is it that dad and half the khaki clad stiffs in Southeast Asia are so chummy?" Bill jokingly pried.

"So how is it that you're so interested Mr. Frog legs Cook?" countered Angela, kidding about being interrogated.

"Ah hell, no reason. Just fascinated with our new global world, I guess."

"While we're at it, just what is it that you do Mr. Green Beret?" She turned to Anderson. "Thailand seems pretty calm to me; at least I thought so until I saw you men come into the Colonel's rooms last night."

"I'm not exactly sure what we're doing, or why we're doing it." Anderson hedged.

As the night wore on, the bar became crowded with Special Forces personnel on R & R, bar flies, and a few other odd balls. Bill was too busy serving drinks to pay much attention to Anderson and Angela. As soon as the table in a far corner came free, Anderson jumped for it, anxious to spend time with her in a more secluded, if even a bit darker, spot than under the bright light near where Bill hurried to keep up with the drinks.

Once seated, they both ordered another drink and took in the noisy and boisterous antics of the GI's around them.

"Tell me about yourself," she asked.

"Not much to tell I'm afraid. Born and raised in the Rocky Mountains. From high school to college. Hit the road for a while and then here."

"OK. That didn't work. Let's try this. What's going on?"

"What do you mean?"

"Is that what they taught you in the Green Berets?"

"What?"

"How to avoid answering the question," she scolded.

"Not exactly. I guess you're talking about the war? What we are doing, I'm doing? I thought I knew once. It all seemed so simple, straightforward. But now I'm not so sure. It's getting crazy."

"What do you mean?" Angela coaxed.

"I'm not sure what I mean. After two and a half years of training and even through the first part of this assignment, I was certain that what I was getting myself into was right, patriotic, morally and philosophically correct. Most of the time I still think so, but there are other times ... Most of the people here smile and are polite to the point of obsequiousness, but behind our backs they openly hate Americans. Can't blame them I guess. American's are thoroughly convinced they are superior and act that way in front of them, treating the indigenous personnel, indigs as we call them, as though they were an inferior race.

"Bill is a two tour Navy SEAL and finally quit because he had had enough. Married and bought into the life here. I haven't asked him, but I think he feels some of the things I do, the way I do. The mis sions that are going on here are out in left field. I don't think anyone is asking why or gives a shit except for a few liberal assholes, cowards, college professors, and actors stateside. The people I work with are pros; I'm a pro when you get right down to it. What I've come to learn is that pro just means we will keep our mouths shut and do as we're told, anything we're told." Anderson's monologue trailed off. He sat staring at his drink, his tan, hairless arms etched with wiry muscle that flexed as he gripped the glass.

Angela looked at him in silence, wanting to know what he was talking about, but knowing in her soul that he had gone as far in this direction as he was going to. She put her hand on his, kissed his cheek lightly, and then moved her lips to his, extending a long passionate appeal to return to her. But her mind raced all the while, trying to understand why they would send a short-timer back to the States for two weeks, then to return with only a few days left before he mustered out of the Army.

They sat, poised in thought, silence surrounding the space that insulated them from the noise of the bar. Anderson's eyes, fixed on the glass in front of him, shifted to Angela's hands that lay relaxed on the table in front of her. He marveled at their smooth elegance, tanned like the rest of her. He felt like everyone was looking at him, knowing him, the quiver in his gut, the burn in his thighs. He lifted his head and looked at her. Her gaze was steady, burrowing concern and attachment into his soul. He could see her at once, the almost imperceptible pulse in the little hollow in her throat, the delicate, vertical lines in her lips. Her hair was jet black in the subdued light and clashed suddenly against the whiteness of her teeth as she broke into a self-conscious smile, knowing his thoughts.

Angela rode to the airport with Anderson the next day. Their relationship, though brief, was sincere, growing, and they felt a need to stay close. Parting felt plain uncomfortable. They both knew they had fallen in love.

He watched her as he boarded the plane that would deliver him to Travis Air Force Base and the world. Would he ever see her again? She had not been able to reach her father by the time Anderson had to leave. Neither of them knew if she would still be there when he returned.

He closed his eyes as the plane roared down the runway, his back pressed hard against the seat as the angle of accent increased. He didn't see the cobalt sky rush toward him nor the gray-green water of the China Sea splash against the shores to which he, a pro, knew he would return. He slept ... finally.

CHAPTER SIX

Travis Air Force Base was a marathon walker's paradise. It could only have been designed by an engineer who fell asleep during planning and layout class. At customs, Anderson looked at the strange sight as the confusion of the place rubbed off on him. Several gates were arranged like supermarket checkout stands. To his left, several Army privates and specialists were busy dumping everything they owned on the floor while guards poured over every item. All were young, alive, and back in the world, safe. He stood watching this amusing activity when he heard a voice call to him from a stand on his right.

"Hey Sarge, can I help you over here?"

Anderson lifted his bags to the counter in front of the customs official.

"You got anything to declare?"

"Nope."

"Go on then."

Anderson breathed a sigh of relief. "Where's a telephone?"

"Up the hall on your right. Can't miss it."

Anderson thanked the man and hurried to the booths, wondering why he had been exempt from the invading search the others were having to endure. His beret and Staff Sergeant stripes maybe, or just a lazy agent. He listened as the phone rang, over and over. The voice he had hoped for answered at last.

"David, is that you?"

"Dead nuts, cuz!"

The beginnings of Anderson's military service had left him occasionally interested but for the most part bored. Boot camp, MOS, and advanced infantry training found him, although in good shape, anxious to get to where he wanted to go: Fort Bragg, North Carolina and the Special Forces compounds. Only seven men in his battalion had been selected to begin training to qualify as a "Green Beret." He had already suffered the humiliation of KP and guard duty with the weird smattering of American mankind whose association he was forced to endure. He had been ready to get on with it.

He had arrived just after Christmas, awe struck in his imaginings. In reality it was just another group of buildings: barracks, CP, training classrooms, mess hall. But in the minds of the men there, and in the minds of the nation, it was a place the elite met and did whatever it was that such men did. This pride, this fear of failure drove them to excellence. Year after year they strove to acquire skills that would serve them in the most remote locations of the world. They learned to trust in and work with small teams, to make the most of the very little they would carry on their backs. Each team was crossed trained in the disciplines that would best serve both individual and team needs. Languages, demolitions, intelligence, medicine, light weapons, amphibious operations, scuba, and on and on were learned in a way that complemented the team. If a team member was taken out, another could take his place and his job, filling the void. A 12 man team could be split and still be whole. Training took nearly three years to be deemed a Green Beret. Left in remote locations on their own, they were forced to be independent of the rest of the military's logistical machine.

Individual skills of survival in any situation had to be learned. The psychology of each member had to be extraordinary, stoic in the face of pain, indifferent to being totally alone. It all fit Anderson's personality. He had found his niche at last for it put him in touch with whom he was. The feel of the equipment and the mission suited the predator, the hunter in him. The long hours and tough training regimen kept Anderson growing in the skills he was best at. He had tried to leave behind the burden of lost love, turned inward, and now gave himself to the single emotion of the edge, the means to stay alive. But now, Angela. Would he let this relationship lead him to the depths of despair once again? He vowed to forget her, and just as quickly the snake he had come to know intimately twisted and snarled in his gut.

The automatic weapons the Berets used were tools that had a definite place in the scheme of things, but Anderson still preferred the purity of his long range weapons. He spent every available hour honing that which he truly loved: testing techniques of loading ammo, practicing in the wind and mirage, keeping track of new stock and bedding techniques. It kept him sharp and happy.

His training had gone on for three years. Troops from the 82nd Airborne and the Communication Group near them had already been to hell and back, and some had even gotten out during this time. Anderson had begun to plan for a career with the Force. He didn't have to listen to too many rumors about the extra pay and fringe benefits the officers got to realize that was the way to go. He had submitted requests for Officers Candidate School and Flight School. But the Army, in its infinite ability to screw up paperwork, spent a year processing it. It was only days after he had volunteered for Southeast Asia and gotten orders to ship out that his acceptance to both flight school and OCS came through. In the end Anderson decided it was for the best.

Now, back home, he realized the Army's screw up had been a blessing. Safely on the ground at Travis Air Force Base, Anderson made the second of many phone calls.

"Afton, is that you? This is Anderson."

"Hey, how are you?"

"Ah, man, still alive and kicking."

"I haven't heard from you in a while."

"Yeah, I've been kind of out of pocket."

"What's going on?"

"Listen, Afton, you got some time? Can I come over to the house?"

"Sure, glad to have you. Can you make it about four this afternoon?"

"Damn straight. See ya then." Anderson was relieved. So far, so good, he thought.

On the ride over to Afton's, he reviewed in his mind the rifle he hoped the master gunsmith and stock maker could craft for him. He wondered how he would answer the obvious questions that Afton would surely ask. But his mind kept switching to David and the rendezvous they had agreed on for the following day. He was still undecided about Afton when he pulled into the driveway. He'd have to play it by ear.

"It's good to see you again, Anderson."

Afton Seven's easy and genuine smile shone through as soon as he recognized Anderson. Afton was the type of person that would go out of his way to help anyone, especially when it came to pure rifle accuracy. Self-made, he had carved his mark in the industry by starting an operation in his garage with a now equally famous friend, Ted Black. Though not as yet established throughout the shooting world, Afton was already a legend among benchrest accuracy purists for his innovative fiberglass stocks.

Members of the benchrest community understood the advantages of the material over traditional wood. Fiberglass is inert compared to wood, and, to a great extent, overcame the problem of stress due to the warping and thermal growth characteristics of wood. Water did not affect fiberglass, another problem inherent in wood stocks. New designs advocated floating the barrel instead of letting them rest on the stock's barrel channel. This reduced the differential stress and the altered harmonics on the barrel, often induced by a climate or temperature related warped stock. Gluing the receiver to the fiberglass stock instead of bolting it overcame differential stress in the receiver due to similar problems associated with bolting and wood. And strides had been made to understand the change in point of impact when the rifle was transported to varied environments and changes in temperature and barometric pressure. These and other accuracy enhancing discoveries were only known to benchrest shooters in these early years. Traditional rifles could not compete with the precision instruments used by hard-core benchrest competitors. Groups less than 2 tenths of an inch at 100 yards were now commonplace in the rifles crafted by purists such as Afton Seven. Top competitors were shooting 3", 5 round groups at 1000.

Anderson had enjoyed Afton's friendship over the years as fellow competitors. He felt badly that he had to push the conversation toward his needs, but time was short if he hoped to accomplish all that was necessary before he returned to Colonel Langlinais.

"Afton, I need a rifle put together inside ten days. I know that's asking a hell of a lot, but I'm prepared to make it worth your while if you can possibly suspend what you have on your plate for that long. The design's a little different but not impossible. I need brass, dies, powder, primers, scope, the whole ball of wax. I've got five thousand dollars. Can you manage it?"

"That's quite an order and a hell of a lot of money. What do you have in mind?"

Anderson began to unveil his vision: a combination of benchrest and sniper rifle for a very specific job. Afton and Anderson talked until nearly midnight about the design. Afton became more and more intrigued with the concept and functionality of the instrument. He read the list back:

Hart barrel chambered for .243
  1 in 8 twist
  18 inches long
  heavy varmint contour
  black matte anodized
Modified composite/fiberglass stock
  shorten forearm 4 inches
  sharpen chine at edges to ride front sand bag
  remove pistol grip
  embed aluminum bar stock in forearm for rigidity
  modify butt and cheek piece to allow telescoping from
  shortened to normal length
  black matte finish
Two ounce Burns trigger
Lyman scope boosted to 32 power by Siebert
Scope covers
Remington 700 short action blue printed and glued to stock
black matte anodized
Weaver bases and light Bushnell scope rings
black matte anodized
Eleven degree crown at muzzle
Use Ackley improved chamber reamer with .261 tight neck.
Fireform 100 rounds of Winchester matched brass and turn necks to .0086
500 Remington 7 1/2 small rifle primers
500, 80 grain match bullets
Set scope for 450 yards and select 50 rounds of best brass
Set neck dies to seat bullet with light pressure
Set Wilson seater die with bullet touching lands when pressure ring in neck
Gap gage to adjust seating depth
Two pounds each of 4895, 748, and H322 powder

Construct front guiding sand bag held by short, light jib suspension with integral rear bag. Collapsing capability.
Cartridge block for 15 rounds with hinged lid
Black canvas bag to carry rifle, rest, flag and cartridges
Shoulder and waist straps

Afton looked up at Anderson. "That about it, or do you have more surprises?" He smiled affably.

"Man, I'm sorry, but I'm pressed for time. I'd do most of this myself but I can't. I need the items on the list ready next week. We'll take it to the range and complete the tuning. We can find the final seating depth, powder, and load then. Can you do it?"

"I'd feel safer if someone did the steel work while I complete the stock and the other items. I've got several of the components you need here at the house. I've got a 700 action as well. Let me contact Bracken and see if he can do the steel. If not, maybe I can find someone else. If they don't have a 700, I'll ship them the one I have on overnight mail. For the right bucks, someone can do it. I'll have the wife get on the phone in the morning to locate the other stuff. There are a few problems though: the Siebert modified scope, the .261 tight neck reamer for a modified .243, the Wilson dies for a wildcat round, and a neck sizing die. I'll have to call some competitors for the scope and make them an offer they can't refuse. The rest is too tight a time frame. I suggest we find a cartridge in the same class that we can find the dies for."

Anderson looked at Afton. He knew that the gunsmith was right. Rounding up his exact request in a week was going to be next to impossible. He'd have to settle.

"I suppose you're right. But don't settle for just anything. The case has got to deliver 3500 feet per second with the 80 grain match bullet. It has to have good brass, mild recoil, and efficient design. I've got to get quarter minute or better accuracy out of this piece. It's got to stay inside 1 to 1.5 inches at 450 yards in good conditions. The 6x47 is too finicky, and it won't give me the velocity I need with the bigger bullet."

"Your choice of cases may be too big to get what you want out of an 18 inch barrel. You need a more efficient case. Let me think on it and make a few calls. I'll get it done one way or another. I've got a couple of friends who can help. If we stick with it, we might have a chance."

"Thanks Afton. Here's the money. If you get Bracken to do the steel, just keep it. I will make it worth his while also. I'll be back next week. I've got less than eleven days to get three months' worth of business and running around done."

CHAPTER SEVEN

David had agreed to meet him the next day in Seattle. Anderson turned in the rental car and purchased a plane ticket at the airport. On board he struggled with the madness of what he had in mind. Maybe he should not ask David to help. The whole damned idea was crazy anyway: traveling twelve thousand miles around the world and back, taking advantage of friends - master gunsmiths - all to kill a man, someone he knew, when half the logistics in the world were already in country. But what the hell, he wasn't a trained sniper and had no other idea what to do except that with which he was familiar.

David stood near the gate, same old Levi's and plaid western shirt. He could read the sparkle in his eyes.

"Hey you ole fart knocker! How's it shakin'?" David said.

"Aw, so, so. How are you? Let's find a quiet coffee shop." Anderson urged, not waiting for an answer.

"I saw a quiet bar on the way here. That ought to do," he said, as he put his arm around his smaller relative. David smiled at the drama and urgency in Anderson's voice.

David and Anderson exchanged gossip and small talk on the ride to the bar. They enjoyed each other's company and the chance to catch up on the hometown folk, though they both knew little. They found a secluded booth in the back of the run down tavern and ordered Crown. The laminated wood table was covered with a thick layer of epoxy. The wood grain and color were enhanced and magnified through the glossy surface. Anderson looked at it and noted the small ring of moisture left by the whiskey glass on the table's surface as he drank deeply.

I know he'll do it. I'm a shithead to be here, swilling courage and taking advantage of his skill and friendship.

"How's the Army treating you, pard?" David was sincere. Obviously Anderson didn't have him travel all the way down here with such urgency in his voice for nothing.

"David, you'll never believe what I'm about to lay on you. I need your help, man. Something's going down over there. I can't get a handle on it. I'm not sure who I'm fighting anymore." Anderson talked nervously, quickly.

"What the hell are you talking about?"

"Listen to this shit," Anderson leaned forward, looked around, and lowered his voice. "Some spooky Bird Colonel just laid nineteen thousand dollars on me to waste some asshole who went over to the other side. It was an order, a mission. You know what I'm saying? This lifer's got his own penthouse in Bangkok, hosts American society in it, has a cabinet full of liquor, and a safe full of cash. He opens the damn thing and hands me this wad. Not only that but this son-of-a-bitch has been feeding the green to my team leader for months. He gives me two weeks leave in the States to get my shit together before taking this guy out."

David pulled deeply on a Marlboro. "So, who's the unlucky sumbitch?"

"That's the weird part. I went through a bunch of training with him. I know him as well as I know you. We weren't big buddies or anything, but then we didn't hate each other either. I donno, maybe I'm full of it, but it doesn't feel right. I keep getting this "set up" feeling in my guts. And there's this girl whose old man is chummy with the Colonel. Not only that but the Colonel has some nutty Major sidekick with lizard eyes. Something's fishy. I'm looking for a way to cover my ass."

"So what do you want me to do?"

"Hey, David, I know you've got family. It's safe. I mean you'll be in a safe zone all the time."

"You gonna tell me or what?"

"I want you to back me up in a chopper. I mean, give me a ride out of there when I finish the job."

"Are you nuts? This is the States. You're talking half way around the world. There's a war on with GI Joes everywhere. I don't know shit about flying in that damn place. Not only that but what the hell am I supposed to do about work, you squirrel?"

A pasty-faced, blond waitress dressed in Wranglers, boots, and a white blouse, tied to expose her protruding navel, approached them. The bartender busied himself switching a keg of green, bar-beer while the jukebox played country western. Neon signs hovered above the booths, their blurred luminescence throwing smoky, rainbow patterns against the oily wooden walls.

"You boys ready?" She asked, her manner bored, her voice husky, rolling with phlegm from years of chain smoking Lucky Strikes. Both nodded acceptance.

"Look, cuz, you remember the old days. Nothing spooks you. I thought maybe you'd jump at this shit. You always wanted the excitement without the military riding herd on your ass. Here's your chance. You're a bush pilot and a pretty good one from what I hear. I've got topos, the works. I've thought the whole thing through."

"Yeah right. What do I do about a passport, stick up some Army post?"

"No problem. I had them made by a friend before I left for the States. I'll pay the airfare, expenses, and a chunk of the nineteen thousand is yours. Leave it with the family before you go. There's eight thousand for you. All you need to do is arrive in Thailand twelve days from today. I'll take care of the rest. You fly into a safe zone, pick me up, fly me out, and go home five days later and eight thousand dollars richer. Surely your boss and Monica will let you have five days. It's no big deal to you, but it's my ass if I'm right about this."

"Let me make a couple of calls. Man, sometimes you're a squirrelly cowboy, you know that." David walked to the abused phone tacked precariously to the wall next to the men's room. He had a smile on his face. Anderson knew he would come through. David did whatever he wanted to do; he always had and Anderson didn't expect this to be any exception.

Three minutes later Anderson watched as David strode toward him, his face upturned in an effort to keep the smoke out of his eyes that curled up from the cigarette between his lips.

"So where's the tickets, cuz?"

Anderson's next stop was Brooks Army Hospital in San Antonio, Texas. He had told Colonel Langlinais to send his muster out orders there. He knew the territory and a Lieutenant who worked with short timers. His guess was that he would help him pull a few strings. After all, his wife was the only person in the world who didn't yet know he was making it with the Post Commander's daughter on a regular basis, outside of the girl's parents, of course.

Anderson called the post several times asking about his orders. He finally got an affirmative from some CP clerk with Corporal stripes and a yellow streak up his ass so far it made his voice sound like Hanoi Jane coming to a two bit radio antenna in the jungle. Anderson hurried to the base after the Corporal told him the Lieutenant was in his office.

"I understand you're wanting out. Is that right, Sergeant?"

"Yes sir, Lieutenant."

"Why don't you stick it out? You've already got four years in. I notice from your paperwork that you were accepted to OCS and flight school just before you went over. Why didn't you take it? You probably could get in now if you still wanted to. It's a great career."

"I've got other plans, sir."

"Wait a minute." The Lieutenant looked puzzled. "The way I add it up, you're supposed to return to Thailand and then muster out after being there three days. If this is right, you'll be over there when you turn civilian. We can't allow that!"

"Yeah, it's screwy, but Colonel Langlinais' got some unfinished business for me. What the hell, it's just a plane ride."

"Look, Sarge, I can't authorize this. It isn't policy. I don't give a shit who the Colonel is."

"I know it's a bit fouled up, but it's not a problem. The Colonel gave me some leave. He told me to go ahead and draw up the paperwork here, and he would let me go home after I finish the work. I don't mind at all."

"No dice. You'll have to wait until you get back to get the proper signatures."

Anderson looked at the officer. He thought about the mission, David, the file, the money, the girl. No, his plan counted on this discharge if things went sour. If he was being set for the fall, this might be his only way out. He had to go for it.

"Listen Bruce, old Dub, you remember, the Warrant Officer, he was telling me you were still sweet on Pam. How is that going anyway? Do you and Liz and Pam have a ménage a trois going yet? We had a bet."

"You piss-ant noncom." The Lieutenant handed Anderson the signed papers and told him to get the hell out of his office.

The next stop was the one Anderson dreaded the most. His mother, the town, the old friends. He'd rather fly back now than face them.

But he needed his gear. The army's shit was just that: shit. He decided to fly in, rent a car, and drive the three hours it took to get to the small mountain community. If he timed it right, he could ride in after dark, visit with his mother a few hours, pick up his gear, and leave before daylight.

Anderson hated himself for leaving his mother in the middle of the night. He knew he was a rotten coward when it came to answering the hundreds of questions his people would ask. Her tears welled, as he knew they would, and his heart wrenched when they spoke their good-byes. He loved her, but he couldn't listen to her. She too would dull his edge. She wouldn't know it or understand it, but she would, just as the girl would.

His mother was overweight, but it didn't seem to dampen her energy nor her steady conversation and injunctions. She fretted over him as he poked here and there for his gear. He found himself apologizing as often as he said, sir, in the presence of the Colonel. Her eyes sparkled, and her face was a constant stream of gray animation. Her arms flailed, hands complementing the arguments and justifications she sought to keep her son from leaving. But there wasn't time. In the end she had to let him go. Her face was contorted with anger, fear, and sadness as Anderson threw his gear in the back seat, climbed into the driver's seat, and turned the key in the ignition. He continued to watch her through the side mirror, waving, and crying while the rental car's lights grew dimmer and faded into the darkness. He had avoided the others in the town of his childhood. He felt like a coward but relieved. He turned south and then right down the lane. He stopped for a moment in front of the house he knew so well, but he knew she was gone forever, only a demon in his memory now. A demon who had torn his heart from his weakened body, turned on her heel, and walked away with it still beating in her hand. He shook his head to dispel the anger and pressed the car's pedal.

Anderson headed for Arizona. He had phoned ahead and found out that Bracken was doing the metal work for him after all. He couldn't complain about this development. Many considered Bracken the premier gunsmith in the country when it came to metal. His work was meticulous. He'd turned out many National Championship rifles in the past decade. He could square a receiver, chamber a match grade stainless barrel, and marry the two to millionths tolerances.

"One thousand dollars? Afton sent me a thousand dollars. I can't take that kind of money for this. Besides, he also mailed me a Burns trigger and this 700 action." Bracken had a conscience.

"It's OK, Bob. I need the rifle right away. I know you're busy. I can't expect you to drop everything you're doing just for me. I want you to have the money."

"I can get it done, and a guy over in Scottsdale will get it anodized for me. I do have a question though. This barrel is too short. You can't get over the end of the bench with this. I don't even think it's legal on the line. It sure as hell will make it stiff though, interesting to see how it shoots. You expecting to win any matches with this caliber or are you just going to use it on coyotes and whitetail?"

"Yeah. I got a chance to go hunting. Once in a lifetime deal, you know. I got a pack for it. Needs to be short and light. Got to be dark so it doesn't scare off everything in sight. But I only have this one chance. I'm probably going to regret it, but what the hell, I'm just experimenting."

"Well, settle in. You can help. No sense just sitting."

Anderson watched the gunsmith work his magic.

Bob Bracken was a CPA by day and had been for years. He led two lives: the first eight hours he poured over figures and supervised several employees in slacks and a tie; then he changed clothes to work at the lathe for five or six hours at night. That is the Bob Bracken that Anderson knew: quiet competence dressed in Wranglers, boots, and a long-sleeved, blue shirt. Tall and slim, he moved like the erudite aristocrat to the oil and steel shavings of his craft, unless, of course, he was sailing through the skies in his glider, showing his Jag, or proving his skill on the rifle range.

Bracken checked the bolt lift and adjusted the firing pin spring until the bolt could be opened easily with only the index finger. He squared the bolt face and lapped the lugs until they had equal and uniform contact. Next he measured the receiver and trued it to perpendicular with the axis of the bore. The threads were chased to square with the receiver.

While Bracken worked with the buttoned rifled barrel, Anderson adjusted the trigger to two ounces with no creep or over travel. The let off was crisp and clean.

Bracken centered the barrel in the lath and started the rougher in the bore. Metal shavings issued from the deepening hole as the machine turned slowly. A constant oil supply bathed the reamer blades. When this was complete, he installed the finishing reamer and completed the chamber to the correct headspace. He was ready to cut the threads that would tie the barrel to the receiver. Bracken cut an eleven degree crown to protect the lands at the muzzle.

"Afton called about the caliber. Seems you wanted an Ackley Improved .243." Bracken's voice broke the silence of their labor.

"Or something like it. I just want a 6mm bullet of approximately 80 to 95 grains doing 3500 feet per second."

"Well, the only thing I have is what I just cut your barrel for. Can't do any better with short notice, not with a tight neck. This is something new that Jim Pinard and Doc Palmero asked me to try. You won't get exactly what you want, but after you see the results, I don't think you will kick too much. It ought to be one hell of a round. I have never seen brass this good in my life. I can only let you have 50 rounds though; I don't have a hell of a lot myself. Here, take a look."

Anderson reached for the tiny brass case. It looked like a short 22-250. The damn thing had a Russian name on it. He wasn't impressed. He didn't think he could get more than 2500 feet per second out of the little piss-ant case. Shit, what could he do now? He was running out of time and the barrel was already chambered. He couldn't tell

Bracken why he needed the rifle, and he couldn't bring himself to look this master gunsmith in the eye and ream him out either.

"Don't look so hurt, son. I've been doing some testing with this thing. I think you'll be surprised. I've got a few pounds of powder of the same lot. Load it hot. You'll get about 10 firings out of the case. That should be enough to get you started. There is supposed to be plenty of brass coming over from Sako. Start out with about 25 grains of 4198 powder. H322 will work well, but this lot of 4198 will give you 3450 feet per second. Try seating in the lands to make a mark about as long as it is wide. Then pull it out to not more than .020 inches off the lands. Somewhere in there you will optimize a harmonic node once the velocity is right. I've got a neck sizer for you with buttons from .257 to .260. The chamber neck is .261. Use the expander there and bring the neck up to 6mm. Then turn the necks to .0088 inch thickness. That will give you .002 inches of clearance. You'll only have to bump the shoulder about every 5 firings, but you probably won't have to size the neck. Have at it boy."

Anderson sized and cut the brass. He measured the case wall, and was amazed to see how uniform it was. No American brass he had ever seen could match it. He trimmed the overall length to 1.49 inches.

"When Afton gets this thing stocked, you will need to fire form the brass," Bracken pointed out. "Use 49 on the Culver with 4895 powder. That will blow the case out to the chamber. Use light tension on the bullet. There aren't too many good match 6mm bullets out on the market yet. You can get some, but it would be impossible in this time frame. Try running these Sierra 70 grain bullets through my press. It will reform them to a 7S shape and give you much better long-range results. I also have some custom-made 68 grain boat tail bullets. Try those as well."

Anderson was skeptical about the new cartridge for the use he intended. There wasn't enough bullet or case to deliver what he needed at the range he would be shooting. He decided he had no choice but to give it a try as he said good-bye to Bracken and left for California. His only way out now would be if Afton or one of his friends had another reamer and could quickly re-chamber the rifle to a more appropriate cartridge.

Anderson watched the skies darken in front of him as the sun dipped into the western horizon and led him toward the coast. The Big Dipper made its ascent into the darkness, and began its revolution around the North Star. Anderson felt for the small compass that dangled together with his dog tags from the chain, which always reminded him of the one that held the drain plug in his mother's bathtub, assuring himself of its presence. The night was clear and brisk, and he drove with the window down. The air that passed his nostrils and infused his lungs was fresh and fragile, like a fine china goblet, ready to shatter with dawn and the oppressive heat of day.

CHAPTER EIGHT

When Anderson pulled into Afton's driveway, he was still worrying about his new rifle. He could see that Afton was busy inside making history. When he knocked, the gunsmith looked up with that annoyed expression that says he wished the intruder would go away. But that irrepressible smile came over his face when he recognized Anderson. Afton opened the door.

"Hey fella, you didn't waste any time did you. Bracken called me and said you were on your way. Come on in. I've got a surprise for you. Is that bundle under your arm what I think it is?"

"It's the barreled action," Anderson informed him as he unwrapped the instrument.

"Beautiful work as always." Afton ran his fingers along the fine, polished, metal surfaces as he walked to the workbench to unveil something of his own. "Well, should we see how it fits?"

Afton laid the Bracken piece into the modified stock gingerly. It fell into place like Bonnie and Clyde.

"I thought you were going to get it anodized?"

"Yeah, I was. But I figured I could get it done here just as well. I donno, I'm feeling pretty antsy about the caliber. I've been thinking about it all the way here. I don't see how this thing can get 3450 feet per second out of even a 70 grain bullet let alone anything bigger. This brass will be pushed past the limit. Besides, a 70 grain bullet won't hold enough energy to hurt a dead dog at 450 yards. I figure I'll only have 600 to 700 foot pounds of energy with that small bullet. Wind drift will be too great. I need over 1000 foot pounds of energy and less than one inch of wind drift per mile per hour at 450 yards. Out of this short barrel, that's going to take some doing."

"What do you suggest Anderson?"

"The bullet's got to be at least an 80 grain boat tail with a ballistic coefficient between .3 and .4. Out of this short barrel the case has got to be at least a .243 Ackley improved or maybe even bigger."

"Well, let's get the book out and see what we can find. Then we will have to locate a barrel with a different twist, probably 1 in 9. This thing's got a 1 in 14. We'll lose approximately 20 feet per second velocity per inch from a standard 24 inches. That's 24 inches minus 16 is 8 inches. Eight times 20 is 160 feet per second loss in velocity. We'll have to look for a case that can deliver 3600 to 3700 feet per second with a standard barrel, and the powder's got to be gone by the time the bullet exits the muzzle."

Afton began looking through his library of loading manuals. Hours later the two men carried the rifle, barrels, and newly loaded brass to Afton's range. Targets with tiny bulls used exclusively by Benchrest shooters were hung at the 100 yard line. Traditional front and rear rests were positioned on the bench. Wing flags were set between the bench and the target completing their range preparations. Afton set up a table for loading ammunition to be used for testing until the optimum load could be found. Afton also set up an Oehler chronograph to measure the velocity of each round fired.

Anderson fired groups of three rounds into the bulls with the .243 Ackley improved case. Tuning the rifle to its optimum produced half inch groups. Anderson was not too happy with the performance, but the larger 85 grain bullet showed velocities in the 3400 feet per second range to be easily achievable.

"I don't know, Afton, I guess it will do, but at 500 yards the error will be over 2 inches. What do you think?"

"Let's give Bracken's case a try and then decide where to go from there."

Afton placed the barrel of Anderson's rifle into the small vise, inserted the action wrench and gave a tug. He removed the action and stock from the barrel, then inserted the new barrel in the vise and screwed the stocked action on to it.

Anderson decided to try Bracken's advice and start with the newly shaped 70 grain bullets placed at a depth in the case to make marks on the bullet from the lands of the barrel as wide as they were long. He placed a round on the loading platform, drove the bolt home with his left thumb, and lowered the bolt handle with his right. His first round fell 2 inches high and 1 inch to the right of his point of aim. Anderson looked back through the powerful scope and adjusted the cross hairs to the exact point at which he had aimed for the first round. While holding the rifle absolutely still on the bags, he turned the knob on top of the scope until the horizontal crosshair cut the bullet hole. He then turned the knob on the side of the scope until the vertical cross hair cut the bullet hole.

Anderson sighted on one of the tiny bulls. The wind was blowing right to left at 5 miles per hour. He moved the crosshairs to touch the bull's outer edge at the 3 o'clock position. The wind was steady. He squeezed the 2 ounce trigger. The rifle moved back to touch his shoulder. As it did so, Anderson cycled the bolt, removed the spent brass and inserted a new case. Three seconds. The wind held. He moved again to 3 o'clock. The hole did not enlarge after his second round, nor after the third, fourth, or fifth. Anderson continued through four more five round groups. Each was smaller than he had ever seen in all his years of shooting. It was easy to see that the aggregate would not be much larger than .2 inch, if that.

Anderson turned to Afton. "Did you see that shit?"

"I sure did. Pretty accurate little case ain't it."

"What velocity am I getting? Have you been checking? I got so absorbed I forgot about it."

"Well, you're averaging 3150 feet per second with that short barrel. If you want more, you might have to go to a longer barrel. We could go up a bit on the powder, you might get another 100 feet."

"I need the short barrel. Let's try the powder."

Anderson struggled with the load, but the rifle could only produce 3300 feet per second, the next higher harmonic node, and still hold the same superior accuracy. He was amazed that this tiny case could push a 70 grain pill at such speed. Accuracy was phenomenal. Anderson was impressed.

"Let's move to 450 yards and see what it can do."

"OK, but do you want to look at the other equipment you had me build and give it a try?"

Anderson marveled at the contraption Afton had built to his specifications. It was strong and functional. He realized it would do the job he needed done.

"It looks great! But there's no place to set it up here."

"I already thought of that."

Afton dragged a 4"x4"x4' length of wood out of his truck and strapped it to one of the steel columns that supported the roof over the benches. He proceeded to screw the portable rest to the wood.

Anderson had loaded another ten rounds while Afton finished securing the contraption to the post. Anderson placed the small rifle on the rest and sat on the ground beside it. A couple of slight adjustments put the rifle in a comfortable position for him. He slid the rifle back and forth in the rest to settle it in. With his left elbow resting on his left knee, Anderson squeezed the small, sand filled, leather bag supporting the rear of the stock with his left hand. He slid the rifle forward again until the cross hairs rested just above the 450 yard target center. A slight squeeze of the rear bag again brought the cross hairs into the exact position. Anderson's right elbow rested on his right knee as he brought his trigger finger into position without toughing the rifle. His cheek was the only point of contact, and that only so slightly.

Anderson watched the flags. Conditions were ideal with a slight, steady breeze prevailing. When he began shooting, he did so with amazing speed. Anderson sent 5 rounds down range in just 14 seconds with the small, single shot, bolt action rifle.

"Let's walk," the rifleman said.

Afton had been watching through the powerful 60 power spotting scope, but said nothing as they walked the distance. Anderson did not speak either. He knew it was good, but both knew that a bullet hole may have printed in the black portion of the target making it impossible to see. They strained to see an errant bullet hole in the black as they grew closer. There were none. All five bullets were no farther apart from one another than one and one quarter inches. The center of the group was one inch to the left of dead center and slightly low.

Anderson and Afton spent the rest of the day loading, shooting, and working out small problems they found. By the end of the day, the bugs had been worked out of the rifle and the support. The rifle was tuned, and Anderson loaded the fifty matched pieces of brass.

"Afton, where did this round come from?"

"I donno. Bracken says it's made by Sako."

"But it's called a .220 Russian. I guess they developed the round, and Sako makes the brass. Blown out to a 6mm diameter it shoots pretty damn good. Have you ever shot it in .22 caliber?"

"Hell, Anderson, I've never even seen the thing before."

They rode back to Afton's shop, talking non-stop about the new rifle and the cartridge. Afton guessed he would chamber a barrel for one of his rifles and shoot it in the upcoming matches around

California. Anderson agreed it was a good idea. Neither had ever seen brass to equal this stuff. A match grade bullet ought to blow the competition away.

At Afton's shop, Anderson carefully packed the rifle, rest, and ammunition in the black cloth case that Afton had found.

"Oh, one more thing. Do you have a small wooden loading box drilled for this size? It only needs ten to fifteen round capacity."

"Hey, it was on your list. I forgot. I made one with a lid and hinge. It locks also."

Afton located the small box and handed it to Anderson. The rounds fit perfectly. Anderson threw the black case into the rental car.

"Thanks Afton. I hope I didn't put you out too much, and I hope you made some money."

"No problem, partner. I made out like a fat rat. Come around again, hear."

With that Anderson headed for the airport and Southeast Asia.

And Angela?

CHAPTER NINE

Boots wagged his tail with a vigor that moved his whole body. The boy took a dog biscuit from his right pocket and handed it to the red and white pointer. From the opposite pocket he extracted another and began to munch on it himself. Ten biscuits each, and what better way to make sure the share was even. He stared into the river bottom, searching ponderously for suckers.

The willows along the bank were thick and green with new growth and young leaves. Vivid pink petals adorned the blooms of spring morning glory vines that wound their way through the maze of verdure. He sat in the small grassy hollow of a birch stand, mesmerized by the slow moving stream, watching each tiny leaf, insect, and twig float by like boats upon an ocean. The fetid odor of the biscuit robbed his nostrils of the scent of dogwood and sage nearby, the taste as pungent on his tongue as it was on his olfactory glands. He chewed methodically, mashing the contents into a fine, saliva infused mass filled with fat, protein, and carbohydrates. He had become quite used to the hard, green-brown canine morsels.

He moved slightly and cocked his head. He could make out a familiar sound, far away. A whistle. Dave. His cousin tumbled down the incline that formed the bank of the river, landing like a cockroach stuck pitifully on his back, legs clawing at the air.

"Whaddaya say? Any suckers?" Dave yelled with an overabundance of energy and enthusiasm. He popped to his feet like the whole chaotic episode had been a planned event.

"Na. Got to wait for summer til the water goes down and forms some puddles," Andy replied laconically.

Dave sat down beside his cousin, put his hand on Boots' neck and looked into the water. Andy could sit this way for hours, he thought. He didn't understand how he did it. Dave could last about three minutes and then his knees would flex, carrying his body to an upright position whether he willed it or not.

"How long ya figger?" Dave chided.

"What?"

"How long ya figger yer gonna sit here?"

Andy got to his feet. He looked at Dave and smiled. Dave rose to his feet and together they started down the trail along the bank, the soft earth cool, caressing their bare feet. Their jeans made raspy, hollow, flicking sounds with each step, like sandpaper lightly striking a screen door.

Dave watched his cousin's back contemplatively for a moment as they moved.

"You alright?" he asked.

Andy didn't answer.

"I'll be ten tomorrow," David announced, changing the subject as though the other had never existed.

Andy stopped, turned, and then put his hand on his cousin's head.

"Whatcha doin'," Dave asked, surprised.

"Wondered if I could feel yer head grow."

"Huh?"

"Well, I figure if you're nine today, and yer gonna be ten tomorrow, you got a whole year of growing to do in twenty four hours. That's pretty fast. Wondered if I could feel you getting smarter right under my hand."

The boys laughed and broke into a run. They were still running when they entered Andy's house, barging through the door like hungry kittens in a chic nursery. They bumped into each other, trying to slow their momentum to some sort of polite stop.

He knew. His mother's eyes held the answers without saying the words. Relative's eyes, too, bore terror down upon him, lowering a weight upon his shoulders until it suddenly shot pain into his gut. He turned and bolted through the door and into the spring air, running back toward the river. He knew. His father was dead. Anderson was twelve.

The drone of the plane's turbines churned in Anderson's ears. He watched the ghostly characters begin to fade as they continued to act out his past on the tiny window beside him.

"Hey, Sarge, ETA fifteen minutes," the navigator yelled.

The matinee of his life, reality in the porthole style window, stopped suddenly and his thoughts returned to the mission. Had he forgotten anything essential? He decided to check his gear again. He examined the paracommander and reserve parachutes. They were neatly packed. He had assured himself of his rigging the day before and again prior to boarding. No sense messing with them now, he thought, though he considered leaving the reserve behind. He turned to the backpack and the canvas case perched beside it. The case was not strong enough to protect the delicate instrument it contained. It worried him: an accident waiting to happen. He rummaged through the plane looking for something more solid. Pieces of thin wood crating had been left behind from an equipment drop, and he fussed with them. He began to fashion a crude splint from the few boards that remained. The navigator donated a roll of tape, and within minutes the case had taken on the appearance of a mummy. He felt a little better about the security of the instrument, but knew that it was far from perfect for a drop through the blackness of the night sky to an unpredictable landing.

He opened the backpack's top cover and surveyed the contents. Several items filled the large center partition of the pack. He studied the food, medical equipment, and other sundry items. All had been put together, in their place, with years of thought and preparation. The outer pockets contained a compass, signaling devices, sewing gear, and maps. The gear was not Army issue nor American made nor labeled. All the items were the best that could be had for the job they were designed to do, and all were his personal equipment purchased or bargained for over the years. And since he could carry no identification he knew that he was supposed to be non-American made as well.

He moved his hand over each of the pockets in his jungle fatigues to reassure himself that objects that belonged there were each in their place. Those were his running gear, each designed to satisfy a particular need should he have to cache or abandon his pack and run, maybe for days. He removed the plastic soap container from the pocket next to his calf. He amused himself with the thought that it must represent the smallest self-contained emergency medical kit in existence. Wrapped and waterproofed, the soap container's contents were of his design also and carried extremely strong drugs, shortened surgical tools, and modified hypodermics. Anderson had modified everything for size, lightness, and functionality: drugs used to curb the ravages of pain; infection, dysentery, and enough Benzedrine to run three days without sleep were included in the tiny soap dish. He checked the stiletto style switchblade that resided in a pencil pocket on the left shoulder of his fatigues. He sighed. The Rolex watch, the ruby ring, and the Randall knife, all the marks of his Special Forces brotherhood had been left behind.

Anderson seated himself again and turned his eyes to the glow of the red light to increase his night vision. The eerie light had a mesmerizing affect, and he looked back toward the window and his thoughts of the past.

The image reminded him of the television in the Opera Hotel lobby in Bangkok only a few months back. He had glanced at the tube as he passed on his way to his room. The picture caught his interest. He immediately perceived it as a broadcast from America, but there was something very strange about the man on the TV and the mannerism of his speech. He stopped momentarily to listen. The man had long hair and a disdainful, aggressive attitude. Anderson listened as the man spoke out against the war in Vietnam and the American war mongers engaged in it. He felt a personal attack in the things this man said. Anderson had received enough news from back home to know there was dissension, but he had not thought it worthy of even national television, let alone international broadcasts. As the camera intermittently panned the audience, Anderson became aware of the many faces in the crowd with the same demeanor and dress as the speaker. He recognized their fervor and what appeared to be genuine commitment to the blasphemous outrages of the longhaired man. As he watched, he grew more uncomfortable, angrier with this man, and even more so with the crowd that cheered his words. He recognized the ideas and the manner of presentation as the kind that breaks the backbone of middle-of-the-roaders and dilutes the commitment of the strong. They were the sayings of a palm reader, filled with logical generalizations aimed at subverting America's decisions and pointed efforts. He could already count the extra dead that would result from this man's converting salesmanship.

God, he must not listen; he must erase this man from his brain. Survival depended on his becoming the war and his surroundings, on his never questioning his actions. To ponder these issues in combat was to lose one's edge, to die. Don't think, do, and then forget.

Desensitize. He did not recognize the man's name or that of others when they were introduced. He left the room committed not to remember them. But the night was long in the Opera Hotel, and he could not help but ponder. The knowledge of escalating dissension hurt him, and he knew it. He must reaffirm his position. He must take the time.

As he peered out the small window into the blackness, he felt that his entire life had been driven toward this point. His years in the mountains, his skills as a predator, his ability to withdraw into a world of detail of the mind, all seemed to be training for this mission. Anderson had taken inventory of his gear. He would soon be at the doorstep of the black night into which be must hurl his gear and himself. What about himself? The phrase ran over and over through his mind: "The life they knew, the people they are." Who was he? Did the packing of his own being, the selection of his own emotional and essential gear, make sense? Did any of this make sense?

His past, and the people in it, played before him like expressionless marionettes in the glass. Painted crimson by the plane's interior light and blackened by the night, the scene seemed cast in surrealistic pyre.

Anderson stepped through the door and out onto the sidewalk of San Bernardino, California. The street and the concrete glared after the hours he had spent in the bar behind him. He pulled at the pack of L&M's until one was free and lit the cigarette while he waited for his eyes to adjust. He knew what he was about to look at. He had seen it before entering the bar. He did not raise his head from its position above the cupped hands in front of him as the fire kissed the tip of the cigarette, but his eyes moved up and across the street to the familiar sign. It was a poster occupied by a peculiar man, an apparition. A tall hat, a strange colored coat, and an outstretched arm, the index finger of which seemed to point directly at him, surrounded the goateed face and serious eyes.

Anderson picked up the pool cue and tattered suitcase. The August sun was hot on his back as he walked out onto the street and slowly approached the sign. He was still undecided, yet felt the pangs of depression as the thought of hustling another stake began to form in his brain. No, this was it, the beginning of a new way out of his dreams of the redheaded beauty who had abandon him, driving him through the tattered back doors of America's most forsaken. He kept a steady stride as he passed Uncle Sam and was soon at the door of the recruiter's office.

What the hell, the guys over there could use his help.

Inside, he held on to his loads and surveyed the interior. The office was small and filled with young men. They seemed too young. The recruiter, in familiar sooty green clothes and dirty, colorful patches, was busy filling out forms. There was barely room for another body. No unoccupied chairs presented themselves, so there appeared no other choice than to approach the green clad sergeant.

"Just a minute and I'll get to you," the man said without raising his head from the paperwork.

Anderson's urge was to leave, and he probably would have if he had known where the hell to go.

"OK, what can I do for you?" the sergeant finally asked.

"I understand a guy can sign up for certain assignments when he joins the Army."

"That depends," retorted the baggy, olive green uniform, "on what exactly you want to sign up for. What strikes your fancy?"

"Special Forces."

Anderson had ended up in California. He was twenty five years old.

David, Monica, and he had spent long hours talking. David had told Anderson of his adventures in helicopter school and his expectations for the future. He told Anderson that several of the students were talking about becoming bush pilots after graduation. Canada, maybe Alaska.

But Anderson had come for personal advice. The Army. David knew something about the Army. They talked of it for hours. David told Anderson about Special Forces: So called "Green Berets."

"Damn straight. If I had to do it over again, that would be it. They were just down the road from us, from the 82nd Airborne. I used to watch them. They did some great shit, man, a hell of a lot more than we did. They were always going places and learning new stuff. The thing I like most about them, that I didn't like about the 82nd, was that they operated in small teams. They didn't have to mess with a whole shit load of kids and freaks like you have to in a conventional outfit. They're cloak and dagger. Yep, that's what you ought to do."

Anderson had been pulled to the adventure of it all. This sounded like what he was looking for. But the underlying reasons were different. He had wanted to escape his dreams. He had also felt a gnawing away within himself, something that bothered him: young men fighting for something, him not helping. His father, his brothers, those he respected had served. He could not respect himself if he did not. And yet, he was not sure why America was fighting at all.

The bus had finally pulled up to a building, the likes of which Anderson had never seen. It was more like a cattle holding area than a place for humans. Anderson chose a bed and sat. It was not long before an authoritative Army type began shouting instructions.

"You men settle in for the night. Tomorrow you'll be heading for Fort Polk, Louisiana. You're going to love it there. Heat, humidity, mosquitoes, mean ass DI's, and venereal disease are waiting for you boys. Y'all can walk across the street for chow if you're hungry. The Army'll feed ya tomorrow and from now on. Breakfast is at first light. Better be up or it's your ass!"

A young recruit seated not far from Anderson, who he estimated to be nearly a decade younger than himself, spoke up.

"Hey Sarge. What time's first light?"

"First off, my name ain't Sarge and neither's my rank. Second off, if you miss first light, you miss one of Uncle Sam's great breakfasts.

Anyway, don't worry about it; I'll get your sorry ass out of the sack in the morning."

With that the man had departed the building and left Anderson and the pack of misfits to their own devices.

The kid had pissed Anderson off with his question. Mostly, he was pissed because he found himself with these kids, in the same position, their equal, no better, no worse. Everyone was lined up at the starting gates, ready for the race, from the same line. Anderson could barely tolerate it. But he guessed it was his own fault, and began to situate his gear near the bed. As he did, he felt an aloneness like never before. He heard himself begin to speak. It was to the youth with the big mouth.

"What's your name?"

"Howard," the kid answered.

"Well, Howard, you play any pool?"

"Sure."

"It's going to be a long night. What do you say we go across the street there and play for some coins? Not much, say a dime a game. You got any money?" Anderson urged.

The kid thought a moment and then nodded his head. They left the squalor of the holding pen and walked across the road. Anderson noted that this pool hall was on the same side of the street as the one he had walked out of earlier in the day. It seemed ironic: all patriotic shit was on the west side and all low life shit was on the east. Anderson had relieved the kid of ten dollars in an hour or so by teaching him the merits of "double or nothing", betting on the 3, 5, 7, and 9 in Nine Ball, and other niceties of the pool hustle.

Anderson had felt a little relief having some money on him again, no matter how small the amount. And the kid didn't seem to mind. He apparently had more where that had come from. Anderson had smiled to himself at the hustlers he had come to know over the years who could leave a man's wallet empty and send the victim away laughing about it.

"Hey kid," Anderson began, only to be interrupted.

"My name's Howard."

"OK, Howard. Where you from?"

"Here. Where you from, man?"

"Originally from Utah, but I have been on the bum for years."

"Oh yeah. My old man says that's where all the polygamists live. You a Mormon?"

"Well, not exactly, and they are not polygamists." Anderson replied. "They gave that stuff up long ago. There are fundamentalists, not part of the Mormon church, who do practice it."

The boy paused, pondering momentarily over what sounded like bullshit, then said, "I heard some of em's got horns."

"Jeez, kid, get real. You think there's any humans walking around with horns? Never mind, don't answer that. Sounds like you and your dad want to return to Salem and the witch hunts."

"Well."

"Grow up kid. They are God fearing Christians like most in this country." His voice becoming louder.

Anderson had felt badly about his attitude with the boy. He made a resolution: be a nice guy.

CHAPTER TEN

Hey, Bud, you're on!

Anderson looked up at the navigator, his thoughts of the past suddenly interrupted. He swiveled in his seat and stood up. His gear was near, and he began to pack it onto his body. He hoisted the para-commander above his head and let it drop down and onto his shoulders. The weight felt good, and when he pulled the quick release buckle into place and snapped it together, a familiar feeling of security came over him. He pulled the backpack up to his midsection and tied it firmly. It was time for the reserve chute. Anderson glanced at it and thought of the probabilities. He passed over it and grabbed the soft case he had earlier wrapped for extra protection. He situated the altered case on top of the backpack and proceeded to batten it down as well. Two items remained to be attached to his body that would increase the load to the point that he would have difficulty walking. The ten minute oxygen bottle went against his chest above the case along with an altimeter. He swung the Madsen M53 9mm submachine gun over his left shoulder and tied it firmly. Anderson put the goggles on but then tossed the helmet into a heap with the reserve chute. The plane bounced softly on its cushion of air, and Anderson had to hold on to exposed pipes near the roof to steady himself. He felt more like a working pack animal than a man. The weight and tightly bound packs made it hard to breathe, but his legs and upper body felt strong and ready. He was in tremendous shape and eager to get on with the job.

Hanging on as he was, a last cigarette proved difficult to light. He would edge the tip toward the flame and then be bounced away. He grew irritated knowing that this would be the last he could indulge himself in for a few days. He managed finally and dragged deeply on its filter. The three men flew through the air in the darkened cylinder at tremendous speed. The bulb's red glow played over them, bathing their odd forms in the crimson light. He looked around the cabin and let the last evidence of a high tech world greet his eyes, and like the cigarette, the last he would see for a while. Remembering, he opened his throat, and used his diaphragm to pull even more of the hot smoke into his lungs, regretting that the cigarette had reached the filter.

The navigator spoke again. "Hey cowboy. Can I ask you a personal question? Why the HALO-spook, all-alone shit? I mean, why not just use a chopper in the daytime?"

"Where's your spirit of adventure, sir?"

Anderson thought about the Laotians, the Hmong, and other tribes, primarily the Pathet Lao. The problem with friendlies is: some of them aren't so friendly. Besides, he did have friends down there that he didn't want mixed up in America's personal problems, nor Vietnamese and Pathet Lao retribution. Simple as that. Guerrillas were infiltrating the area east of Nakomphanom and in Laos and Cambodia along the Vietnam border, and North Vietnam Regulars ran safe encampments from which they hit South Vietnam I Corps troops on a regular basis. The trail remained open despite American bombings to the south and the interdiction operations inside and outside of North Vietnam. Laotian commando teams operating out of the Thai city and led by American Special Forces personnel put the Laotian people in extreme danger. It was certain that the Vietnamese would extract revenge when and wherever possible.

Top secret CCN SF Recon teams in Laos were reporting NVA buildups further to the south - to the west of Ashau and Lang Vei - in an effort to warn their Special Forces brother's camps all along the border. But Anderson was too far north for that to affect his mission, even though traffic would be high. He had to infiltrate without detection.

The interior of the plane went dark momentarily. Then, slowly, the plane's interior light began to blink its persistent signal that the time was near. The lifeless herald would soon turn green telling him that this ride was over, the big one about to begin. Anderson lumbered toward the door when he felt the plane begin to slow. At 180 knots, the navigator opened the starboard hatch. He let go of the pipe and with his right hand maneuvered the mouthpiece of the oxygen bottle over his lips. He bit down. He eased the valve open and looked up into the blackness. Anderson struggled and stumbled the last steps forward and grabbed onto the ice-cold jams. He could feel the wind, twice that of a hurricane, blanket the doorway like invisible, rushing water. Adrenaline hammered at his body in the awful darkness as he felt the oxygen flow into his lungs.

The light turned green.

Anderson jumped with all his strength to clear the plane. He was overwhelmed by the sudden blast of cold against his body and face. He felt the resistance of the air and tried to control his hurling body. He flung his legs and arms out far enough to gain a semblance of stability and then brought his right arm toward his chest as he let his left rise slightly. His body rolled slowly over and he lay on his back on the bed of air. He watched as the plane roared into oblivion. Its running lights were out, and it disappeared like a ghost into the night. The roaring engines grew fainter until he was enveloped by the awful silence jumpers experience amidst the blast of rushing air.

Anderson rolled again. An icy, ebony ocean of nothingness surrounded him. Only the pressure of the air let Anderson know his orientation in space. Nothing was visible. He turned his head to the left and peered quizzically at his hand. But even as he brought it closer to his eyes he could not make it out. He forced his hands into his chest and prodded the case. His body began to roll in a forward somersault. Finally the altimeter attached to the top of his pack came into view. The soft glow was almost too faint to read. He had exited the plane at nearly 30,000 feet - a typical High Altitude, Low Open jump. He was now at 22,000 feet and falling out of control. He forced the edge of the case riding atop the backpack under the rim of the altimeter. Quick glances afforded him ample recognition of his altitude. He fought the urge to assume a terminal velocity position as he again went into a standard frog and settled in for the ride.

The cold grew worse as he rushed through the wind chilled air. He waited for the break line and the ever pleasant feeling of warmth there. As he passed the 15,000 feet mark, floating with relaxed control, he searched for lights below. Still no evidence of anything familiar, just the sea of black, and cold, and emptiness. Phantasmagoria amidst the inky nothingness began to grip him like the dreams of a boy. He indulged the weird stream of consciousness that engulfed his mind. Gargantuan gargoyles from pages of the past rushed passed him and disappeared into the ebony soup. Screaming faces appeared before his eyes, melting into the red blobs of youthful imaginings.

Anderson closed his eyes tightly. He tilted his head forward until he felt his chin touch the cold steel of the oxygen bottle; he opened his eyes expecting the familiar glow of the altimeter. Twelve thousand and falling fast. Eleven thousand two hundred ... He felt warmer air and knew he was near. He welcomed the changing sensation and the return to a familiar and less threatening atmosphere. The ramblings of his mind were gone and he knew from experience that they would not return. Anderson had made it through the barrier of madness whole again without passing out. It was back to business as usual. He checked the chute's pull handle, the case riding atop the pack, the Madsen M53, and then glanced again at the greenness of the gauge. Eight thousand. He turned the valve on the oxygen bottle and removed the mouthpiece. The air filled his mouth with a thump. With childlike curiosity, Anderson let it force his cheeks out and listened to the low whistling sound change pitch as he slowly rolled his head from side to side.

When he came to the two thousand feet mark, Anderson began to stabilize his position in the sky and readied himself for the chute's familiar, soft tug. He surveyed the earth, searching for the inevitable light, but he found none and wondered at the topography below him. Maneuvering the paracommander in such blackness was futile, and he wished for any object to appear so that he could get his bearings. He would have to rely on the altimeter and luck. At the one thousand feet height, Anderson placed his hand on the steel handle that resembled the triangular dinner bell of cowboy camps. He pulled hard and brought his knees slightly up and toward his chest. He felt the tug at his shoulders as the nylon fluttered up and out of its packing. The crotch straps pulled tighter as the thought that only an imbecile would allow himself to become caught in such a situation nagged at him. Deceleration was a blessing for it meant another milestone in the decent toward terra firma. He floated below the single wing made famous by the Golden Knights. Tethered by a nylon spider web that eased his once adrenaline ridden body softly downward, he waited for the feared echo of gunfire that would bounce back from the chute's canopy. But there was no sound save the soft ruffle of the air against the woven cloth.

Close to the ground now, Anderson's premonitional ability ripped the message of the landing loudly through his being. Instantly his feet felt the welcomed increase in gravity as his body settled onto the earth. It was no more than luck that kept him out of the trees or worse. In the darkness he only knew approximately where he was. He had not side slipped through the air on decent; he had to trust the ability of the pilot and navigator when they switched the light to go.

Anderson pulled the quick releases on the chute, letting the wind settle it indifferently to the ground. It was three AM, and the black nylon of the chute was still imperceptible in the hot, humid, Southeast Asian night. He pulled the chute toward him and rolled it over and over around his forearms. His hand found the last of it, and he knelt on the parachute while he hit the harnesses' chest release. He fought it over and off his shoulders, then let it slip to the ground used, thanked, and soon to be discarded forever.

He untied the rifle and then maneuvered the pack onto his shoulders in similar fashion to the chute earlier. He picked up the rifle and parachute and walked quickly in search of cover. The jungle had to be close in any direction. Securing himself and his equipment before first light was paramount. If his position were as planned, northeast would be the direction of choice. He checked the compass and began walking under the heavy load. The feeling of the damp air was welcome. Moisture laden grass pulled at his boots, resisting his progress. Anderson felt good. He always felt good after successfully falling out of the sky and landing on his feet untouched but for the ride, the spectacular ride through the abyss. Arrive alive, the lasting criteria.

Anderson found dense cover after only two hundred yards of slogging in the wet soil. The ground was higher and the vegetation lush. He penetrated it to a safe distance, and after caching the chute and oxygen bottle, let himself relax in what remained of darkness. He was wet to the knees from the heavy dew on the tall grass and wet from his crotch up to his armpits with sweat from the exertion and humidity.

Fantasies of Angela mixed with thoughts of David accompanied his slumber as unconsciousness overcame him and sleep renewed his body for the morrow.

The bus continued on, bouncing and jarring its occupants for hours as it made its way toward Fort Polk, Louisiana. His life changing radically and his emotions numb, Anderson's mind slipped back to the small mountainous area where the three of them had been born and had grown up. Anderson recalled the first time David had spoken of Monica as they rode through the Canyon.

David had grown into a dichotomy of self. He was at once both immensely dedicated to goals and yet dedicated to nothing of any real importance. Dedication to David had always meant getting his own way, of being the center of the universe. The fact is: he was. When David was there, there was no one else. He was larger than life itself. His personality was overpowering: humorous, courageous, insensitive, generous, greedy. Inconsistency was David's forte.

Anderson watched David look at the field. The expression in David's eyes said it all. It wasn't the words that were moving, it was the change of tone in his voice, the sensitivity of the body English that made Anderson know what David meant and how he felt. It was also the awareness by Anderson of a complete change in the attitude of a lifetime.

Yes, David had indeed changed that summer. The mischievous merchant of good times had succumbed to the fairer sex. Anderson had been changed also. The love of his youth had dismissed him like some plaything she had picked up to dispel the boredom of her high school years. Just four months before their vows were to be taken, she had asked him to come to the college campus to pick her up, the college he had been forced to drop out of for lack of funds. She "wanted to talk" she had said. In fact, she had said little as they rode the long miles back home.

He drove past her sister's house to a field near the end of a dirt road. It was a quiet place with the privacy of birch stands at one end. The moon was full, and he could see the shine of her red hair. A winter chill remained in the air. She was bundled in a long coat with a color to which he had never managed to put a name.

She was silent. Anderson looked at her hands. His long standing fascination with her hands played on his mind as he watched her ball them up in her lap. The fingers curved upward; the pads at the end of each finger were large, much more so than his. The middle finger on her right hand sported the familiar bump from too much writing with school pencils. It was not a pretty sight to most, but to Anderson it was beautiful. Everything about her was beautiful to Anderson. He felt uneasy somehow. He knew of nothing wrong and did not want to ponder any such thing either, but she was not acting her usual self. She was generally affectionate: touching, smiling, and acting like someone who is young and caught up in the extraordinary emotions of new love. But tonight she was distant, nervous, thoughtful.

As the moments dragged on, Anderson become more worried and finally broke the silence.

"Finished the invitations? I can help if you like, but my writing is not so spectacular. I know it's tough for you with college classes in full swing."

"I need to tell you something." Her voice broke the awful silence of her being. She toyed with the diamond he had given her and then began to extract it from her finger.

Anderson's stomach turned over, grabbed at him unexpectedly like snakes grinding and twisting in his gut, forcing his whole body to move. He felt the worst coming before it ever completely reached his consciousness. He found it difficult to speak or to swallow his own saliva. He had felt like this only once before, when he saw his mother's eyes and knew that his father was dead.

"What's the matter, something wrong?" He heard himself say with great difficulty.

Her head was down, her eyes on the ring in front of her, her attitude apologetic and obsequious.

"I am giving the ring back. I don't want to see you anymore."

She laid the ring in the palm of his hand.

His mind reeled. He reached for a reaction with some sort of reason, with calm. But his essence was hysteria. He tried to get hold of his emotions. He stared up at the moon, bright, a globe, and tried to nail his concentration to it. He could feel his throat tighten and tears well in his eyes. Anderson's throat and jaw were in pain as he fought to control his emotions. He could feel pressure build in his head as he fought to control his body as well. He knew she could see his pounding temple. He wanted to run.

Instead, he started the late model Oldsmobile, put it in reverse, and backed out onto the farm road. He looked straight ahead as he drove toward the main highway. He could not bear to look at her. His only thought was to control himself - or better, to escape the situation altogether. It was the battle of his young life. He did not speak even as he pulled the car up in front of her older sister's house. He opened the door and walked around the front of the car. Even as he opened the door for her, he could not look into her eyes. He knew that if he did, something even more terrible would happen. If he hid maybe this would go away.

She stepped out onto the moist grass of the parkway and turned to him, the slight sound of coming frost rising to his ears. Snow on the north side of the house glistened, reflecting the yellow gleam of the moon and accentuating the silence of the night. Still he could not face her. It was only when she began to speak that he finally raised his head and looked into her eyes. She seemed so sincere, without any intent to hurt him. But it only hurt worse to see her this way. She was saying with love that she didn't love him. He was a throw away, good practice for the real thing, and the real thing was elsewhere.

"We can still be friends, can't we?" She urged.

His emotions changed abruptly. It was anger, an anger he had never felt before. This was an emotion he could deal with. How could she say that? Everything had been a lie!

"Friends?" he heard himself say, his voice rising even as he finished the word. "No we can't remain friends as you call it. In fact, you'll never set eyes on me again!"

He turned and started back around the front of the Oldsmobile not realizing that what he had said would really be true. As he drove away, his mind and body rocked to the pangs of adrenaline surging through his veins and hurt flooding his emotions. He was betrayed. His vision blurred and he nearly drove off the road. He passed by Sugarhouse Park on the way to his tiny apartment. Almost involuntarily, the Olds came to a stop. He opened the door and moved to the edge a small pond. The ring was still in his hand. He watched as light caught and flickered on the twirling ring, arching high above him. The pond was calm, like glass, and the sudden eruption of its surface sent circular rivulets expanding ever outward. He turned and walked away. He felt his life was over.

The days, weeks, months, and years that followed were hell for Anderson. Incessant dreams of her haunted his sleep. Anderson knew that he was obsessed more than others. He knew that he had to hang on to sanity. Sanity became not a gift but something to be worked for with his whole being. He could not have known then how the next few years would take their toll. The Melrose bottle became a familiar friend, bars his sanctuary, and the street his battle ground where he fought to stay together, whole, to not let everything go, to dream the better dream. As each day began, he waited for her to return, to announce that some mistake had occurred. She never did. Now he simply waited for each day to end.

He had been quiet as David drove the few miles back toward the field. David was only too familiar with Anderson's problem, and had, in his own way, tried to comfort him on occasion. David loved Anderson, he thought sometimes more than David loved his brothers. But David approached the subject with logic, with answers of how he ought to view the affair, and with how he ought to look to the future. Anderson knew that David wanted to speak the words that would heal him, but these were not them. David seemed to feel this and, for the most part, usually said nothing.

Anderson often felt that he and David shared every emotion until now. He knew that David could not really feel his pain. Anderson had thought about Monica. He knew more about her now than he had known in high school. He had only hours ago met her again, but he had felt in his heart that she was not capable of hurting David. No, he was more afraid for Monica.

He had seen clearly the way she looked at David. He had searched his brain for a memory, that look for himself? He had realized, as they left the farmhouse and climbed to the main road, that he had never gotten such a look. How was it that he had missed it? He had realized then that Sarah had never really loved him at all. He felt worse than he ever had over the last three years. While he had always, in the past, believed that she did love him, he had always, in the back of his mind, wondered if that were true. How could she have just walked away from him? Even when she had married not long after the date that Anderson and she were to be married, it never really satisfied him to think that she had not loved him, until now. Not until he had seen how Monica looked at David, not until he had seen her eyes.

CHAPTER ELEVEN

Unspeakable heat from somewhere annoyed his escape from reality. He opened his eyes slowly to find a single ray of sunlight penetrating the three canopy jungle. How it had chosen to land squarely on his face could only be attributed to the gods of chance. He blinked and shuffled his position slightly, freeing himself from the hot, yellow fire of the sun. He began to let his surroundings sink into his brain. The overpowering vision of strange vegetation was everywhere. The stimulation of solitary green, the color of pea soup, closed in around him. He shut his eyes tightly, breathed deeply, and pulled himself noiselessly to an upright sitting position. He sat, staring at the broad leaves laden with clear droplets. The ground below him was damp, his clothes still saturated with moisture from the night.

From his pack he extracted a long plastic tube, untied the top, and reached inside. His fingers felt the hard smooth surface of the rock hard candy. He laid it on his tongue and began to roll it in his mouth. The hint of sweetness flowed toward his throat, refreshing even his attitude. He pulled the water flask from the pack and added a portion of it to the contents of the plastic tube. Small, dead fish swam among kernels of instant rice, staring back at their dinner guest with beady little eyes stuck in the heads that the Okinawans, who prepared the rations, left attached to the bodies. Freeze dried vegetables competed with the fish for space. Anderson's breakfast, lunch, and dinner would soon be ready.

He stood and tried to recognize his location. He had to stick to the safety of cover. Another guess must be taken. If his premonitions remained correct, he would find higher ground farther to the northeast. He slung the gear to his shoulders and looked for an opening in the jungle. He checked the compass suspended from the beaded metal necklace, then slowly made his way through the growth. Though the harness of the jungle impeded his progress, he felt more at home. The primitive environment was sanctuary to his soul.

The Hong Cong made camouflaged jungle fatigues were soaking wet from exertion and dew by the time he reached higher ground. The premise of success now rested on Anderson finding out where in the hell he was. He circled the small hill, locating openings through the trees that afforded him glimpses of the surrounding forest top and azure blue sky. In time he found what he was looking for: the peculiar limestone rock formations that jutted almost egotistically up through and above the forest roof. He placed a map of the area on the organic matter that had accumulated on the jungle floor and removed the compass from around his neck. He oriented the map to north using the compass and back triangulated the azimuth of each limestone finger.

His position now known, he proceeded to what would be his base of operation. Though it was not a direct route to his goal, sticking to the ridge of the hill made going easier. By noon Anderson was in position and had cached his main pack. This accomplished, he was eager to complete phases two and three scheduled for this day. Anderson moved quietly through the jungle toward the compound. At the halfway point, he carefully hid the M53 submachine gun.

Anderson knew that success, and his life, depended on being careful, and on the predator that was so much a part of him. North Regulars ran the compound, but it was the locals that he had to fear. Like faithful watchdogs, the indigenous little bastards could pick up a single molecule of an American's scent wafting in the air. Years spent living in the jungle had given them incredible abilities. Their senses of hearing and smell could not be underestimated.

He was a klick from the border. The target was another klick beyond that. He cut west for one hundred yards and found a small area into which he could crawl. It opened into a ten by ten clear space large enough for him to stand, hidden from view of any angle. He removed his clothes and found the small flask of water. He carefully washed under his arms, his neck and face, and his genitals. With a small handkerchief, Anderson dried the best he could, wringing out the small cloth frequently. He carried, in the bloused pockets of his jungle fatigues, a bag of cornstarch and a plastic bottle of unscented deodorant. The cornstarch went between his legs to ward off the terrible chafing he always got in this climate. The deodorant helped keep his American odor in check.

When Anderson finished dressing, he carefully placed the pant legs of the fatigues in his boots, drew olive-drab, shock cord around the cuff of his shirt sleeves at the wrist, and buttoned his collar tightly at his throat. The only exposed flesh were his face and hands. From his pants pocket, he retrieved a flat dish, opened it and with his right index finger began to put the charcoal based substance on his left hand and then his face. He drew lines with the viscous mud to cover the broad surfaces of his face, nose, and ears.

Anderson reached for his case from which the bandages had now been removed. From it he withdrew an eighteen inch long by three eighths inch diameter rod. The end had been flattened and sharpened. At the edge of the clearing he began to dig a small hole, placing the excavated earth next to the opening carefully. When it was approximately eight inches deep, he proceeded to dig five more just like the first. He knelt and urinated into the first and quickly filled in the hole with the dirt piled near it. Soon, he knew, he would be wringing bloody liquid from his socks into the hole. Leeches would pull the stuff from his body, the rancid odor of the dying cells pungent to the indigs in the sweltering heat.

Normally he enjoyed animals and birds and tolerated insects to a degree, though in the jungle they badgered him endlessly. But now they could spell his end. Animals and birds could give his presence away to a passing patrol or to the camp with their squawking and taking flight. The insects gnawed and sucked, creating festering, bloody sores that could be smelled.

Anderson made his way out of the shelter and back to the small trail he had used earlier. As he cautiously moved back along the trail, he kept his eyes and nose alert for something he needed. But he was not successful by the time he reached the spot where he had first taken the detour. Anderson took the time to cover the area that exposed the trail to the shelter. When he finished, Anderson moved on toward the border. He stopped where he determined the border to be and rested for a short time.

Just a few steps and Anderson would be in North Vietnam, Land of Ho, and just beyond, the old man's trail. He knew the area not far to the North of his present position well. He had led commando teams over it and to the trail many times, times of fear, and sweat, and exhilaration. But he preferred by far to be alone.

And then he smelled it ... Water Buffalo.

He followed the scent until he came to a clearing about one hundred yards across. Anderson was elated to find the sweet, but strong smelling, gruel near the jungle's edge. From yet another pocket, Anderson withdrew three, eight inch pieces of tightly netted cloth. He piled the dung in the center of each, pulled the corners together, and tied them with a string. He tied two of them to the back of his boots and one around and just above the rear of his knee. His scent now partially disguised, Anderson was soon on the trail moving toward the compound again. It took him only thirty minutes to reach it. He approached carefully, checking the wind as he went. At fifty yards he lay flat and began to crawl.

It took another thirty minutes to advance to the clearing's edge, and when he did, he was at last able to see the compound for the first time. It felt familiar, very familiar. The hours spent studying the aerial views had paid off. It was four in the afternoon, and Anderson got busy. From the case, he extracted the rod he had used earlier, along with another. The latter had a bearing at its top end and was threaded at the other. He screwed the two together. Inside his case, he found a small ribbon of cloth, camouflaged to match the tan grass prevalent in the field shared by the North Regular's camp. Again he began to crawl, this time into the field. When he was twenty yards out, he planted the rod in the earth and set the small weather vane looking device on top, from which he hung the ribbon. This done, he turned and crawled back to the shelter of the jungle.

From the tree he had picked, the wind flag was now visible only an inch above the long grass except along the path over which he had crawled. Working from a laying position, Anderson pulled a third short rod from the case. This he threaded into the tree twenty inches above the ground. At its free end, he attached a short piece of blackened aluminum bar. At one end rested a small, flat piece of leather, and at the other a V notched piece of the same material held fast to similar pieces of flat black aluminum plate. Anderson located the cornstarch and covered each with the powdery substance. He pulled the custom made rifle from the case and placed it on the two leather pads. The rifle's flat fore end settled on the leather, and the rear of the modified stock fit snugly in the V notch at the rear. Anderson slid the rifle back and forth carefully to ensure that it was settled and that it moved freely. The case held yet another piece of equipment. This he clipped to the rod to the right of the rifle. He opened the lid of the wooden block exposing fifteen rounds of the wildcat cartridge. The head of the case was exposed to the afternoon sun while the projectile rested safely within the protective shelter of the pre-drilled wooden block.

Anderson scooted under the device and locked his elbows with his knees. The rifle rested untouched by him. He placed his head alongside the stock and took hold of the rifle's grip-less body. The view through the thirty two power scope appeared immediately, and he set the parallax for four hundred and fifty yards. A slight movement of his hand on the rear bag and the elevation of the rifle increased. A slight push forward and the rifle's point of aim lowered slightly. Pushing the rear of the stock from right to left pivoted the rifle horizontally. He was nearly ready.

Man is the ultimate predator, and Anderson was a master predator of the old tradition. The target would be taken as it had to be. It was neither sport nor blood lust. Predation was his nature like that of all other men. Since time began for man, it was their way, and it was his. Anderson subscribed to the action, letting it ride in his being like a part of him. Suppressing it was hypocrisy.

He set about his task. Notes had to be taken and studied. It was five in the afternoon. A quick traverse of the compound through the scope indicated that no changes had been made to its layout. The command post was situated in the center and faced Anderson. From the doorway at his view, he could monitor the movement to and from this nerve center. To his right, slightly south, were the troop's barracks, and just to the north, the training area. To his right were several smaller bamboo structures that appeared to be less than five feet tall. In front of them were slight humps in the ground over which appeared to be a structure much like the hoist above a well. It did not take long for Anderson to confirm what they were as he watched a young man dressed only in a pakima advance to the edge of one of them and throw food down into it.

He watched the tiny shacks for some time until two men appeared at the door. One of them had a grip on the other and began marching him forward to the pit in front of them. They were both

Caucasians. When they reached the second pit, the man in control yelled to one of the Regulars. The brown skinned man turned and trotted toward them. As he reached the two, the man directed him to action by rolling his hand. The Regular began to turn a crank situated at one side of the derrick. Within seconds a cage appeared from out of the ground. Constructed of large bamboo poles, the small enclosure began to turn freely on its axis once it cleared the pit. A guard opened the door and thrust the smaller of the two men inside. Unceremoniously, the contraption was lowered into place again.

Anderson watched the men retreat, one much larger than the other and with a characteristic walk. Though it was now too late in the day to see with much clarity, Anderson knew who it was. He could not mistake the practiced choreography of the man who exuded ego even in his physical movements: Deliberate, contemptuous.

Anderson removed the rifle and placed it back in the case, but he left the wind flag to flutter and switch in the changing afternoon air. He pulled vegetation over the rest to reduce detection, maneuvered the harness of the case over his shoulders, and began to crawl back the way he had come. He raised his body to a crouch when he reached the fifty yard point. Though he still proceeded cautiously, he could cover more ground now. He stopped at the hide on the way back and relieved himself again, carefully and quickly covering the deed with the moist earth of the jungle floor. He rubbed the dung on his pants where the insect's bloody prints were already beginning to show. He knew it would draw more of the infernal little bastards to him.

Anderson noted the Madsen M53's location as he passed, keeping the spot firmly in mind. He moved on and was at the main cache site just after dark. The time was 1830 hours. He opened another of the Okinawan long range reconnaissance patrol rations, added water, and lay back waiting for the brittle morsels to assume the familiar, distasteful mess that it was. He saved the hard tack candy for another time. While he dined on the mummified remains of fish and rice, he tried to keep his mind focused on the mission. He knew something was wrong. What was missing? He felt he was being played, but what was the scam? As much he as disliked Colonel Langlinais' bravado and staged environments, he believed him to be an honorable man. He dismissed the idea and turned his attention to Colonel Langlinais' second in command.

Major Elliot McCauley was normally a quiet man with a medium build and a steely blue-eyed resemblance to a security boss Anderson once worked for. He hadn't trusted that guy either. McCauley never tired of being the Colonel's shadow, or so it seemed. Self-effacing to the point of obsequiousness when in Langlinais' presence, he changed to 'the man in charge, the tyrant' when he wasn't. Played to the point of straight backed absurdity, McCauley danced around giving orders that seemed to emanate from his puffed up chest. Fascinated, Anderson had watched the Major on the few occasions he had had the opportunity, watched as the Major's eyes flicked to the Colonel's for direction, caught and tried with desperation to hold the Colonel's eyes for praise and acceptance like a child to his father when the child attempted something new. Beads of sweat formed on the Major's forehead when he thought the Colonel disliked something the Major had said or done.

No, it just didn't fit. The hair stood up on the back of Anderson's neck. A movement to his right. He watched carefully, every sense adrenaline driven. Nothing.

There, there it was again, low to the ground moving from Anderson's right through the dense jungle. The Madsen M53 was on the trail and the rifle cased. He had made an error. He didn't make many, and now he cursed his own over confidence. It was late and difficult to see as the sun had already dipped below the hills. Suddenly a fleck of gold passed through a small opening. He strained to see and hear. The evening shadows played tricks on him. Suddenly, there it was: the huge cat stopped in a clearing and surveyed his territory. Anderson was stone, his camouflage blending in with the background. The cat was at ease, yawning, his jaws opening widely, huge teeth uncovered as the cat's head stretched high. He lowered his head finally and looked at the ground as though in lazy contemplation. His left hind leg bent under his right as he lowered his hind quarters to the jungle floor with a bouncing thump. He walked his front paws forward a few inches at a time until he was laying on his chest with his paws spread wide.

The cat panted heavily in the sultry heat. Anderson did not blink. After several minutes the cat rose and walked lazily, seemingly bored, to the opposite end of the clearing. He stopped, surveyed the area again, and then jumped into a large tree near where he had stood. Anderson reached for the case, withdrew the rifle, carefully, slowly, and put the scope on the cat. He watched the animal's claws dig into the flesh of the tree as he approached a V formed by two branches. There lay the feline's recent kill. The cat crouched over it and began to feed. Anderson saw clearly the black spots on the cat's golden hide move as the defined muscles underneath flexed powerfully, ripping chunks of bloody flesh from the slain deer. He was adaptable, resilient, at peace ... the leopard.

Anderson moved slowly, imperceptibly to a more comfortable position facing the cat. He draped the rifle across his legs and thought of Angela standing naked in the early morning light in the Opera Hotel, the blinds painting her body with black and golden hues that reminded him of this beautiful cat. He let his eyes fall to the rifle, suddenly aware of his use of it for protection against the leopard being so similar to his first desire for protection when he looked at the girl. His acute desire to live for her would in turn increase the probability of his own demise.

The first day's tasks were complete and Anderson needed sleep. The cat disappeared with the darkness. Filled with confusing dreams of the girl in the Opera Hotel and the fantasies of his early years in the mountains of his birth, Anderson's night dragged on. He thought of David's arrival in country.

CHAPTER TWELVE

It was nearly 0900 when David reached the chain link fence. He drove the car into a grove of trees a hundred yards from it. He pulled on a Marlboro and thought once again about what the next few hours would bring. What the hell, he thought, no better time than the present. David looked in each direction and made a break for the fence. He tossed the AWOL bag over and followed it. He raced to the chopper. Damn, the door was locked. Apparently Anderson hadn't thought of everything.

Anderson had driven him by the enclosure three days earlier. He had told David about his observations over several weeks of passing along this road earlier in the year.

"Slow down. This is it. These choppers were brought in here a few months ago. Uncle Sam gave them to the Thai's, but they don't have a pilot who knows how to drive the damn things. I know they're fueled because I saw them doing it myself."

"That model is packed with electronic goodies, but I'll bet my bush pilot's ass they're layin' light."

"What are you saying?", Anderson asked.

"I'm saying there ain't no bang, bangs on board."

"Listen Dave, we don't need it. You'll be coming from the friendly side. You're not in this war, and I don't want you in it. You got that?"

David's back straightened, his chest puffed, and his head moved back. He peered down at Anderson through those mischievous eyes in his characteristic way. "Jeez, cuz, just an observation. I don't personally give a shit anyway. The assholes have to catch me to wax me. Would you just settle down and let me run down my end of this trail?"

"I know you, you sumbitch. We ain't fishin' for trout under a culvert with our hands anymore or trying to get a look under a girl's skirt with bullshit stories or buy Melrose in a whore house at fifteen. This is serious shit. I know you can't handle authority, and I'm not trying to dish any out. I'm asking for your help. This is my turf. Be smart and listen." David stared at him. Daggers traveled the short distance across the front seat of the rented car. "Asshole," David mumbled, turning to look again at the choppers all lined up like sleeping dragon flies.

"Alright, alright, give me your pitch. Am I just supposed to crawl over the fence and steal one of these iron birds?" David asked.

"Simple huh." Anderson retorted.

They made their way toward Lop Buri but turned off from the highway that led back to Bangkok.

"I've got to take care of something and now is the only chance I'll have. Pull off the road up ahead there." Anderson pointed to an opening next to the dirt road. David stopped the vehicle as Anderson reached for the duffel bag he had brought with them. From it he extracted the black bag to which were attached shoulder and waist straps and then walked to a nearby tree while David watched with idle curiosity. He carefully withdrew the bag's contents and laid them on the ground.

"What in the name of Sam Hell is that thing?" asked David.

"Pretty spooky, eh?"

"Is that a rifle or what?"

"I think I'd call it more of an instrument, ole buddy."

"So what the hell does it do?"

"Well, I believe it shoots dead ass zero at 450 yards, and I'm about to see if I'm still right. There's a spotting scope in the duffel; set it up and get it on that tree out there. Stay here. I'm going to step it off. I think it's about 450."

It's the same old shit, thought David, as he set the scope up and moved it toward the tree. Ole cuz just can't seem to shake his fascination with bizarre rifles. As he watched Anderson prod his way back, he noted the plush grasses and the rice paddies beyond. He had no idea what the plants were nor the bird that suddenly fluttered across his view, settling on a hump in the field some thirty yards away. He could see red flowers behind Anderson, discrete dots in a sea of green that kept appearing and then disappearing from his vision like the spots that plagued the backs of his eyeballs after a night with the Muscatel bottle into which had been poured a half pint of Everclear. He drew on the cigarette, shook the mesmerizing hold this strange land had on him, and returned his attention to his cousin.

"445. That's close enough. Spot me. Do you see the white mark I made in the bark?" Anderson directed.

"Yeah, I got it."

Anderson made ready. It was nearing 10:00 AM. The winds were light, blowing from right to left. Mirage was just becoming perceptible in the morning heat. Anderson watched intently. The rifle barked. Three seconds and the rifle barked again.

"So?" asked Anderson as he peered at David.

"Dead nuts, both shots. Can we go now?"

As they rode back toward Bangkok, David was curious.

"What's with this Hanoi Jane? You seem to have a real case of the ass about her."

Anderson thoughts turned to fire as they always did at the mention of her name.

"Look David, people don't really understand what some of these guys go through and what they continue to go through. People don't understand what facing an unknown enemy under these circumstances can be: a strange land filled with death, strange people, strange customs, and situations that you can't comprehend or control.

"You've got to endure and survive. So you develop an edge. Think of an edge as a psychological positioning that allows you to do what you would not do under normal circumstances. If your edge gets dull, your chances for survival are greatly reduced. People don't understand this concept, how the soldier keeps the edge honed: you've got to believe fiercely that what you're doing is right; you've got to believe that your fellow Americans stand behind you 100 percent; you've got to know they are willing to take the risks. If you don't hold this belief deeply and without reservation, you can't conduct yourself as you must, and do the job that you must, and survive as you must."

"Yeah, but what's that got to do with her?"

"OK, look, as long as a soldier is in Southeast Asia, keeping an edge is possible because he is insulated from the changes taking place back home. The war doesn't have to make sense if no one tries to make sense of it. With self-doubt about the war, he can't react properly to help ensure his or his buddy's survival.

"Hell, we all know there is some sort of movement against the war, a national movement within the borders of our own country, within the borders of a nation free to follow constitutional law protecting our rights for self-protection, for freedom of religion, for freedom of speech, for freedom to protest, the very reasons for which any soldier believes he faces the unknown and fights an enemy he can't see.

"But, man, it is emotionally devastating for an American soldier sitting in the jungle, secure in his belief that he can endure, that he can survive because he has the edge, to hear the voice, feel the breath, smell the scent of a beautiful American woman floating through the misty morning vegetation, surrounding him with repudiation, reprimand, doubt, and insult.

"Part of the American soldier's very essence was the Fonda family, and Henry was part of them. Fonda's young daughter, Jane, continued in his fine tradition to give us pleasure and entertainment as her beauty shone on the huge screen portraying American life, her features, movements, and speech an uncanny reflection of her father.

"But now try to think of that soldier as he sits, his body, his clothes, his equipment wet in the humid surroundings. The voice of her sings out from North Vietnam, from amidst the enemy. Man, you've got to know that his brain whirls with confusion and conflict. His edge dulls; he lets down his defenses; his chances for survival are jeopardized because he hesitates, tries to decide. In fact, many of them are doomed because of it, and they don't even know why. Most of them are young, barely out of high school. They don't give a shit about purpose, cause, or any of it. They're barely holding on as it is, pot, cocaine, their only relief. The only reason they keep going is because they don't know what the hell else to do. A little peer pressure and a whole lot of survival instinct is all they can hold on to.

"It's a terrible American legacy and won't be forgiven by most who serve, who understand, and whose buddies gave their lives the next day or the next week because of her, because she brought about the decay of resolve, the hesitation and restraint of young reflexes, instilled self-doubt, and stole the vital second it takes to react and live. There's no time for questions here, only reactions. That's not to mention what she has done to the POW's.

"America should respect and take with utmost seriousness the feelings and actions of those who serve our nation with patriotism, self-sacrifice, and love for their country as well as those who were caught up in it through nothing more than chance or stupidity.

"Damn it, David, young guys, seventeen to twenty years old, sit in the jungle, not old enough to vote for their president, or to drink legally, yet old enough to sacrifice their lives for him and for the country. These guys remember the soft, feminine voice that strikes out at them in insult from the north. Some will die because of her. I don't see our country there beside these guys, supporting them anymore. I don't see her there beside them fighting. She is a coward.

"A hell of a lot of guys have given their lives, their legs, and their arms for her right to do what she did," Anderson was nearly screaming. "God save us all if they infer sanction on her actions later on, but I know damn well they will. Shit, sacrificed to protect our constitution, our right to protect ourselves, our right to freedom of speech and protest, and then..."

"OK, OK, I get the picture. Jeez, don't trance out on me. I'm sorry I asked."

"No, man, she took the wrong path to protest. She could have gone to the South to push her dirt or better still, the Alamo; that would have been bad enough. But to go to the North? No, she's a traitor, or just plain dumb. Nonetheless, she was giving comfort and aid to the enemy. What else can I say?"

Anderson paused, his emotions vented for the time being. Drained, he spoke again, softly.

"Shit, David, I'm no sniper."

"No, a hunter," David said.

"But he's American."

"No, a traitor. Look, cuz, you're not doing anything a hundred other guys didn't have to do in the Civil War, or in a dozen other wars. Don't sweat it. It's OK."

They rode on in silence for a few minutes. Then David asked, "What power scope you got on that instrument as you call it?"

"Thirty two," Anderson replied. "Why?"

"Too bad. With a lower power you wouldn't see his eyes when you wasted his ass."

CHAPTER THIRTEEN

Anderson never tired of roaming the streets of Bangkok. The city teemed with sights and sounds and smells that were forever new to him. Buddhas appeared in unlikely places, the golden pledges stuck solid to their great stone bellies. The edges of these tiny, thin, gold squares fluttered in the breeze. More and more were pressed thumb tight into the pores and crevasses until, over the years, the Buddha was metamorphosed into the elegance of a jeweled Gargantua. Temples complemented the common streets and forbidden hideaways alike. Graceful, falling, flowing roof lines spoke of ancient ways and societies that remained a secret to all but the few. Beautiful women were adorned in silk and hats that pointed to the heavens. Sedate, demure, and mysterious, they danced to musical octaves that were as strange and haunting and beautiful to him as the undulations of their sensuous choreography.

Everywhere there lurked a deal. It was said that Bangkok had it all. If there was a desire within you whether material, sinful, lustful, or larcenous, it was there for you or it was nowhere.

Anderson watched the city speed by as the car flew through the now familiar city, honking its horn to gain the right of way. The Opera Hotel came into view on their left, and as they passed it he thought of the girl. Should he tell David? She seemed now a passing in the night, the vision in a thousand fantasies. David should know because David was he, and because he told Anderson of Monica in his secret way, his soul exposed, vulnerable. He decided to wait until there was closure to their purpose. Selfish, self-protection.

The pair pulled up to Bill Baedeker's Cellar Bar. Bill was an ex-Navy SEAL with several tours in 'Nam under his belt. He didn't dislike the States, but he had fallen in love with the orient and with a woman who was helping him make his way with the Cellar. Bill was a husky incarnation of the perfect-Italian-gentleman-roughneck, but he wore jeans and a tee shirt when he could get away with it.

The Cellar was the hangout for "Green Berets" stationed anywhere inside the Asian Campaign. You could be assured that whether they wore their colors or not, they were part of the brotherhood. And so too was Bobby, the Siamese woman who took the best of care of these young men for the ring of a couple of quarters lazily spinning and singing their way to the silence and stillness of bright buttons laying on the mahogany bar. Bobby took her man's hand and, head bowed in the characteristic politeness of the Thai's, led him to the men's room and to the enchantment of the fifty cent head job. Spitting and coughing into the ashtray, she drowned out the intermittent lyrics of songs that wafted through the streets of one of the oldest of cities, practicing one of the oldest of means.

"Hey, Anderson, how goes it!" Bill called out as the two entered.

"Hello, Bill. This is my cousin David. You'd never believe me if I told you what he's doing here."

"You think it over while I get you a Chevis. What for you, cuz?"

"Crown. Is there anything else?"

Anderson exchanged the small talk that constituted one of the few reliable taps into the network that flowed throughout Southeast Asia serving the grapevine.

"How's old Carolina's wound healing? Heard you were with him when he got it."

"I donno." Anderson replied. "Haven't seen him in a while."

"I understand he had $10,000 on his head. What happened anyway?"

Anderson resurrected the story about Carolina. A rough and tumble character from the South, Carolina was a forty five year old Platoon Sergeant who refused to return stateside. He grinned and drank on when the subject of the amount levied against him by the Cong was broached. As Anderson recalled, they had been talking about it when it happened.

"Carolina was sitting in our team's small mess. We had strung wire netting above the louvered boards to keep the air flowing but the mosquitoes out. He was leaning back in the chair and resting his shoulders against the netting. I noticed someone outside walking parallel to the wall. When the guy got even with Caro, he turned, lifted something shiny over his head, and plunged. I was half drunk, and the whole thing seemed to move in slow motion. Next thing I know, old Caro had about three inches of bloody sword sticking out of the center of his chest. He was three sheets to the wind also and just stared at the thing. He finally looked up and told me maybe I ought to do something to keep 'ole Caro' from kickin' the bucket.

"Now ain't that the damnedest thing ya ever seen?" he said, a faint, sardonic, pitiful smile in his eyes.

"I asked him what the hell I was supposed to do? He told me that pullin' the goddamn thing out might be a good start. I ran outside the door. Man, it looked weird sticking out of the wire netting like that. The thing had a long handle with string wrapped around it. I had to heave it over my head to get it out. When I got back through the door and over to Caro, he was still just sitting there. I grabbed him and hauled him out to an Army ambulance we had in the camp. I got him in the cab, and we high tailed it to the dispensary to get my bag. I stripped off his shirt, stuck a thoracentesis needle in his mid-back, and filled it with blood a couple of times; each time it ran all over the seat when I opened the spigot. I smeared Vaseline over the wound, slapped plastic bags over it, and taped it down.

"I headed for the Malaysian border to a hospital they have there. I didn't think we'd make it. Fact was, I didn't. About three quarters of the way there, the adrenaline wore off and the booze got to me. Caro had to take over. I evacuated more blood, replaced the plastic bandage I'd put on him, and let him take the wheel. The tough son-of-a-bitch drove himself the rest of the way."

Anderson dragged deeply on an L&M. "Anyway, that was a long time ago. Right now I need your help."

"What's the problem senator?"

"I think some shit's going down. I think I might be the pigeon. What do you know about Colonel Langlinais?"

"Nothing much. If anybody's clean, he is. He'd sure as hell have turned off the bullshit if he's not."

"How about his flunky, the Major?" Anderson asked.

"Can't say, but I do know he spends one hell of a lot of time in here with those boys from Kanchanaburi," Bill responded. "You spent some time up there with the Karen's too didn't you?"

"Yeah. Shit. There's American justice for ya. I don't know what's worse, Air America or that bitch on the radio. Listen, Angela's at the Opera. Can you get word to her for me? Dave and I are headed over there in a few minutes, but I might miss her. Tell her I'm standin' ten. Let her know I'm on her six like hair on a beaver. But on a more serious side."

"What's this shit?" David's ears were moving up over his head, ready to clash when they met.

"Whaaaaat?"

"The squeeze, who's the squeeze? Come on cuz, give me the lowdown."

Anderson stopped. He asked himself about the hard ass attitude he had about the girl. But he needn't ask. Fear was the answer. Fear of putting his feelings on the table. Fear of getting in over his head, of dulling the edge. He was up against it. He had two choices: fight the emotions he was not allowed, or let it all hang out to the man who deserved to share his vulnerability.

Not yet.

"Hang it for a while, bubba. Back to the job at hand. Bill, can you line up a small wooden crate about one by two by six feet for me and stash it at Bobby's place for a few days?"

"Sure. What else?" Bill answered.

"Well, that's the hard part. Here's what I need you to do..."

The Major glared at Colonel Langlinais and paced the room, his finger in his nose scratching the interior, a constant and disconcerting habit he fell into when he was agitated.

"You let him go back to the States, gave him nineteen thousand dollars? What the hell for? Is that some kind of coonass strategy you didn't bother to tell me about?"

"Hold your temper, Elliot, and listen to me. We've gone over this before. He's your pick in any case. There's no one else in country, no snipers. We can't conscript one from Vietnam or the States, can't afford for anyone else to know. If we have chosen this method, then we, by default, have also put ourselves in a risky position: the shot must be just that, one shot. There's no chance for more and no chance for a repeat later. This kid is confident of his skills. And he's a survivor; it's in his eyes. The problem you didn't bother yourself to become familiar with is that his considerable skills are tied in with some kind of specialized equipment." The Colonel paused a moment. "Is there something sacred about the timing? Are sixteen days outside some window of opportunity that I don't know about?"

"No, no. It just seems an unusual thing to do." The Major left it at that and sat down, wishing he had kept his mouth shut. The sudden excitement combined with the insufferable humidity had drenched his fatigues, causing them to stick to his body, and he tugged at the shoulders to relieve the tightness. He sat silent, his mind reaching for any part of his plan that might be compromised by this unforeseen stupidity, any changes that had to be made, any losses that might result. Fear and anger had made their way to his hands. He glanced at them, saw the mild tremor, and placed them on his knees. He thought about the scotch in the Colonel's bar.

CHAPTER FOURTEEN

At the Opera Hotel Anderson grilled David through the night and into the early morning hours going over the route. He continued to convince himself that David's knowledge of running the bush and his bravado would carry him through.

Anderson inquired about the girl and, although they had learned that she was still in country, she was not expected to return to the Opera for a couple of days. David kept up his jabs about the relationship, frowning when Anderson stood his ground, promising to continue the discussion when they made it back.

The cousins finally slept, exhausted, twisting fitfully in their chairs with a subconscious, anxious anticipation about the future, the days to follow: a danger in the heat with insects, interminable wetness, snakes, and gun infested jungle greenness. Fear, skill, and the confidence of youth seemed their only allies.

David let Anderson out at the entrance to the airbase in the late afternoon. He watched Anderson talking to the guard, pointing northeast, and gesturing threats. Anderson pulled some paperwork from his shirt pocket and thrust it at the sentry. The helmeted soldier relented. Anderson turned and nodded to David.

They were each on their own now.

It only took five minutes for the jeep to arrive.

"Where to Sarge?" The private lurched forward halfway to the windshield as the jeep squealed to a stop just feet from Anderson.

"Hanger B104."

The austere, olive drab vehicle jostled across the alternating packed earth and pock marked asphalt runways toward an obscure Air Force hanger. Once there, the boy let him out, turned the jeep in a tight circle, and sped away to continue his fun.

Anderson stood amid his gear, digesting his aloneness, thinking of the absurdity of what he was about to do, then turned slowly and faced the door to the hanger. He was reminded of the day he walked into the recruiter's office in San Bernardino four years ago. He hoped to hell he didn't meet the same crowd of people inside. He left his equipment and stepped through. A small office, whose only contents were a desk loaded with old flight manifests, an exposed light bulb hanging precariously from the ceiling, and an inefficacious, bald Air Force noncom, greeted him.

"Wadaya need chief?"

"Orders." Anderson replied with authority, shoving the paperwork at him.

The stubby man studied the papers indifferently. A frown began to take shape.

"You're a day early, chief. What kind of bullshit is this anyway?"

"I got stepped up. No time to cut new papers. No big deal. Today, tomorrow, what the hell's the difference. You guys got a pony for me?"

"Shit. Maybe. I donno. Gimmie a minute. I gotta make a call."

It took five minutes for the hanger operator to get through. When he did, he talked to what was obviously the pilot.

"Here, the Cap'n wans a talk tya."

"Yes, sir." Anderson said into the field telephone.

"He says you're Special Forces. That right?" The voice queried.

"That's right, sir, Staff Sergeant Anderson." Need a ride in tonight. You got a high flyer I understand."

"They told me you were due in later. I got a squeeze going tonight. You sure you know what you're doin'? It really don't make a shit to me, but I was countin' on tomorrow or the next day."

"Yes, sir, I understand. But things have changed. It's got to be tonight." Anderson stayed calm, convincing.

"Alright, alright, I'll be over. Give me forty five minutes. Hand the box back to Sergeant Landers," the officer ordered. Even as he extended the phone to the little man he could hear the pilot. "Jeez, I didn't even get my rocks off."

Anderson watched as baldy took orders, shaking his head affirmatively until he finally looked up, slammed the phone down, and began busily filling out paperwork.

Anderson lit a cigarette and waited.

David languished in the hotel, enjoying the Asian atmosphere and sucking on Mekong but missing Monica and the kids just the same. He was excited about the upcoming, new adventure. Finally, without having to take orders from the chicken shits in the Army, he could get in on a little of the action his-damn-self.

His cousin was not telling him too much, but then there was not much to tell that Anderson knew either. David knew that Anderson had to waste somebody, another American, and he knew that Anderson smelled something wrong with the deal. That was about it.

David glanced at the AWOL bag and wondered if that were enough. A helmet, a dark green jump suit, a head set, and a change of clothes for Anderson were inside. To hell with it. He decided to hit the night-lights. There was still time to waste, and he sure didn't want to waste it in the hotel when a world of decadence waited just outside.

Bangkok teemed with nightlife. The bars were legendary. He decided to take one of the Thai taxis and see for himself.

"Sawa de krup," greeted the Thai driver.

"Bars, girls." David told the diminutive man.

The driver smiled, put the fifty-seven Chevy in drive, and they lumbered on their way. David noticed the man's driving was a bit unconventional. With his right hand on the steering wheel, he constantly honked the horn with his left. Traffic seemed to be regulated on a "he who honks first and loudest, commands the green light", a light that didn't exist. The system appeared to work as long as the driver understood that large trucks do whatever they want.

David began to think that every fifty-six and fifty-seven Chevrolet ever made must have ended up in Thailand. As he watched, fascinated by the masses of human flesh pedaling along the klongs and small streets, David was sure the driver was taking him in circles. But presently they arrived at the exterior of a rowdy saloon. GI's were everywhere. Girls, attractive girls, paraded in short, silk skirts, flaunting their wares.

David stepped out of the cab and handed the driver some money. He decided it must have been enough because the little fellow grinned and hit the gas. At first it was too dark inside to see. Some seconds passed before his eyes adjusted enough to make out human shapes in energetic activity. There were girls everywhere. The hall was huge and filled with young women. Tall, short, slim, fat, the girls laughed and moved and threw their straight, jet-black hair to the right and then to the left. The black silk moved as though in slow motion, covering their tawny shoulders and then falling slowly, sensuously to hide their muscled backs.

David's eyes fell on a woman who looked to be in her early twenties. She wore spiked black heels. The lack of hose was not apparent as her muscled calves flexed under olive skin. Small boned, her thigh rippled golden in the light and carried enough sinew to make the knee appear small. Her heart shaped mid-section cut sharply to a tiny waist and then angled upward to wide shoulders atop which rested a beautiful, fine featured face. He felt the animal in him stir. She moved toward him, her eyes never leaving his. Her lips curled; her eyes burned like smoldering embers, reflecting the bar light. She tipped her head slightly forward and to one side. He knew it was all over but the shouting.

Three days, twelve thousand miles, and an unfamiliar society away, David held his breath and prayed for strength as her seductive touch slid silently along his thigh. Her brown fingers were delicate and long, punctuated by crimson knives that dug into his flesh, softly, urgently. He felt his loins stir with response.

"GI want sucky, fucky?"

David felt the knot in his stomach twist harder and the hair stand up on the back of his neck. Jeez, he thought, that's it? The essence of human female beauty seduced me by just being alive and then reduced it all to, "want sucky, fucky?" If Monica saw me now she'd fry my shorts.

"Thanks, but me married GI. No sucky. No fuc..."

Her expression changed like Texas weather. The girl turned so fast his eyes shot to her heel to see if it would screw into the floor. As she sped away her whole aura changed, but the seductress in her was soon revived as she repeated her performance once again on a likely prospect across the room.

David ordered Crown and sipped it slowly as he thought of Anderson. Who was this Angela? Got to see this gal. If she were so damned great, why was Anderson reluctant to talk about her? In fact, he didn't seem to be thinking much about her at all. And the helicopter ride into nowhere? David hoped Anderson knew what the hell he was doing.

CHAPTER FIFTEEN

Dawn was three hours away when Anderson awoke, sweating in the humid vegetation that engulfed him like some suffocating and imposed surrealistic re-enactment of biblical suffering. He thought back.

The Captain had arrived with his navigator, and together they had pulled the huge, winged tube off the runway, pointed it northeast, and waited impatiently for their crazy passenger to jump. He had almost decided to call the whole thing off, waiting like a fool at the hanger, suffering the impudent glances from the balding non-com. Shit, maybe he should have.

He squeezed the last of the paste into his mouth and stuffed the remains in his pocket, folded to trap the odor. His clothes and body were wet, added to by the early morning dew once again. He stood and began to move toward the target, more sure this time of his route and the obstacles along the way. Again he stopped at the hide to relieve himself, deposit the wrapper in the hole, clean his body of the night's accumulation of human-ness, and to rehearse the actions he would take tomorrow.

Anderson crawled into position before dawn. He slipped the mosquito netting over his body, then sat comfortably and waited for the first rays of the sun to penetrate the field and turn the grass to a golden blanket of silent, mindless beauty. The field moved not at all with the rising sun. No breath of air stirred the jungle's eerie domination. The greens of the forest waited to flow into the field and overtake it in an insidious bid to cover everything and every place.

Anderson noted the time, 0630, when there was enough light to fire by. It was 0730 when the first rays touched the far side of the field. Anderson watched carefully now, for it was not long after that that the air would begin to stir. He watched the wind flag intently. By 0830 the ribbon began to flutter, then pick up, and finally take a definite position pointing to the northwest.

He counted thirty seconds until the first shift of the flag to southwest, then build again, drop, and swing back to the northwest, switch, drop, switch back, and build up, count thirty seconds and repeat. The pattern held reliably with only small variations. Anderson knew that the flag only indicated conditions at its position near him. Because trees surrounded the large clearing, there would be swirling movement producing opposing directions - vortices - of the wind at various distances from his location. Anderson kept his eye on the main building fashioned by alternating vertical and horizontal bamboo. His attention was on the horizontal pieces. Not until 1000 hours did he finally see what he was waiting for, mirage. Slight at first, it soon gave Anderson another necessary indicator.

Anderson watched the movement of the hot air play across the bamboo, its wave giving away the velocity and direction of the wind as assuredly as an anemometer with a wind vane. The high power scope magnified the effect. The wind slowed, increasing the amplitude and decreasing the frequency of the telltale waves, then boiled vertically as the wind decreased to imperceptible, now switch to run the other way, switch again, slow at first and then build with the wind, the waves now decreasing in height and lengthening. The flag steadied to the northwest and the mirage followed. One, two, three ...

The wind flag near Anderson and the mirage some four hundred fifty yards away would match one another for 20 to 35 seconds at approximately two minute intervals. At noon the wind direction began to drift in from the north, and by afternoon the predominant wind was blowing toward the southeast. But at dawn Anderson found himself looking directly into the eastern sun, and not until after 0900 could the shot be taken. This gave him a window between 0930 and 1130, two hours to be safe. This matched studies supplied by Colonel Langlinais' sources. The long hours taken to ensure the hit were paying off.

Anderson carried no information to the site with him. He had committed all the necessary details to memory prior to deployment. Notes made at the site were destroyed at the hide each day after they had been looked at and reviewed three times, lessening the probability of mission compromise if he were captured. Anderson had selected the site where he now sat after careful study of the predominant winds, exposure of the field of fire, most probable locations of the target, and withdrawal strategy. Now, after nine hours of surveillance, he was pleased with his decision. He began to feel confident of the hit.

He waited patiently, ever the accomplished hunter. He watched as the camp came to life, daily chores of automatons like ants on a bed but with less discernible purpose. It was 0900 when the moving bodies within the confines of the remote clearing began to exhibit more defined activities. He could clearly make out parts of training exercises he himself had labored through. And at their helm, the target. Anderson moved his head slowly forward until the three inch eye relief of the scope presented a circle of view nearly the size of the lens itself. He looked at the students momentarily and then smoothly moved the rifle to his right until their instructor was centered in his view. It was his first sight of the target in daylight. Alex sported a baseball cap, a worn tank top, and the tired old jungle boots. The only apparent disconnect with his past was the full, black pajama pants. A dog followed his every move. He noticed a movement of the man's hand. It was Alex all right. He had worried that little piece of plastic constantly during training at Bragg as well.

Alex spoke to the students in fractured Vietnamese. He got most of the point across, but stumbled occasionally and had to ask one of the lieutenants who spoke English to translate. Even as he stood there talking, a part of his brain was somewhere else. He was more anxious than ever about the feeling he couldn't shake. He was at the point that he knew he had to do something about it.

Anderson's stomach wrenched suddenly, followed by the familiar hot pain in the top of his thighs. The adrenaline rush turned to a mild quiver that, albeit quickly subsiding, disturbed him as an act over which he had no control. The sight of the familiar American, a comrade from another time, now the mentor of the one who vows to destroy you, was combined with the knowledge that he was also the target. Anderson lowered his head until his cheek rested on the rifle stock. He closed his eyes tightly and heard the cry of his generation swelling within him, "What in the hell am I doing here? What in God's name are we all doing here?" He wanted to run and to keep running. He wanted to be anywhere but here.

Anderson forced himself back on task. He could not allow these thoughts, thoughts that destroy the warrior. Survival must not stumble over obstacles of social consciousness, landing in a pit of self-deprecation, self-pity, and philosophical meanderings. He could not afford to lose his edge. He was not a draftee; he was a trained professional. Horseshit!

It was just past noon when Anderson heard the unexpected. The familiar whop, whop, whop of a chopper flying at treetop level sounded behind him. He did not move, but waited for the bird to advance over and past his position. He watched as the compound came alive with curiosity. Though strangely marked, it was definitely of American make. The pitch of the props sent dust first down into itself and then exploding in the only direction it could, up and away from the powerful wash. The machine came to rest near the anxious students. Anderson glimpsed a motion to his right and followed it to the door of the command shack. The commander of the jungle outpost stepped from the porch and began to stride in the direction of the helicopter. Anderson quickly swung his scope back to the left. The sliding door of the chopper opened smoothly, rolling on its bearings. Cautiously a crouched figure appeared in the doorway and jumped to the hard ground; his knees buckled slightly, giving away the man's years. Anderson blinked. It was Colonel Langlinais.

CHAPTER SIXTEEN

It was Anderson's second day out. He had felt confident that the mission was going as planned, but now his gut churned. Something was wrong with this whole deal. Was Colonel Langlinais the bad guy? It didn't compute.

He watched through the powerful scope as the men exchanged words, gesticulating like puppets. There was no sound, just the movements of toy soldiers in the scope's field of view. He could not make out what the tall, lanky man was saying to the smaller, straight backed militant in dirty, khaki field gear. Finally, they stopped and turned to face the helicopter. From its bowels a perky Buck Sergeant stepped out and began running, crouching, toward the Colonel. Langlinais took a case from the young man and raised it in front of the pugnacious camp commander.

Anderson almost heard the guttural command emanate from the thick lips of the little man. From the right he saw two wretched American Air Force officers pulling carts over the pitted, hard earth, behind them the target. Just as swiftly, the loads of small, brown wrapped bags were loaded from the cart into the chopper.

When the last one was aboard, the Colonel handed the smiling bandit the case. Anderson could see the Colonel watching the target. There were both fear and anger in his eyes as he switched from the prisoners to the confident stride of their tormentor. Anderson could also see the disgust on the faces of the ill-treated wards. The Colonel exited as swiftly as he had appeared. Anderson couldn't believe it. An American Colonel had flown into North Vietnam, made a drug deal under the noses of American prisoners, and left no shadow, as though he had never been there. The camp returned at once to normal. The target went on with his instruction; the commander had once again disappeared. The prisoners were gone, hastened back to their bamboo cages. Anderson felt like it had all been a dream.

He tried to will himself to purge the scene temporarily from his mind. There was still the mission, the job: hit the target, disengage. He looked again at the wind flag in front of him. Characteristically, it had moved to indicate the northeast quadrant. The velocity was stiffening, and the mirage, running wild, made objects jump and tumble sporadically. The target went on exploiting his secrets. The commander stepped from the hut to survey the world under his control. Life was good.

Anderson stopped near the hide, his mind vacillating between scenarios. It had to be explained. The Colonel had talked him into a last mission. The Colonel also knew the time for the hit.

That was it! Langlinais expected the hit in two days. He hadn't heard from Anderson and thus didn't know Anderson was in position. He had shown his hand because he didn't realize Anderson would see the whole thing. Does that mean there won't be a pick up? And even if there were, would it be a pick up or a put down, for good. Dear God, he thought, what the hell is going on?

Safely in the hide, Anderson washed himself with small gifts of water. As he stepped through the ritual that helped him avoid detection, he assessed the situation. At the training center in Fort Bragg, the counter insurgency instructors went over it again and again.

Humanitarian, economic, national security: the good guy slogans in a bad guy disguise. They played an international game of falling dominos, democratic freedom, and bravado at these young men's expense. True? Did it matter at this moment?

Anderson crept through the night waiting for the hour to pass until he could rest, drink, and let down his guard a bit. At the cache, he stood silently before letting himself relax. He tested the air for telltale smells, the sounds of the unfamiliar, the clink of a rifle bolt, but there were none. The night was a black, impenetrable phantasm again, and he was part of it. Fetid air from the rotting jungle tinged his nose; insects began their incessant humming, buzzing orchestrations, and soon the terrified screams of birds and beasts of prey would begin to fill the night. A light rain began to fall.

Sleep would not come. He had to make the hit tomorrow. It would be his last day as part of the American guerrilla machine. It would be legal, and then it would be over. No more commando raids across the border; no more fearing the rifle shot that would end the life of a team member or himself. His run for freedom would be that of a civilian. The Colonel would have no direct jurisdiction.

But the hit? Why should he make it now? Anderson had pondered the act for some time with a final feeling of resolve before this last incident. Yet, when he had looked into the eyes of the American defector, the coldness of his act had struck him. Anderson had always been thankful for his decision to make war on the ground against the enemy in fair chase. The men who must send the missile, guide the bomb, or give the order against an unseen enemy were removed from the severity of the act, disengaged from the personality of it. The men of the Enola Gay busied themselves with the technical aspects of their job. The bombardier carefully watched the crosshairs for the aiming point, referred to by the crew only as the AP. The meaning was lost in the letters: AP, AP, AP, not aiming point. The bombardier watched as they approached the triangle formed by the rivers and let the "Gadget, Little Boy" go at the precise moment. But he saw only the river, not the eyes, only the indistinct shapes of the topography, not the man, not the child. He knew that something different would be the result of his actions, but not what. Distance buffered the act.

To promise death and to look into the eyes of the defender is to embrace the horror of it within the act itself. The choice to give oneself to reticent, probable endings in support of a cause is to behold the masters in their greatest conversation. The voices of existential argument haunted the souls of those who partook. Anderson searched for the lines, the pages of Sartre, of Kierkegaard, of Dostoyevsky, and of his beloved Kant. Did or did not the ontological argument forbid and disallow the act of man in sentient predation against man?

No. The answer lay not in philosophy; the answer lay in his breast, in basic axioms, mottos of the Green Berets: "De Oppresso Liber" must remain the goal, "Honor Before Advantage" the way. After all, the Colonel was not Special Forces; he was military in league with the Agency. He issued the orders to borrowed elite troops without having to participate in their ethic or their fate. Anderson's aiming point would be his rifle's cross hairs clearly imposed on a human head, Brenner's head. Just another target.

Prisoners. American flyers. What the hell were they doing there? Why so close to the Laotian border instead of further inland where the politburo could parade them before the people, gloating in triumph? Because this band of mavericks was holding hostages for ransom: drug money. In all probability these were flyers turned over by Laotians for favors, American bomber crews returning to Thailand after raids on North Vietnam targets drew a high price.

Thoughts of the girl drifted in and out of his mind. He wanted to succumb to them like a struggler in the snow, the cold grasping him in its icy tentacles as a sleepy death drew him to his end. He had to shake his head to clear her from his mind or let fantasy destroy him.

At last it came, the resolve. He would not only take Brenner, he would take the others as well. This traitor was no longer an American. No one could judge Anderson's actions without first becoming the war, the jungle, without paying the dues. He alone directed the outcome; without him there was no war; there was no compound, no drugs, no bad money. He was a part of them all, and he must flow with the river into which he had fallen. Without consummate action, he would drown. Without the AP, there was nothing, but with it there was nothing also. His effort and the world's knowledge of it were nothing, a speck. This was not Hiroshima, not the destruction of thousands, not a world event; it was simply the engagement of one against another, the clandestine execution of a traitor.

His SF comrades never seemed to suffer such reflective bullshit. Why him? They went about their business in a matter of fact, professional way, almost automatons, he thought. His years in seminary and his study of philosophy were detriments he decided. On the other hand, maybe they were just better at hiding their emotions than he was at thinking about them.

Anderson lay sweating, drenched in the salty, wet stickiness of his body and his surroundings. The black stillness of the night was his friend, but he could not enjoy its comfort on this night. He fell in and out of his slumbering until it was time to go, time to fill the orders. He couldn't be impeded by the pack and the items stowed there. He selected only one of the squeeze tube rations and filled his flask from the water jugs. The flask fit neatly in a bloused pocket and would have to last for the meal, a final wash, and the only drink he would take. He had saved the rock hard candy for just such a time that required water discipline. When the run started, Anderson would carry only the cased rifle, the Madsen M53, a small med kit, the switch blade knife, and the black fatigues he was wearing. All other items would be left to rot in the humid air that he hoped to put behind him forever.

CHAPTER SEVENTEEN

The jungle played its quiet song as he moved through the dense, wet, tangle of vegetation. He was thankful that it was the last time. A distant storm roared low and long like a freight train exiting a tunnel, the eerie sound of it making the forgotten snakes deep inside his bowels twist with a knotted loneliness that lay hidden, waiting to overpower him. Even in the dark the way had become familiar, and the hide, easily found, was a welcomed place, his place, where he prepared himself for the last time. As he squatted there in the darkness, he felt a burning sensation in his rectum. God, not now, he lamented. But he knew he was getting sick. Something had gotten to him. He could only wait to see how badly. He cringed at his own bodily noises that seemed loud enough to wake the whole camp more than a thousand yards away.

The digs were carefully covered along with all other evidence of his presence. He was deliberately reducing his essence to the light and swift moving predator, the carnivore that was the basis of man since time immemorial, since the birth of intelligence, like the leopard. And now, finally, after four years, since that day at the pool hall in San Bernardino, he would leave behind the Special Forces paraphernalia he'd thought he wanted and return to the old ways, to run for his life.

Anderson assured himself that the Madsen M53 was still in its place as he proceeded across the border. He moved with added caution. He was too near the end now for mistakes. Crystal water droplets like bits of mercury clung stubbornly to the tips of leaves, and each that he touched adding a tiny bit of moisture to his clothes until they were soaked with it. He couldn't be sure which upon him was the jungle, which was his own sweat from the steaming humidity of the jungle, or which was sickness creeping up inside him. Slivers of light began to play tricks with the mist that floated, soft and billowy below and inside the jungle's canopy. He felt a mild stab of tightness in his gut again as shapes unfolded before him, not quite real, forcing his eyes to try and penetrate the yet un-penetrable. Suddenly he felt as much as saw a flicker in the jungle to his left. Anderson froze. He watched, listened, smelled his environment.

Then he saw them: two indigs were moving toward his trail. Damn, not now; he didn't have time for traffic. He did not move. He did not breathe. He watched.

A man and woman. Both were wearing pakimas. They walked with their heads down, watching the jungle floor. Which way would they turn on the trail?

He did not move.

The couple stopped at the trail and began to converse in Vietnamese. Anderson didn't know the language and was helpless to act until they made up their minds. The woman pointed in Anderson's direction, and they began walking directly toward him.

Anderson couldn't, wouldn't let them compromise him now. If he moved, they would spot him and run. He didn't know where they had come from or which way they would retreat. It was happenstance that they were now caught up in this horror, through no fault of their own, through no awareness. As was custom the man quickly moved into the lead. They continued to look only at the ground in front of them. Carefully, quietly, Anderson's hand moved toward the Randall Model 14 attack knife on his left side. Then he remembered. It wasn't there. He reached for the stiletto and held it in his right hand, the blade under his left arm, and waited. The young man was only five feet from him when Anderson quietly said, "Hello."

The man was visibly startled by the sound of a human voice where he knew none should be. Anderson closed the distance suddenly while at the same time raising his left arm in the air. The man's instincts followed Anderson's hand as it rose over his head. Anderson's right hand described an arc with lighting speed toward the man's neck as it became more and more exposed, following the diversion of Anderson's left.

The cut extended to the jugular and severed the esophagus. The woman stood paralyzed, not believing what she saw happening before her. She watched the man sink to his knees grasping his throat, the blood spurting, then oozing from between his clenched fingers. She looked up at her assailant and realized in horror, her predicament. She turned and ran for her life. Anderson caught her almost immediately. He pulled back on the long black hair. The woman's feet came out from under her, and she crashed to the ground on her posterior. Anderson was on her, his hand pressed deeply into her throat, the knife held in thrust position but at bay. He looked into the eyes of terror and realized he couldn't kill the woman like this. Still holding the knife, his fist crashed into her jaw, knocking her unconscious.

Anderson looked up. The man lay silently in the trail. He brought his left knee up and across the woman and stood up. He remembered the piece of shroud line he had cut from the parachute. He quickly bound and gagged her, then dragged her into a dense area of the bush. He located the man and made a motion to check his pulse, but stopped. He knew the man was dead. He had seen the blood burst from his neck and the man's hand try to stop it.

He rolled the man over on his back. My God, he was only a boy, maybe seventeen. The young man's eyes were open, looking at Anderson, his face contorted with shock. Blood continued to spurt softly from his throat, not making it to the brain, and run down along it until the dark red color painted the leaves below, spilling onto the black earth. He wondered how that could be. The brain must be dead. How could the heart still pulse? Anderson sagged back onto his heels, letting the horror of his act, this murder, sink to the depths of his being.

He was overcome by the significance of the fluid, mesmerized by its continued movement along the dead body it once inhabited. It was like oil in a car: living, lubricating fluid inside a container of muscle, flesh, and skin that enclosed it tightly, protecting every drop greedily. Anderson had opened the container, letting the fluid spill out, stopping the pumping, the piston like, life giving, moving organs within. Just spilling out on the ground. That was all. That was all it took. His stomach bit at him suddenly. He had to disengage. No more than an elk; no more than a deer, a hog. Damn.

Anderson shook his head hard. He had to work fast. He hurriedly dug a hole near the blood and carefully scraped the bright red, oxygen enriched, stuff inside. He returned to the man, removed the yard of cloth he had been wearing, and wrapped it around the native's neck. He hefted the dead weight to his shoulder and walked into the thickest part of the jungle for a distance he thought was about seventy five yards. He laid the body down carefully, looked again at the dead man for a moment, and then turned away.

Anderson returned to the trail, cleaned up again, and covered the hole, assuring himself that no telltale signs remained. He left the trail again and found the woman. He sat down beside her. He had to think. How could he ensure that she wouldn't make a sound, nor move until it was over? Damn, he was running out of time.

He removed the pakima from her young, tawny body. She lay naked, unconscious still. He tied her thumbs together tightly, as well as her knees and big toes with the line. He cut the cloth into strips. With her elbows pulled to the rear, he tied them together behind her back. He removed the surgical tape from the soap dish and placed strips carefully but tightly over her mouth. She lay on her side as Anderson wrapped the line around the toe binding and then tied it to the vegetation. This completed, he stretched her body and tied her head to a sapling on the other side. He finished immobilizing her by placing a two inch diameter pole between her back and her elbows. She would return to consciousness soon, and when she did, she would not be able to roll or move forward or backward. She was still unconscious when Anderson left her.

Sticking to the ritual, he crawled into position after dawn, nearly an hour late. The weather was holding. He sat beside the rifle, waiting. The time passed slowly but relentlessly while the first yellow hues of the Asian sun warmed the sky. The life sustaining globe would make its amber, scorching appearance above the trees just to the right of where Anderson watched the camp, acting as catalyst to the wind. He watched the hidden flag intently.

The wind flag near Anderson was the primary indicator of the wind's effect on the bullet. Once pushed from its primary path, the missile would assume a new angle, and then another lessor angle, and then another, as it sped along. The angle widened the distance between the cross hair and the point of impact. But in clearings such as this, the wind often played tricks. As it passed over the jungle's ceiling, it dipped into the clearing, producing shearing crosswinds. It was the mirage that would provide the second, necessary indicator, the grassy field the third. The wind that the mirage indicated was the wind at the target, and, although it had little or no effect on the bullet at that point, the mirage told Anderson when the wind would most probably be laminar, providing a steady, predictable push between himself and the target. Mirage also bent the light rays that entered the powerful scope, displacing the perceived target from the actual one. Only hours of practice prepared the rifleman for the distance between the two, enabling him to determine the correct aiming point.

Anderson had lain awake through much of the night revising his plan. The drug dealing commander had to go, and his first line of management would follow. This would leave them in confusion and give Anderson the extra yards he needed. The rifle was silenced, and he counted on their shock and confusion to give him the time needed for precise shots at that distance. Anderson knew that he could sustain controlled fire through the single shot rifle at 4 second intervals. Moving laterally would add 2 seconds. Thus he reasoned the time from start to end of fire would consume approximately 25 seconds to hit the four men, including ensuring the primary target with two hits. This was possible only if he could get the men within twenty five yards of one another.

Head shots were chosen for the primary target and the commander. The second insurance shot on the target and each of the two officers would be chest shots delivered above the diaphragms. The latter two shots would not be taken if it were determined that time had run out.

He thought through the sequence again as he sat watching the flag. At 0830 the flag was just beginning to stir. He adjusted the wooden block attached to the support on the rest and opened the lid, displaying twenty matched rounds. The block held the cartridge's projectiles downward, protected by the wood. Positioned close to the rifle's receiver, the ammo was at his immediate disposal.

He adjusted his position for the last time. At this distance, the angle of traverse for all four targets would not exceed six degrees. He placed each foot in the holes he had dug for them to rest with comfortable support. He checked once more the position of his head near the stock and the placement of his hands. His back was comfortably supported for the wait, but a slight movement forward for the shots cleared him of it. He would fire the rifle free recoil. No part of his body would touch the rifle until the butt of the stock reached his shoulder near the end of its natural travel due to recoil. He checked the bolt travel and feel and thought through the process of precision fire that he had so many times before executed.

He took sight of an object hanging near the door of the commander's hut. He fixed the cross hairs on it and without touching the rifle, moved his head back and forth and then up and down while noting any movement of the cross hairs on the target. He moved the parallax adjustment on the front of the scope in each direction until it was most clear, and then bobbed his head both ways again while he studied the cross hairs. When they did not move from the target, the parallax was set.

Time passed, tension grew, and the wind increased. Inexorably, unwittingly, the targets approached the hour of their death. The predator's eyes followed their movements. The silent jungle would draw their blood and their punishment.

CHAPTER EIGHTEEN

The primary target, clad once again in baseball cap, tank top, and black pajama pants, walked slowly toward the training area. His expression seemed empty in the strengthening light of the sun as it slowly changed from amber to yellow as it cleared the trees and the morning breeze tempered the wet heat. His walk was slower, more labored, less confident than Anderson remembered. Anderson wondered where the tan dog was that never left Brenner's side. He watched Alex and remembered the friendship they had shared, more of an easy acquaintanceship really. They had taken classes together at the Special Warfare Center and the final struggle to pass the grueling qualification trials at Camp Mackall. Brenner had whispered, as classes went on, about his exploits in Chicago where he had grown up. An only child, Brenner was accustomed to the rewards garnered from the occasional fit only the truly spoiled could master. He had convinced himself that everything was a scam, and anyone who didn't get in on the action was a chump. "Hey, sweetheart," he once exclaimed, "you wouldn't be here if your old man hadn't scammed your momma into having sex. And to look at you, I'd say the best part is still runnin' down her legs." And at girls passing by, "Hey beautiful, before I get home tonight, remember to slide down the banister and warm up my supper."

Once you got past his huge ego, he could be a nice guy, though thoroughly self-indulgent. Anderson had no idea how Brenner had found himself in this situation. Prisoner turned defector, trainer turned sympathetic, nice guy American turned greedy? Anderson could only speculate.

At 0930 the winds began to cooperate. Anderson waited. He wanted the thick-lipped commander of the camp. Brenner gesticulated feverishly as he faced the group of disinterested NVA non-coms. The two lieutenants stood like watch dogs behind the class, approximately twenty yards in front of Brenner.

Finally the door to the command post opened and the commander of the tiny jungle outpost stepped forward. He marched animatedly, authoritatively toward the American and his men. Anderson waited and watched. When the stocky man was ten feet behind the American, he stopped, watching the proceedings with a critical eye.

Anderson slid the bolt back and carefully placed a cartridge onto the floor plate of the receiver. He moved it slowly forward into the coned chamber and locked the bolt. The custom two-ounce trigger had no safety and required only the slightest touch. His eyes shifted quickly from the flag to the mirage, to the grass, to the target, and back again. He was in his element now, traversing familiar ground. Anderson waited for the moment, the moment when the mirage aligned with the flag. The predominant condition was correct. He waited for the next thirty-second interval and the mirage.

He watched the mirage change from left to right to a boil, and finally assume its slow, rhythmic flow from right to left. Anderson's left eye noted the position of the flag in front him. The flag had rotated and now flowed toward the northwest as well. The ribbon hung, and then began to ease up to the correct angle. Anderson moved the cross hairs tangent to the American's head, the horizontal crosshair touching the top of his skull and the vertical hair touching the back of it. The wind would move the bullet three inches to the left of the cross hair's location. Anderson lowered the horizontal cross hair to just touch the top of the man's ear. He saw the target's head turn; he seemed to look right at Anderson. Something was out of place, not quite right. Anderson could not put his finger on it. Still, it was the familiar form of Alex Brenner. No, it was just a target.

The Enola Gay flew on. The bombardier watched as the cross-hairs approached the Aiming Point, the AP.

Then, from the bowels of Anderson's past, came a silent lament:

I was floating down that old green river ...

Intimacy. Machine and man. Fluid. Familiar caress of cold steel, then the flash, orange, followed by pale smoke at the muzzle.

The recoil sent the rifle's butt to Anderson's shoulder. The man's expression changed to surprised disbelief as the tiny hollow point bullet entered the brain cavity, began to mushroom, and then break into pieces. The brain was instantly turned to a blood churned mass of disconnected parts swimming in a thick, dark red soup. He grabbed his head as though to hold it together. His knees buckled and he fell suddenly and hard to the ground; his body convulsed; his legs pumped an imaginary bicycle; his arms grabbed at empty space.

Anderson kept his gaze on the little flag in front of him as he lifted the bolt's handle with the side of his index finger. His position did not change as he drew the bolt back, grabbed the spent cartridge with his right hand, and dropped it as he simultaneously plucked a second round from the wooden block. He tossed a new round through the loading port and into the receiver as the thumb of his left hand began moving the bolt forward. Instantly, as the bolt hit home, Anderson's right hand closed it and moved fluidly to the grip. In a millisecond the rifle was repositioned, moved laterally as he slid it forward, and then his hand was removed from the rifle but for his finger on the trigger.

On the good ship rock and rye ...

The commander came into view; he stared in disbelief at the convulsing American, and just as quickly the sound of the rifle spit death a second time. The commander had not time in these four seconds to even assess what had happened let alone decide what to do about it. As yet, the camp's personnel did not realize what was happening.

A third round sang out as Anderson put insurance into the chest of Brenner. Again, the awful hiss of the precision rifle broke through the air, the projectile boring into the chest of the first lieutenant. He grabbed the wound and struggled forward gasping for air, his lungs and heart torn irreparably. The other officer started to his aid and then thought better of it. He turned and ran toward the barracks, his brain reeling with cognition of his plight. Twenty six seconds had passed when the bullet found the mid-section of the soldier's back. He hit the ground rolling. The flag began to let up; the mirage turned to a boil. It was over. The American and the Viet commander were dead. The officers were either dead or wounded, but certainly in no position to lead their men in an assault of retaliation.

Anderson looked up from the scope. He had thought of them only as paper targets. He had held steadfastly to a practiced indifference. Only paper, no difference, he could hear an inner voice say.

The men in the compound were running about with what appeared to be no semblance of order, like a fire ant hill after being stepped on. No movement issued from the prisoner's side of the field. If the remaining soldiers had detected his position, it would not be long until they were in pursuit of their enemy. He had one last duty. Anderson moved the rifle to the right until the prisoner's shacks came into the scope's view. He found the crude lock on the bamboo door. The rifle barked a last time.

He removed the rifle from its rest, slipped it and the cartridge block back into the halter case, then snuggled the case up on his back. He low crawled for the last time the now familiar path until he reached adequate cover. At last he was on his feet, breaking into a slow cautious trot. He must not panic. Better to be deliberate and enduring than to run recklessly, risking injury and fatigue.

The young woman was still where he had left her, lying in the tiny clearing. Anderson looked at her, again at those eyes of terror. She was conscious and had been struggling, but when she looked at her husband's murderer, she froze. He bent down and quickly cut the line that held her head and the binding that held her toes. Then he was gone.

He could hear no one as he reached the location where the short assault rifle waited for him. He rested momentarily, listening intently. Faintly, but distinctly, he could hear the sounds of men moving through the jungle. He grabbed the short automatic rifle and began to trot again toward the hill in front of him.

Sweat poured from him, into his eyes, into his mouth, the warm, salty taste finding his tongue. As he labored, closing in on the hill in front of him, he thought of the cowardly act. Death had come to them without a face, without eyes, without expression, without warning from a silent jungle. How could there be honor in his act? War is wrong by its very nature. Can any act be right that is a subset of wrong? Oh yes, he reminded himself, he was there because of humanitarianism, economics, and national security. America only did battle with the bad guy; America was never wrong. To kill is to save. Bullshit.

Anderson finally broke through the jungle's steaming mass into a clearing. The base of the hill he sought lay just another four hundred yards ahead. He guessed his pursuers to be more than that behind him. He had to make the base of the hill, and cover, before they did, but he knew also that he had to make them find this location near the clearing, better to fight on his terms than on theirs. Anderson moved back along the trail, breaking limps from the succulent vegetation. He could hear them getting closer. He knew he couldn't win in close combat with the Madsen M53; he had to find the clearing on the hill. Anderson started running, his odds diminishing. His legs pumped, hammering at the tall grass. The Madsen M53 weighed heavily in his hand. The sounds of their strange language grew closer and more distinct. He wondered if they had found his trail. No looking back, keep the pace. Pump, pull the knees high again and again, slamming the shallow water with explosive sounds that disturbed the holy silence.

He heard shots ring out. Bullets broke through the sparse jungle at the base of the hill. He knew the AK-47's were inaccurate, the soldiers winded, and the range long for their offhand firing. All he could hope was that luck was on his side. Then, suddenly, he was swallowed up once again by the cover of the green maze. He fought the hill, his legs burning with lactic acid from the exertion, looking for the clearing from which he had surveyed the area days before. At last he found it, dropped to a sitting position, and simultaneously pulled the rifle case from his back. Anderson reached frantically for the cartridge box. He opened the bolt of the precision instrument and placed a round on the loading ramp. He took his first look at the enemy. He didn't stop to count, but guessed there were ten or so as he took aim on the leader. They were approaching the center of the large clearing at the base of the hill when the leader dropped from Anderson's first bullet.

Anderson knew his first shot was luck. The cross hairs bobbed and weaved as he tried to control his heart and his breathing. He had to struggle to control his body. With great concentration he took a second soldier. By the time he sighted on the third, he was calm again. The tattered men continued running straight at him, now only two hundred yards out. He could now see their faces clearly through the powerful scope. He took aim at a fourth Viet and saw that he was only a boy. God, he wanted them to stop and turn back. He swept the field. They were young, too young, but he had to stop them. His scope found an older man. This guy had to be the power behind the charge, an ignorant rhino who didn't yet know he was in the middle of his own field of death. Anderson knew his bullet would be high at this range, and he held the horizontal cross hair below the man's collar bones. Calmly now.

But I floated too far ...

The bullet entered the man's head between and slightly above the eyes. The scene seemed surreal as the man rolled to a stop and began to convulse; his head arched back as his legs continued running. The beleaguered combatants looked at their comrade in horror. Four men were down; this assailant could not miss. Now, with no leader, the group turned and began running back from where they had come. Anderson grabbed the Madsen M53 and fired a three round burst over their heads to keep them from changing their minds. He had no wish to kill these boys; he just wanted them off his ass. He shouldered the weapons again and started up the hill. Just on the other side was the rendezvous point.

CHAPTER NINETEEN

The Colonel sat looking into the eyes of his second in command and listened.

"Jim, we've got to get up there. I know he'll be there."

"Look Major, we haven't heard from Anderson since he left for the States. We should have gotten some message. I don't know; I thought we could count on that young man."

"Colonel, he'll be there. The guy's Special Forces. He'll be there because he doesn't know any better. Those Green Beanies are so damned patriotic they'd get me off if I told them it would save the country. He's got a job to do. Just because he didn't check in doesn't mean he's not going to take this bastard out. It won't hurt to look in any case."

"All right, do what you have to. Just make sure the kid is OK if he's out there!"

Major McCauley was a worn out man. Fighting to maintain his composure for all these years had left him disillusioned, frustrated, and angry. Being the Colonel's flunky for twenty years screwed at his guts until he had devised a plan to make himself rich. He wanted out so badly he could taste it, but not until he put himself on easy street for the rest of his life. Piss on the Army; piss on the Colonel; piss on the war. He had made it a personal goal to screw Hanoi Jane when he got home just to top the whole thing off. With the kind of money he was making, he just might pull that off too.

The powers that be seemed to think it was OK to haul opium out of the country to endear the Karen and Meo tribes. Why not take advantage of the situation? They were no better than he was.

He got Johnson on the horn.

"We're ready. Get that piss drinking chopper pilot and Joe, then shag ass out to the pick-up. You know what to do when you get there. Don't let that bleeding heart son-of-a-bitch get away, or I'll tear your head off and shit in your neck. You got that?"

He had one more call to make.

Angela was startled by the phone. It was early.

"Hello," she said meekly, knowing it couldn't be Anderson but hoping it was.

"Hello, this is Major McCauley. I'm so sorry to wake you. Listen, your father called early this morning. He didn't want to disturb you. He asked that you return home a day early. He also wants you to pick up a package for him. I took the liberty to make the arrangements for you. I'll see that the package gets aboard in your name. Are you alright?"

"Oh yes, just sleepy. What's the urgency? I was hoping to go shopping with one of the other ladies today. I wanted some brass. Oh well, all good things I suppose."

"I hope you've been able to do most of what you wanted."

"It has been fun. I don't suppose you have heard from Sergeant Anderson?"

"Sergeant Anderson? Oh yes, the young man that was at the party in the Colonel's suite. No, we haven't heard from him since he left for the States. In fact, I was thinking of asking you if you had heard anything. But I guess not. His team hasn't heard from him either."

"Well, thank you, sir." Angela said and hung up, worry making her throat tighten uncomfortably.

The Major sat thinking about the situation around him: the girl's father, the Colonel fat, dumb, and happy. And Anderson. Now that worried him. Where was that shithead? He reached for the horn again.

"Sergeant, is that you? ... over."

"Yes, sir. Go ahead, sir ... over."

"Switch to secondary ... over."

"You got me?"

"Loud and clear, sir ... over."

"Don't screw this up, you hear. That guy can hit a fly on a shit house wall at five hundred yards. Play him in close. Use your friendly position. If you don't take the asshole by surprise at close range, he'll eat you alive. No chances, do you understand? ... over."

"Yes, sir. I understand ... over."

"What's your position? ... over."

"Approximately thirty minutes east of re-fuel point ... over."

"ETA?... over."

"Wind's out of the east, but still less than one hour ... over."

"This is your show, Sergeant. You better make it good ... out."

Angela was worried about Anderson. Could something have happened on the trip or in the States? Neither had known how their situation would work out when he left for home. She felt they might never see each other again if they missed meeting before she had to leave. It distressed her to have to board the plane without some word.

The trip was long and tiring for her. Her father was waiting when the final leg of the flight brought her safely onto the tarmac in L.A. She couldn't believe it; she didn't remember a time when he had personally met her at the end of any trip. He was always in a business meeting or hard at work. It seemed to hang from his neck like a tether. Yet there he was.

"Angela, over here."

"Hello daddy. This is quite a surprise, but a nice one."

"I missed you, sweetheart. Now come on to the car. My men will pick up your bags and bring them along."

"Thank you. My, my, aren't you the thoughtful one."

"How was your stay in the orient?"

"Well, I wanted to talk to you about that. I met someone. He's a Green Beret. He's nice daddy. You will like him."

"Jesus, Angela, not some grunt. Don't tell me I sent you over there just to have you fall for some half dollar GI. Not only that but those guys are losing popularity every day, not to mention the war. What the hell's got into you?"

Angela paused momentarily before entering the limousine. She hated it. The business deals, the coded conversation fret with innuendo, the stuffy business suits and balding men. Somehow the interior seemed more closed-in than normal cars. But she had grown tolerant of it and now sat silent as the long vehicle sped toward her parent's home. Where could Anderson be? At least the rest her life was back to normal. A good fatherly reprimand had seen to that.

CHAPTER TWENTY

The pick-up point lay below him. It was late afternoon as he tried to rest atop the hill, but he could not. His mind kept going over the last few weeks. He simply did not have enough information to formulate anything out of what was obviously bad shit in the making. If drugs were involved, why was he pulled to make the hit? What difference did it make if Brenner was neutralized or not? War stimulates bad feelings among pawns, but drugs always stimulate bad money. Wasting an informer, deserter, and collaborator makes for some small gain in a war. What gain would it make in a drug deal? If the mission had been for the war, the pick-up would be friendly. But tying up loose ends in a money deal was another proposition, and he was a loose end. He seemed left with only the plan he had made after his meeting with Colonel Langlinais. It better work or his ass was grass as the cliché goes.

David would just now be arriving at the alternate location they had decided on. It was a small area situated between two ridges just two thousand yards to the west. David would have refueled at a Laotian village where two of Anderson's Hmong commandos lived. Anderson had trained them for weeks before running interdiction missions on both sides of the border with them, and they would accept any order or favor coming from him.

It was safe and easy for David: fly into a friendly area; fly Anderson out, and then take the first flight back home. Couldn't be easier. If Anderson didn't show, David would fly out anyway, and that would be that.

But what if the improbable happened? Colonel Langlinais' men might have wind of the hit and be looking for him at their designated pickup point, nearly two thousand yards from the one he had given David.

Anderson decided to take one last look at the pick-up point below. He had to call them into an advantage position so that if the worst happened, he had, at least, a chance. He realized he had to call their hand at long range. He knew that if they got him in close, he stood no chance. The problem was the door gunner: the M-60 could rain death in the right hands. Anderson concluded that if he were a target, it made no sense for them to take him back to base to waste him. And if they had to get him, they would have to tip their hand if it looked like he might slip through. The bottom line: he would have to be his own bait.

Anderson walked the area. Six hundred yards northeast of the planned pick up point was an area just large enough for a chopper. A fifty yard gap in the jungle ran from the clearing up a small hill for four hundred yards and then ended abruptly in dense jungle. He turned and melted into the lush, wet vegetation. It was just past noon when Anderson heard the squelch sizzle on his small radio.

"Hunter, do you copy? This is Tangooo, Sierra, One, Eight, Zero. Come in Hunter."

"This is Hunter. What is your approach? ... over."

"Ten minutes out on heading four five ... over."

"Hold your heading. Will bring you in by sight. Wait for instructions ... over."

"Negative, Hunter. Plan is solid. Make your way to primary LZ."

"Primary LZ compromised. Make a run at me. Your window is critical ... over."

"What's your situation? ... over."

"Target down. Regulars on my ass. You'll have to cover me. Repeat, window critical ... over."

Anderson knew that if they wanted him, they would try to strafe him and get the hell out. If not, they would come in for him. He also knew that door gunners had a bad habit - some kind of deep seated obsession - of starting their fire low and then angling up and right when faced with a single target. He figured he had three seconds before the first thirty caliber bullet hit him. He hoped to hell this wasn't some asshole who didn't know the rules.

Anderson heard the chopper before he saw it.

"Tango, you are coming up on my position now. Can you see me? over."

"No sighting. No sighting. Confirm approach!"

"Approach confirmed. Just keep coming. Smoking lamp is lit ... over."

"We've got you, Hunter. Stand steady. Approach and pick up is northwest quadrant, your position ... over."

"Copy. Northwest quadrant confirmed ... over."

Anderson watched the lazy approach of the machine, like a dragonfly stalking a mosquito. He readied himself. His odds were good, but odds are just odds. The chopper suddenly angled fifteen degrees north, and the first crack of the M-60 followed shortly after. Anderson turned and ran directly away from the line of the barrel. At the count of two, he took a hard left into the trees. Damn, he had been right. The bastards were out to waste him. But he had made it. The crew would never come in after him no matter how bad it might be on them when they got back. They didn't stand a chance in the bush with him, and they knew it.

He watched the olive drab bird circle futilely and then disappear. He had four hours to make it the twenty five hundred yards to where

David waited for him. Anderson had only walked a hundred yards when he noticed that his right leg was growing stiff, and he could feel a slight ache. He looked down at his boot. Blood mixed with the moisture of the jungle glittered like burgundy wine. He lowered his pants and saw the damage. He laughed with relief as he realized that he had made that left turn not a split second too soon. The wound was through the outer portion of the thigh muscle. He decided to check it more thoroughly later. He would be back in Bangkok within hours. He could make it until then.

"Set this sumbitch down," Johnson screamed.

"What the hell's got into you, Sarge?" the warrant officer asked.

"We can't leave the area until we decide what we're gonna do. There's no sense flying in circles 'til we do. Sit 'er down and let's figure out what the hell we're doin'."

The pilot eased the helicopter onto a grassy knoll. He shut the engine down and climbed out, enjoying the chance to stretch his legs. Johnson was already out, pacing, thinking.

"We screwed up royal. We gotta get our story straight and make it good. McCauley will check us out permanently. I know he will. That prick is cold as ice. He doesn't give a crap 'bout us. Even if he doesn't waste us, we will be dead when we get back to the States. This is bigger than a bunch a no count assholes like us."

"So what do you suggest?"

"I don't know. Let me think a minute. That snake eater sucked us in. He had to know something. So where the hell is he goin'? And how does he figure on gettin' his lily white ass outta here? For one thing, he's gotta go west. He can walk clear across Laos and Thailand and nobody will ask him one damn thing. But how's he gonna do it dressed in camo, dirty as shit, and by himself. I say we head back toward the Thai border, zig zagging as we go. Maybe we'll get lucky. It's better than doin' nothing."

"Hey, ole buddy, how's yer hammer hangin'? You're early. What's with the blood? Didn't think you'd have time for deer hunting during this gig."

"Come on you silly shit, where's the bag I gave you."

David pointed behind the pilot's seat.

"I'm here to tell you the deer were hunting me this time. Man, am I glad to see your white ass."

Anderson pulled light clothes, a rucksack, and a small camera from the pack. He removed the filthy fatigues. The wound was not bleeding and appeared to be doing OK, though it ached and felt stiff. He wrapped an ace bandage around his leg, shot himself full of procaine penicillin, and swallowed a loading dose of broad spectrum antibiotics that he always carried in his leg pockets. He hid the camo and packed what was left of his equipment in the black canvas case.

"Let's boogie, cuz."

David lifted the helicopter off the earth with characteristic deftness. Anderson knew he must be a damn good pilot. Transporting equipment and personnel into forest fires took nerve and skill. He felt safe riding with his cousin. He could finally relax for a while. David turned the chopper toward the western border of Laos as Anderson leaned back and relaxed for the first time in many hours. He and David had been in a hundred scrapes and taken no scratches. Why would this be any different? Anderson's eyes closed. He was tired, and he felt his conscious awareness ebbing as his body slumped. Then he saw their faces, the officers running as the blackness of sleep overtook him.

"Damn, we've got a bird dog up our ass! Where did that thing come from?" David yelled.

The helicopter lurched.

Anderson was in the execution phase, the officers running. The bolt continued to move forward, his right hand poised to close it, his eyes on the target.

"Damn it, cuz, we got trouble. Get your eyes open, I need help."

Anderson heard the faint cries in the background like someone in the bush far away calling him. No, it was something else, something more real. His consciousness stirred. He could hear the roar of helicopter. He looked over at David and remembered where he was. David's eyes told the story; Anderson knew at once that something was wrong.

"Jeez, David, what's going on?"

"I don't know, but somehow I have the distinct feeling they ain't friendly. See if you can get a look." David turned the chopper abruptly.

Anderson leaned out of the doorway as far as he could.

"Now how in the hell did those dickheads find us?"

"Those dickheads? Just what are you saying ole buddy?"

"I'm saying that I screwed up. I'm saying that we're about to get our peckers fried."

"Hold on to your seat. We're going for a ride." David plunged the chopper nearly straight down, bobbing and weaving until the tree line appeared inescapable. He pulled it out not ten feet above them and leveled off.

"Where's water, a river?"

"Just over that hill you're about to run into."

David lifted the bird over the crest and dove along the slope on the other side. Anderson did not believe a chopper could do what David was making this one do. He banked sharply right again to let Anderson look. The other helicopter was above and behind them. David dove again and banked left into the river bottom, skimming scant inches above the water. The other chopper sped passed them, but was quickly back on their tail.

The two choppers raced along the twisting course of the river, bobbing and weaving like a dragonfly in pursuit of a mosquito.

"Look, cuz, when I go around the next bend, we're bailing. They might not see us. This piss ant machine will hit and burn like a bomb. Maybe they'll think we took the hit too. When I say go, get your ass out of this death trap and into the water. I can see they've got ordinance, and we've got squat."

Anderson saw the bend coming up. David took the turn banking to the left. Anderson got ready, slinging the rifle to his shoulder and grabbing the Madsen M53. He felt the adrenaline course through his veins and rivulets of sweat run down his chest under the shirt. When they lost sight of their pursuers, he jumped. His exit was not controlled, and he tumbled toward the warm, inky-black fluid, hitting it on his buttocks. Anderson struggled toward the surface laden with the weight of the rifles. He broke the water's surface expecting the worst, frantically turning and trying to see through the film of water cascading over his eyes.

David's chopper moved straight away, then banked to the right again. Anderson could hear the other chopper behind him. The hissing sound of a missile approached just as he saw it speed overhead. David's helicopter took the hit. Anderson's brain registered the scene as it exploded with David still sitting at the controls. David had scammed Anderson and drawn fire to himself. Anderson watched in horror as shards of metal seemed to flutter slowly toward the water. He watched the other helicopter circle to confirm the kill and gloat and finally turn to the west and disappear over the tree line. *Damn, it worked. They think I went down with it.*

CHAPTER TWENTY ONE

"Major, the whole thing just doesn't make any sense. We've never heard a single word from Anderson since he left for the states. Your men took a sighting at more than four hundred yards. How do they know it was Anderson? How do we know the kid didn't jump ship when he got home?" The Colonel paced behind the teak desk that sat auspiciously in the center of his office.

"Who the hell else could it have been?" Argued Major McCauley. "First off, why would anyone else take out Brenner? Second, the guy that my men saw killed by the Regulars fit his description: five eleven, medium build. Third, the man identified himself. Johnson split because he was taking fire. The bastard got paranoid. He boogied; the job was done."

The Colonel paused, greatly troubled. Relenting, he looked back at McCauley. "We'll have to issue a casualty report. List him as being killed in South Vietnam as usual. We can't afford to have anyone know what we're doing up here.

"Call that son-of-a-bitch who runs the camp. Let him know that I want my prisoners now. I've paid that thief enough ransom for our boys. No more.

"I just don't understand Brenner. I was so certain Sergeant Brenner would come through. I can't understand why he turned. I've never seen an SF soldier do it. Not them. We shouldn't have put him in that position. What the hell good did it do anyway?"

"Don't be so hard on yourself, sir. It was a good plan, and Brenner was up to it. Manipulating their confidence in order to coordinate the drug money for our men's freedom was the only way to deal with these assholes without letting the folks back home know that we are deployed in Laos and North Vietnam. These things happen. We had to take him out, sir. We couldn't pull him back after he'd turned, and we couldn't compromise our efforts to get our other men out."

"Put him on the list as well, Major. He was a good boy once, and he put himself in a hell of a spot. We asked too much. List them as killed in Vietnam in the line of duty. Give them both their due."

"Yes, sir, right away." Major McCauley turned and hurried out.

The Major was dealing now. The old bastard had swallowed it hook, line, and sinker. Brenner and Anderson, the two golden boys with their bullshit Green Berets, had taken it in the ass. No witnesses, no fuss. life was good! Now on with business. List them; who gives a shit anyway. Get with Little Ho and tell him it's time to let the prisoners go. He had more money now than he knew what the hell to do with. Splitting the offer with Little Ho, diverting half shipments from Kanchanaburi to California, had added up quickly, more than in his wildest dreams.

The Major stepped into his office and reached for the phone.

"Johnson, you sweet son-of-a-bitch, I love you. There's an extra ten in it for you. Let's get on up there and make a last deal with Little Ho, my fortune cookie. Get the chopper ready, I'm going to love pitching this scam myself."

"Yes, sir. Thank you, sir."

The Major hated riding in helicopters. They gave him the creeps. Though he had been doing it all his life, he saw them as spinning death traps, too slow to duck a bullet. He sat quietly, spending his fortune as the chopper sped along toward the border.

"How much longer, Johnson?" The Major asked after what seemed to have been several hours.

"Not far now, sir. By the way, we are comin' up on the spot where we wasted Anderson. Down there. There it is, just past the bend."

"Looks like a fitting place to spend eternity to me ole buddy. From womb to tomb. Did we ever confirm who his sidekick was and where they got hold of a helicopter?"

"Not a clue, sir. In fact, there are no missing reports from any outfit in country. Do know that a chopper we gave to the indigs come up missing over near Lop Buri though. It wasn't signed out. No one seems to know a damned thing about it."

"Well, I don't know how it can be connected to any of us. No one even saw it clear the hell out here. It's neutral ground. Everyone's out of the picture and no one knows why or really gives a damn. Couldn't be more perfect. You're a genius, Johnson."

"Thank you, sir. About my extra ten, I have problems at home. Think there's any chance..."

"No problem. You'll get it tonight."

"There's the compound now, sir."

The chopper flew characteristic insignia that to the Viets meant payoff. The approach was easy. The Major stepped to the ground in a crouched position to clear the lazy, rotating blade and began running until he was out of its reach. He stopped and surveyed the encampment. A young soldier walked toward him with bravado, apparently in charge.

"You have heard then?" The Viet spoke English surprisingly well.

"Heard what? Where's the Colonel?" Tell him I'm here. I don't have long."

"He won't be joining us. We were attacked yesterday. The assassin killed the Colonel, an American, two of my fellow officers, our top sergeant, and a young soldier. If that wasn't enough, he shot the lock off the prisoner's door."

"What the hell are you talking about?"

"Well, at first we thought it might be you Americans, but then we found this. What do you make of it?"

Major McCauley took the small, empty shell casing from the North Regular's hand. One thing he knew at a glance: it wasn't American. Nor did he recognize it as any other round used in this god forsaken war. "Not familiar," he said.

"Look at the head stamp, Major."

The American turned the case over. There he read: .220 Russian. He handed it back to the Viet.

"Look, we don't know anything about the attack. Looks like some Russian. We only want our prisoners. We've made substantial monetary agreements and want you to honor yours."

"Agreement? We here know nothing of the particulars of that. We're only soldiers. Sadly, the Colonel is no longer here to make deals with you Americans."

"What do you want?"

"What are you prepared to offer?"

"This is the last. We expect the prisoners to leave with us when we return. We want to know exactly how many you have, and we want to know their health."

"That can be arranged, Major. Now what is your offer?"

"We have five hundred kilos being delivered from the Meo on the Thai-Burma border in three days. Two hundred kilos will be dropped here. In addition we will deliver eleven thousand dollars in American currency the day after."

"Major, I'm not sure how many prisoners we have. It was not my job to count them."

"Look, I'll double the amount this last time. You can do what you want with it."

"Ieeee, that is good, sir. We shall be waiting. No funny tricks now or we will be forced to eliminate the prisoners. But even worse, Major, we will let it be known that you have land operations crossing Laos to interdict in our beloved North, adding a new and incriminating dimension to the war. Further, we shall get word to your American actress friend that you are dealing in illegal drugs as well. I don't think your home town TV audience would see that as the great American ethic at play. I can see her demoralizing your soldiers now, instilling hesitation and doubt in their cause, just enough for my men to send them to Nirvana."

The Major held the Viet's eyes for a moment, and then he turned to leave.

"Major, there is one more thing you might wish to take with you." The Viet threw it at his feet.

The Major picked it up cautiously. Turning it over in his hand he tried to imagine what it could be for. At the end of a short, pointed stake a broad piece of camouflaged plate had been attached. The two inch wide plate rode on ball bearings and extended a bit farther from the ball bearing attachment on one side than it did on the other. Both sides had been painted a straw camouflage, though black stripes had broken the camo on the other. A length of ribbon hung from the end. The Major had never seen such a contraption before.

"Where did you get this?" he asked.

"We found it near the Russian shell casing."

"What the hell is it?"

"The best we can figure, it is a wind device of some sort,"

The Viet answered.

Major McCauley could not have been more pleased as he boarded the helicopter and began the trip back into Thailand. He would divert three hundred kilos to himself besides another four hundred thousand in cash in the bargain. He would be a silent hero for rescuing American prisoners, who would mysteriously and regrettably end up missing in action.

Once in camp, the Major stopped by his office to make a last phone call to the states. He could tell the Colonel his good news after that.

"Hello."

"Yes, Miss, this is Major McCauley. Can I speak to your father?"

Angela recognized the voice before he identified himself. She couldn't resist asking. "Listen, Major, I was wondering about Anderson? Has he shown up yet?"

"Oh, my dear, I'm so sorry. Staff Sergeant Anderson died in the line of duty day before yesterday. I'm sorry to have to tell you such terrible news. I know the two of you hit it off very well."

Angela could not believe what she was hearing. Anderson was too young, too much alive for this to happen. No, it couldn't be. "Are you certain it was him, sir. I mean, couldn't it have been someone else. What happened?"

"Yes, I'm afraid so. I wish I could provide you with more information. If I learn more, I will call you. Could I ask you to get your father on the line for me please?"

Her heart stopped. Anderson. It couldn't be. A connection had formed. It couldn't be broken just like that.

CHAPTER TWENTY TWO

Safely out of the water, Anderson assessed what he had left. Afton's rifle was still intact. So was the Madsen M53. Inside a pants pocket was the soap dish medical kit and in the shirt two fresh packs of cigarettes and a lighter. Anderson made his way into the jungle's interior. He was exhausted and decided it would be best to get some rest before going on. He found a secure place to spend a few hours, and leaning back, allowing his body to relax, he began to un-wrap the pack of cigarettes. He was relieved that he could finally allow himself the luxury, happy that he'd remembered to include them in his clothes for transport on the helicopter, and blessed the tobacco company for the water proof cellophane wrap.

His mind drifted back to his childhood and to his friend. What would he tell Monica and the kids? Jesus, how could this have happened? He knew these guys weren't that smart. He guessed he'd underestimated their determination or the retribution they would have faced if they returned empty handed, or, maybe, it was just plain dumb luck. His suspicions had been correct, and he had gotten David mixed up in it. That chopper's occupants wanted Anderson dead.

The Colonel wanted Brenner dead. The Colonel passed money to the enemy in exchange for drugs, and he did so in plain sight of American prisoners. Where did the drugs come from? They looked like the opium packets he had seen the Karen working with when his team was helping them stand up to the Burmese, a little sideline calculated to keep the Karen quiet while training the Laotians in the Karen's mountains.

Everyone was aware that the CIA helped the Meo tribesmen distribute their poppy harvest. It was a simple business deal. Both the Burmese and the Thais wanted the revenue that the nomads generated in the mountains that made up the border between the two countries. The Karen and Meo had fought them both for hundreds of years. Special Forces, in league with the CIA, had offered the Karen and the Meo protection from both countries in exchange for favors. It was called "establishing rapport". America wanted them on their side; they wanted intelligence gathering, and they wanted to control the southern Chinese border. Both tribes were more than obliging to this offer. They also allowed the American Special Forces Teams to train Laotian Commandos atop their mountains in preparation for deployment into North Vietnam. That is where Anderson learned that the agency had not only offered them protection but distribution of their poppy via Air America. It was all too sweet for everyone. The Karen got to stay in their beloved mountains. The Meo got to continue growing poppy, and the Karen got to help with, and buy part of, the harvest. They were encouraged to sell it to the CIA. And they didn't have to worry about the Burmese and the Thais. The Americans were able to control the mountainous border without incident and train far from their area of deployment. They were able to operate with these teams in North Vietnam without anyone's knowledge. But the missing link: just what in the hell did the CIA do with the opium, and where did Air America take it? Rumor had it that the stuff was sold to Turkey, was processed, and then ended up on the streets of New York. Or was it processed and made into medicine for the control of pain? What was missing of course was, who cared. Obviously, it was someone who stood to profit handsomely from the black syrup.

Profiteering drove the chopper crew to kill his cousin. Were they acting on their own? Anderson knew better. This operation had to be orchestrated by someone with the authority to deploy, spend, and sacrifice. It had to be the Colonel. He must have sent Anderson in to waste the witness or a stooge gone bad. But why not just do it himself? And the prisoners?

No, thought Anderson, it doesn't add up. The Colonel was obviously authorized by the CIA to pay off drug accounts. That accounted for the money in the Colonel's safe. He had to be authorized as well to pay off Special Forces teams to establish intelligence networks, gain rapport, and generally carry out the dirty work. Although this was not what Anderson would call an ethical American undertaking, it didn't hang the Colonel out as being a crook either.

The Major? The Colonel lived primarily on his laurels, but the Major lived off the Colonel's laurels as well. This must grate on the Major something fierce. As the Colonel's right hand man, he, in fact, had absolute authority to act in the Colonel's behalf. The guy could do, and get away with, practically anything he wanted to in Southeast Asia. It made sense. The Colonel would never suspect that his man of thirty years would incriminate his name behind his back.

But the Major couldn't do it all alone. He had to have trusted, greedy, inside men and a buying organization somewhere, the States most likely.

Anderson thought again about David. He had to take out the men responsible. They couldn't be left to grow fat and rich and have gotten away with killing his friend. He wondered what the reports would be about himself. Anderson knew that to die in Laos or North Vietnam was to die officially in South Vietnam. They couldn't deny that he existed. Too shaky to forge a manifest. No, they would just report him fallen in South Vietnam like all the rest. He knew that he couldn't get to his mother or family before they sent the customary "I regret to inform you" letter. He wondered if Angela would find out or be too far removed from him to be able to.

His need for rest and the desire to sleep fought his conscious marathon. Thoughts of the Colonel, Brenner, the Major, and drugs reeled in his mind. He turned finally to memories of his friend, his cousin, and images of the past.

CHAPTER TWENTY THREE

"Hey, David, you peckerhead, come on over here and look at this."

David knew what Anderson wanted. "Jeez. Let's just get outta here," he yelled back.

"Don't be such a pain in the ass. Look, I hit it again!" Anderson ran toward the impatient sounds of the pickup truck, rifle in hand. David was already moving out as the door slammed shut.

The cousins rode along the rock-strewn, dusty roads near their home, oblivious to the future, to the coming events that would test their pioneer heritage, and to the mad world outside their mountainous sanctuary. They were young discoverers of life, continually exploring the Rockies, the social structure around them, and themselves.

Anderson had returned for a brief visit home. He and David were doing what they spent most of their time doing among the small communities: riding in a car or pickup down and around and up endless mountain roads. Anderson watched the river - familiar, alive, energetic - flow through the canyon and remembered the many things he had done on its shores: hunting, running his dogs, swimming, and just enjoying a mindless cycle of discovery, recovery, and happiness.

"I'm in love," David had suddenly said.

Anderson remembered well the feeling that shot through his insides. It made his hair stand on end like the butterflies he got in his gut when he had to deliver a speech in school. It always happened to him when someone said or did something that appeared so much out of character.

Anderson turned his eyes to David and surveyed his features. Was this David's mischievousness surfacing again? There was the familiar gleam in his eye all right, one of genuine happiness.

"Kingston? Monica? 'Mon, cuz, you remember."

Anderson searched his memory; he ran quickly through all the local girls with whom they had attended high school. Ah, yes, he remembered. He visualized the young girl, not yet grown. His mind's eye saw a small, plain girl with a smiling face, yet just a face in the crowd. She had been a few grades behind him, a non-entity from his school years.

David went on, "Me and Tommy were at a dance. I just started dancing with her and talking. You can't believe how beautiful she is. I'm gonna to marry her," David smirked with self-confidence, "but she doesn't know it yet." He seemed to imagine himself the winner of a game that hadn't quite gotten under way.

Just then the pickup pulled off the highway and onto a small dirt road that sloped steeply toward the river. The road was not long and terminated at a homestead with familiar sheds, corrals, and fences in need of repair. The yard was native landscaping. Lilacs, cottonwood trees, and birch lined the property on the riverside. Mild winds brought the odor and sounds of the water as it cascaded over the granite and volcanic rock that made up the river bottom. The hillside beyond and across the river took a steep ascent to the ever heightening mountains beyond. A hundred yards from the house sage brush and shale gave way to juniper and bedding grounds for mule deer that waited for nightfall and the succulent grasses and the water below. Mustard weed lay thick and pungent, jutting yellow fingers into the gray sage like honey pouring from a beehive. Anderson recognized the area as belonging to the Sutton family. David, without a word, hopped out of the car and was on his way to see his new found love. He stepped up to the front door of the house and received a response to his knock within seconds. Anderson never forgot the young woman that greeted them at the door that day: natural, flushed cheeks, light brown hair, a mouth that was always smiling with a delicate unevenness of the lips, eyes that gleamed eternal happiness and a look for his cousin that broke Anderson's heart. The young woman's wonderful face was held in the air by a perfect figure. He was amazed at the transition she had made since high school. In the next few minutes and over the following months, Anderson came to know well her special light and her gleaming eyes that matched those of his cousin and best friend. He also came to know the jealousy one can feel of another who had something so special, devastated by the feeling that he might never have it for himself.

After some amount of small talk and an agreement between David and Monica when they might next see each other, Anderson and his cousin were on their way, going nowhere. As they rode along, David spoke to Anderson in ways that Anderson had never heard him speak before.

"Been doing some farmin'. Dad gave me the forty over by the Simmons' place. I mean, mine to plant in my own way, do with like I want," David said. "I can't exactly explain, but I really like it. Planting it and seeing it grow gives me a great feeling, like it's part of me, like this is what I should be doing. It's great to see things grow that you planted yourself."

Again, Anderson felt that twinge in his stomach; again, David was being so out of character. He had helped his dad run the farm, the cattle, and the milk herd most of his life. But it was always a chore, something to weasel out of. David was proud that he could operate all the farm equipment, that he was good at it, and that he had the ability to do anything well, that is, so long as it had nothing to with academia. Not that he wouldn't be good at that also, but "hitting the books" never fit in with David's "let's go, we've got an adventure to experience" attitude. He was a person of extraordinary gifts, almost none of which he had ever used to any real good. His reflexes and strength were nothing short of phenomenal. Anderson was always amazed at how David would catch their supper of fish with only his hands, no fishing pole, no spear, just his hands. Anderson tried to match him in what constituted his gifts and his personality, but he could not. David always exploded into Anderson's home like no one else. He left like no one else. He drank like no one else. He fought like no one else. There was no one else, not when David was around.

Anderson thought about what his cousin was telling him and knew that it was true: David was feeling some deeper, more mature part of himself. The girl, the farm, all were stirring in his cousin a new being, a new form of himself. Anderson grew nervous of such realizations and changed the subject by suggesting that they get the guns.

The people from the mountainous area of Anderson's youth were pioneers, Mormons whose ancestors had braved many trials to claim the land and settle it in their own way. They were farmers and ranchers and third generation mountain folk. They were also hunters and had for a hundred years supplemented their diet with fresh game. Pheasant, deer, and elk were indigenous, and in the fall and winter, the area lay in the flight path of mallards and geese. To youngsters, the guns were like a tractor on the farm: the first few times using them were a thrill, something new, an adventure of sorts. But in the end, like the tractor, the newness wore off, and it was just a tool, rarely used unless needed.

Not for Anderson. Guns remained the fascination of a lifetime, a never ending source of enjoyment. Anderson never regarded these feelings as out of the ordinary, but there were those who did. In particular was David's father, who surprised Anderson one day when he burst out, "You are too fascinated with guns boy, it ain't healthy." Anderson had often pondered over the truth, or lack of it, of his uncle's statement. He had finally come to the conclusion that it was only the declaration of one who did not share his feelings about much of anything. No one understood why Anderson bothered with so many of the finer points of his rifles. None of them hand loaded their ammo.

The men's regard for their weapons was strong. They enjoyed talking about the various calibers and which might prove best for deer in their mountain ranges. They prided the ownership of reasonably priced, scope mounted Remingtons and Winchesters that had become popular during the early 60's. But in the end, the guns really had only their singular use for these pioneers: harvesting the animals in which they took great enjoyment and pride in hunting. The men's routine was the same year in and year out. The rifles languished in a closet for months without being cleaned, then they were pulled from their dark resting places a few weeks before hunting season. They purchased cartridges from the local general store and sighted their rifles in over some nearby object used to steady their aim. The men often took time to assure themselves that the bullets were impacting an inch or so above the bulls-eye at one hundred yards. Perception dictated that the bullet's trajectory with such a one hundred yard point of impact would allow them to be on target at some vague, longer distance.

The mountainous west often presented long shots. These pioneers had become accustomed to taking such shots and being successful. As the early sixties presented themselves, so did the .264 Magnum, the .270, and an assortment of other mid-range cartridges. The 30-30's and .300 Savages of old began to disappear. It was the conversation of the time, and time was what they often had plenty of, along with venison.

To Anderson the rifles became an obsession. He poured over everything he could find. He spent long hours making each cartridge a thing of precision. Each had to match the next. Hours of testing went into bedding the rifle, squaring the action to the barrel, and the myriad technical items that were a part of solving the harmonics of the barrel. Cartridges were loaded with various powders, bullets, and primers until the correct velocity and pressure were established to produce a combination that sent each bullet into phenomenally small groups. The bullet's depth in the case was varied away from the barrel's lands and then toward and into them until the repeatability of impact was even more finely tuned.

Anderson prided himself on being able to place a bullet within hundredths of an inch of a designated point at one hundred yards. He and David called such feats "DAZ" for Dead Ass Zero or sometimes just "DN" for Dead Nuts.

At their make-shift range, David watched with boredom as Anderson proved again that he could take the flag off the U. S. Treasury building on a ten dollar bill without touching the pole.

At the one hundred yard target line, Anderson would ask his cousin to choose the right or left eye of Hamilton. Anderson never tired of performing such feats: The eye on the pyramid of a one dollar bill, the four numbers on the bill on either side of the faces, the little men in front of the Treasury, the old Ford. All were potential targets.

"Which wheel, come on, which wheel?" Anderson would urge.

"Who gives a shit? Don't you ever get tired of this bullshit? Let's go get a bottle of Melrose and suck up some attitude."

"Come on. A few more rounds and I'll be through. Then we'll go look at your damn field. I want to see what's got you so fired up. If it's half as good as that skirt you're so nuts about, it must be something."

"Damn it, I'm serious about this. Give me any shit over her and I'll drop your water works and hit you over the head with the bloody end of 'em," David shot back.

“OK. OK.” Anderson replied meekly. “So you’re love sick. I can handle that. But you ain’t got a pot to piss in. What about that? How are you going take care of her?”

Anderson fired again. Hamilton’s left eye disappeared.

“Hey, dude, look there: dead nuts!”

As they rode away, going nowhere in particular, Anderson thought of the girl and David and Monica and felt the hurt and the jealousy bite deeply into his gut.

CHAPTER TWENTY FOUR

Anderson finally succumbed to sleep thinking of David and the look he had on his face as he told Anderson to jump. Only David had known of his plan and his decision to be the life giving bait.

He woke hours later, feeling sore and weary. He managed to find room in the case for the Madsen M53 short assault rifle. He had a long way to go, and the rifles sure as hell weren't going to help him out of this situation. Anderson checked the compass that hung from his dog tag chain. He knew his position and the approximate azimuth to the village where he had befriended, then recruited and trained, the Hmong commandos. With luck he could reach it in two days. First, he had to have something to eat. The last thing he had put in his stomach were those damnable LRRP rations. Except for bananas, to which Anderson was deathly allergic, the jungle was full of vegetables and fruits for the taking. Water was always available in the fleshy plants that grew almost everywhere. If one had to exist with just a pocketknife, the jungle was the place to do it. Anderson had a slight problem, however. He had a bad gash on his left forearm, and the punctured leg was not looking as good as he had hoped. The opening in his arm could be stitched but he had to do something else with the leg. He had hoped to get back to Bangkok to get help. Now he had no choice. He extracted the soap dish from his pants pocket and laid it on the black case that held the rifles. He carefully removed the tape used to keep it closed as well as to second as a bandage closure. Inside were needle and suture. He prepped the area around the wound with the antiseptic, careful not to get any inside; killing the delicate tissue with antiseptic invited infection. He threaded the catgut in the needle. Carefully, he closed the bottom of the wound and worked his way toward the top. He placed a small piece of iodoform gauze in the bottom, and then ran it up and out onto a clean area of the skin. This would act as a drain to help prevent any bacterial pockets from building up inside the closed wound as it healed.

Anderson paused, lay back on a rotting tree stump, and tried to regain his composure. The pain and the act of suturing his own arm without topical anesthetics had left him weak and sweating profusely. Shaking his head violently, he tried to force the alertness he needed to finish the job and push on.

He threaded nylon into the needle to complete the final closure. Anderson proximated the edges of the skin and took a stitch near the center. He continued this procedure until the wound was closed, leaving the gauze protruding from between two of the stitches. He tore part of his shirt and wrapped the wound with it.

But now came the more difficult wound. Gas gangrene was the fear with any wound in this hot, humid climate. Not even a day had passed since the door gunner had nailed him. He hoped he was still safe, but he knew there was dead and traumatized flesh deep in his leg. Debridement down to viable tissue was necessary. Cauterizing would stop the bleeding and kill bacteria temporarily, but not for long. No, there was a better way to treat the deep puncture. He replaced the items in the soap dish and secured it with the remaining tape. Tugging the black case to his shoulders, he struck out, stiffly, in the direction of a village he knew well.

Anderson kept a look out for what he knew would keep his leg free of anaerobic bacteria until he could find help. He had fought the jungle for more than two hours when his nostrils flared from the pungent odor of dead, rotting flesh. He turned until the wind was in his face and then proceeded slowly. It did not take long to locate the offending carcass.

Anderson removed his pants, tore the entire bottom from his shirt, and removed both sleeves with his pocketknife. He laid them carefully on top of the black case. He tugged on the dead carcass until it turned over with a flop. There they were, hundreds of them: maggots: ugly, squirming, living in filth. But, ironically, they represented the only chance Anderson might have.

He scooped the larva up in his hands and deposited them on the bandage he had fashioned. Quickly, he tied the shirt around his thigh over the wound. The insects would eat only nonviable tissue. The bacteria that required such tissue could not gain foothold enough to produce systemic effects nor could anaerobic bacteria survive the larva's onslaught.

Anderson took four tablets - a loading dose of Tetracycline - and left the remaining bottle out of the homemade medical kit. There was no more that he could do except get back as soon as possible. He could feel the squirming insects against his skin, laboring to enter the puncture wound. He could also feel the dull throb in his leg grow worse. He looked again at the miniature medical kit. This and the sickness he felt coming on were beginning to rattle him. He knew it was there inside, small and green like a tiny tube of tooth paste with a humming bird's tongue flicking from one end, dripping the clear salve: the morphine syrette. No, not yet. He had to think, to walk without the stupor that the drug would produce.

He walked into the small village in the Laotian interior near Phou Bia, one of Lao's highest peaks, on schedule. It took all he had. His balance seemed off, his legs were weak, and he had stopped sweating. Anderson was perfectly built for such a challenge. He was not so big that his endurance suffered, but he was not so small that he lacked strength. The combination complemented and balanced the attributes he needed to survive under such stress. But even the best could only go so far.

The Hmong were happy to see him. There was nothing he desired they wouldn't produce. But they never tired of watching his strange American customs. They lamented at his putting halazone tablets in the water. After all, they had drunk the water all their lives; it had to be good. Yes, he explained, but they were strong while the Americans were weak and could not survive as they could.

The natives looked upon some American habits as unsanitary. It never ceased to amaze them that Americans blew their noses into pieces of cloth and then stored them in their hind pockets like jewels, or that they took baths in tubs and sat in the very water that was washing the dirt from their bodies.

Anderson was relieved to finally find a safe haven. While the area often crawled with Viets, Pathet Lao, or collaborators, he was friends with the village chief and several of the younger men. They prepared a hut for him, and once the greetings were obliged, Anderson felt he could get some rest.

He woke in the early morning hours feverish. He took more antibiotic and drank a quart of water. His appetite was gone. By late morning, Anderson was nearly delirious with fever and pain. The Chief tried to help. He wanted Anderson to let his wife clean the wound and apply some local herbs, but Anderson wouldn't hear of it. "No. You must leave the bandages on," he argued.

Anderson hovered near death for two days before the fever broke. Fearful, madding dreams had filled the long hours. The sudden release from the alternating heat and chills left him euphoric. He felt that he was going to make it.

He had lain there, drenched in his own secretions for more than an hour when someone entered.

"You feel better?" Chi You asked.

The village patriarch was a diminutive man, slim and gaunt. His smile was as big as life itself, filled with black teeth from years of chewing beetle nut. A mild tug would have severed them from his mouth forever. His weathered body was exposed above the waist; a colorful pakima covered the rest of him above his knees. His feet were wide and callused and afforded him good support on the sloped hills that surrounded his community. He carried the traditional Gurkha style knife at his waist. The handle was fashioned from rosewood to match the scabbard that was thrust between the cloth and his stomach. From his neck hung the Buddhist priest's carving to ward off evil. Crafted from human bones, they were revered more than the heavy gold chains from which they dangled.

"Finally. Guess I'll live," replied Anderson. "I do have a touch of diarrhea though. Please boil some water for me and bring coals from the fire. Grind the charcoal into powder. I will add the charcoal to the water myself."

"You need the opium, Andy."

"Thank you, Chi You. That's even better."

Chi heated a ball of opium on the end of a small metal rod. He worried it into the pipe. The two men lay facing each other, smoking. The tranquility flower's precious gift soon flooded their bodies with delicious indifference to the world's madness.

But even the poppy couldn't overcome the old man's worries. Chi finally spoke.

"Death is very close to us in these hills. A snake or a tiger may bite you, or you might fall off a cliff or drown in a stream. If men do not behave, disaster always follows: disease, death of chickens, pigs, and water buffaloes, or poor crops.

"We have no medicine or doctors like the Thais and the foreigners, so we must rely on the spirits. When something goes wrong, we divine with the aid of chicken bones. If the divination says that the spirits must be fed a pig, we sacrifice a pig. A chicken won't do.

"We are glad to help the Americans, Andy. But I am afraid. When you leave us, the Viet and Pathet Lao will come after my people. Our problems are small here in the mountains. We do things that we have done for many generations. But we know we can't stand up to the Viets ourselves.

"There are political factions here in our country as well. They are terrible people. Even the Cambodians to the south are hungry to rule.

"I don't know, Andy. I fear for the future." The old man's face was grim. He shook his head, depressed by his predictions.

Anderson peered through the smoke filled hut. Chi's face seemed softer than he had ever seen it.

"Chi, listen to me. Protect your people. Stick to yourselves. Don't help the Americans or anyone else."

"No. We were glad for the chance to help against the Viet and Pathet Lao. They are tyrants. They treat us like cattle."

The conversation lapsed as the two men pulled again on the pipe. But amid the haze, Anderson could not get the past events off his mind.

"Chi, where do you get the opium?"

"I am not sure. A man brings it from the east. He says he has connections. He is very proud of himself. It is good. No?"

Anderson had no comment to such a question, but instead smiled for the old man's benefit while thinking of how he would get to Vientiane. He knew he could not do so without their help. Could they help him, he asked?

"Yes. Yes," Chi answered. "We can arrange that. There are many cousins along the way. They will help."

Chi chose two young men to accompany Anderson to Vientiane. They had worked with the American's secret war before and were anxious to help. Everything would work out they explained. Not to worry.

The trip was a cacophony of half-naked human souls, arguments, payoffs, and sour food, but after four days they were at the outskirts of the great city, the city where young Americans came to lose themselves in the filth and squalor of the opium dens. Once at their journeys end, having traveled north through Malaysia and Thailand, they settled into a life of dreams and escape. At thirty cents a hit, few ever survived their money.

Anderson asked his companions to go into the city for new clothes, a backpack, and regular shoes. He told them they must find a large U bolt, a strong pair of pliers, and a small length of pipe, showing them the diameter required. When they were gone, Anderson settled back to rest and wait.

The Hmong shook Anderson from a fitful slumber. Backlit by the afternoon sun, they looked surreal to his waking brain. When he regained his senses, he began to examine the bundles they had laid before him. As the young men from the mountainous jungle laughed about the sights of the city from which they had just returned, Anderson busied himself. He noted that they had managed everything but the pliers. He thought it strange that they had found a U bolt but no pliers. He glanced at them about to ask but then saw that they had changed into their traditional pakimas. No, if they had found pliers, he thought, they would have given them to him.

He located a small branch just short of waist height. With the machete like knives the natives carried, he hacked all but a foot of the branch from the tree. While he attended to the Madsen M53 he asked the Laotians to build a fire. When the flames took hold, he withdrew a small rod from the case and placed the end in the fire. He had removed the barrel of the M53 and also removed the magazine and swiveled the stock forward. The already short rifle was now only half the size it had been when assembled.

When the steel rod was red hot, Anderson pushed the heated point into the stubby branch, repeating the process until a hole was pierced through. The rod was heated again and another hole created. He pushed the U bolt through the holes and attached the nuts. To adjust the length he needed the bolt to protrude, he cut flat spots on both sides of the branch. At last the U bolt fit, leaving more than an inch of the U portion above the wood. Anderson slid the barrel of the precision rifle through the U bolt. When the nuts were finger tight, he used his belt to tighten them as much as he could. Anderson raised the bolt handle, pulled it to the rear approximately a half inch, and ran the small pipe over it. With a quick tug, the receiver began to turn. Anderson knew that the bolt handle, which was only silver soldered to the bolt shaft, would have broken off before the barrel threads gave in any normal rifle. But this one was made to easily switch barrels. With very few rounds through the barrel since it had last been installed, he stood a good chance of success. It was luck and he knew it.

Anderson placed the two shortened rifles and the rolled up case in the backpack, changed clothes, and tried the new shoes on. Far be it for him to complain that they were leather clappers. At least they had a leather heel strap. He truly hated ones without.

"How do I look?" He exclaimed.

The boys laughed, explaining that Americans always looked pretty strange to them. After he thanked and said farewell to his saviors, Anderson struck out for the city, turning around once to find them grinning and bowing exaggeratedly. It was the polite way, but he knew they were jibing him a bit also.

He hoped he looked the part of a down and out white man. Squalid appearance, limping slightly, unshaven, and disheveled hair added to his authenticity. The backpack and clappers were the final touch, just another harmless, addicted American. He was on his way home. The military was behind him, and they no longer carried any jurisdiction. Besides, they thought he was dead.

Anderson finally located the train that made its way from Vientiane to Bangkok. He sat among the peasants with their chickens and vegetables. Life would truly be great if he had a bottle of Chevis about now, he thought. He could not sleep on the hardwood, pew-like seats. He didn't care. He was alive. He had only to put the names on the list. Each would pay for David. Each would pay for treachery and greed. Of course he knew that once they realized he was alive, it didn't matter much anyway. It would be them or him until it was over. The war had not ended, only the players, the reasons, and the sides.

He watched from the window as the train passed ornate temples, golden in the fading sun, the rush of objects nearby that sometimes failed to register any identity in his brain, the klongs that moved like melted, flowing amethyst across the country side below a blue sky fleeing from the onslaught of nightfall. Blackened silhouettes of stick-men dipped their blades beside dugout canoes and sliced through the water, returning home amid the shimmer of nightlight.

Features of the shapes and sounds and life in the car around him began to haze and disappear: the cluck of a chicken, the impatient clatter of hooves of an anxious goat against a hollow floor, the haunting cry of a baby in a distant car beckoning his mother to press her breast into his mouth, the touch of the soft, oily surface of the seat giving way to the hardness of stone. Smells invading his nostrils with human-ness, garlic, spices, the cauldron of animal, vegetable, and drying fish, grew dimmer. The imprint of rhythmic, monotonous flashing of lights through the window and the thump of steel wheels against the edge of each rail joint threatened permanence like the sun's white yellow globe behind closed eyelids. Surreal impressions boiled in his brain as Anderson gave into fatigue, his chin bobbing against his chest.

CHAPTER TWENTY FIVE

Angela paced her bedroom floor. She was not willing to accept it. There must be some other explanation. Anderson couldn't be gone. He just couldn't be. She tried to remember his voice. The last things they said. There must be a clue. Someone doesn't call and tell you that someone else who existed just doesn't exist anymore. Why had he gone to the States and then returned? She knew GI's seldom came home for R & R; why did he?

Then something flashed across her mind. Bill Baedeker.

"Hello, is this Bill?"

"Sure is ma'am. And who might this be?"

"Angela. I was with Anderson. Don't you remember?"

"Oh hell yes, little lady. How's it shakin'? Where's Anderson?"

"Oh no. I was hoping you could tell me. I got a call from Major McCauley. He told me that Anderson was dead."

There was silence on the other end. "I didn't know that, Angela. I'm real sorry. Anderson was good people. I hate to see it happen. I know he was crazy about you. In fact, he wanted me to give you a message but you were already gone."

"Message? What? What did he say?"

"Only that he wanted to make sure you knew he liked you, and that he might miss seeing you at the Opera. It was pretty clear that he is, or rather was, crazy about you."

"Thank you so much, Bill. Please call me if you hear anything more. I'm counting on this not being true."

"I sure will. Don't you worry."

Bill hung up, laid down the phone, and looked toward the table in the far, dark corner of the bar. Anderson nodded. It would be alright.

Bill closed the bar about fifteen minutes after the phone call. He came over to the table Anderson had chosen.

"So, what's the story? You look like warmed over dog shit. Come on up and put yourself back together, then tell me all about it, paisan."

"Bill, I need lots of penicillin, bandages, iodoform gauze, and other supplies. Where is the crate, still at Bobbie's?"

"OK, OK. Come on upstairs and get in the tub. I'll get your stuff and you can work on smelling better. Heww, what is that anyway, eau de cologne of pig sty?"

Bill's wife, Peanuts, helped Anderson with his clothes. When they removed the bandage from his leg, both stepped back. The sight was incredible, horrifying. Maggots crawled in and out and around the wound looking hungry and gaunt. His friends were paralyzed by the sight.

Anderson laughed. "Hey, meet my little friends."

He asked Bill's wife if she had a normal size straw or a piece of small, hollow bamboo. She produced the latter almost immediately. Anderson forced the wood into the wound.

"Now, Bill, light up a cigarette and blow the smoke inside."

They all watched as a half dozen more of the insects crawled out of the hole in Anderson's flesh. But the wound was clean and pink, and drainage was nonexistent. After they had him languishing in a hot bath, sipping on Chevis, Bill left to collect the supplies Anderson had requested.

Anderson was not finished soaking by the time Bill returned. Everything was there. Anderson administered two million units of procaine penicillin to his thigh, and he would continue to do so on a regular basis until the supply ran out. Bill's wife helped bandage both wounds. Anderson began to resemble his old self once again. Bill donated some oversized clothes, and the refurbishing was complete.

"Where you going from here, ole man?" Bill inquired.

"I'm wondering if it's smart to tell you. If they find out that I'm alive, they might come over here and put the hurt on you."

"What the hell difference does it make? They'll kick the shit out of me anyway if they find out that I've helped you as much as I have."

"I'm sorry about that. I appreciate your help. I'm not military anymore. I scammed that out of the bastards. So I can't ship out on anything military. I don't want to be seen near any airport around here anyway. I think my best bet is to take the train to Singapore and ship out from there. Most people will take me for a junkhead who's lost or made it back from the dens."

"You're probably right. That may be your only way out. We can put you on the train at night. Maybe we ought to take you south by car a hundred miles first and let you board there."

"No, I'll be alright. I could use a ride to Bobbie's though. I need to put my black case and a couple other items in the crate. Day after tomorrow I would like you to send the crate to my place in the states. With a little luck, you won't have to fool with me anymore.

"You never got around to telling me what Angela said on the phone. Did she sound OK? What was the deal?"

"She said Major McCauley had called for her dad. He told her you were dead. She's not inclined to believe it. I think the truth is: she's simply not in a position to let herself believe it. She told me to call if I found out anything. She sounded alright under the circumstances."

Anderson watched the incense burning below a small Buddha that sat bull-like in the middle of a tiny teakwood table neatly covered with a linen cloth. He turned his gaze to the Nescafe in front of him, absentmindedly fascinated by the separation of the instant coffee from the thick, Danish cream. Beside it lay the zippo lighter with the dagger and crossed sword emblem brazed to its front. Completing the triangle, the L&M cigarette lay perched in the ashtray and burned faithfully, its blue-gray tendril moved slowly from side to side, rising and twisting into vertices that spiraled outwardly in opposing directions, widening with height until they disappeared.

"What's going down here, Bill, and who are the players?" Anderson said, looking up and into Bill's eyes.

"Anderson, it's the same ole stuff, drug money. And it's got to be big. You don't just sit this crap out on your friendly roadside stand. Big money means an organization, front men, buyers, sellers, daddy warbucks. It starts here, but no telling where it ends: Seattle, Los Angeles, New York, you name it. It's common knowledge what the Meo and Karen grow, and it's common knowledge that Air America is flying it out. Nobody but insiders knows where it goes. But it doesn't take a lot of brain power to realize that somebody's got to be skimming along the way. You know that the assholes who tried to waste you are under Colonel Langlinais' control. That shit couldn't go on without his knowledge or someone in a position to insulate him from it. Will ya listen to me. Missed my calling. Shouldda been a detective."

"These pricks waste everything they touch: my cousin, good men in country, the Karen, the indigs, the kids they pedal it to, and me. When they find out I'm alive, and they will, I'm a dead man. I'm the only link they've got over here. The Colonel's flying fat and happy not knowing shit. But they tried to waste me. They'll realize that I know something, and anything is too much for them to chance. Guess there's only one thing left for me to do. Take as many of those assholes with me as I can. Who knows, maybe I'll get lucky," Anderson smiled.

"Which leads me to another couple of favors I need from you. Call flight control at the base. Ask for the manifest of the chopper that left last week and logged 1200 miles. Tell the guy that you're from payroll and can't find out if they were on a hazardous duty run or not. Tell them you need to know because some CO has got them logged for extra pay, but there's nothing to substantiate it. Ask for the names on the manifest so you can verify that it's not a mix up with another flight.

"And last but not least, and certainly not the easiest, I need to know what is inside a file in the Colonel's office. The file is labeled Operation Deja Vu. It was lying with all the other stuff I saw when I got into this whole mess. I think it's CIA based. It was pretty common knowledge that the Colonel's activities were directed and funded by the Agency."

"Are you nuts? How in the hell do you expect me to do that?

If they don't kill me, they'll ship my ass off to Leavenworth."

"I don't know Bill. I thought you might have an idea. I'll call you later to see if you've found out anything."

Anderson said good-bye to his good friend before dawn the next morning. His goods were safely packed in the crate and would be on their way home soon. The train was a familiar, mobile hard spot, and Singapore was a long way off. As he rode the rails south, Anderson planned. It crossed his mind that he could simply stop in some place like Jakarta and spend the rest of his days. He would probably have a lot more of them left if he did.

But he had a message to deliver and a few payoffs to make. Somebody was going down; they just didn't know it yet. It was beginning to look like the good Major would be one of his targets. But who else? Who was on the manifest in that helicopter? Who were the State side contacts?

Anderson went over and over what had happened, trying to put it all together for the thousand odd miles it took to get to the southern tip of Malaysia. Plans, options, and alternatives were beginning to formulate as he finally approached the city's station.

A few hours later and he looked at the southern peninsula for what he hoped would be the last time as the commercial airliner lifted off the ground and headed for blue sky and the open ocean.

CHAPTER TWENTY SIX

"Major, let's go over this again. I don't understand Anderson's actions. You say he eliminated Little Ho, two officers, and some noncoms? What the hell for? His only official target was Brenner." The Colonel didn't wait for an answer; he went on.

"Manipulating the Meo's opium harvest solves many problems for this area, for the military, and for the world. Being ransomed by some damn renegade North Vietnam Regulars for American prisoners had us stepping out of bounds for a while, but this last request is bullshit. I ought to blow them out of that stinking jungle!

"Now that Brenner is out of the picture, we can't waste any time. This negotiation crap has got to come to an end. I want our boys out of there now!

"And what is this stuff about a Russian case? What the hell was Anderson doing with a Russian stamped case, shooting everybody in sight? It doesn't add up. That helicopter pilot was two hundred, maybe even three or four hundred yards out. How did he know it was Anderson? Somebody in camo and striped face; it could have been anyone. Besides, the hit was a day early, and we never did hear from Anderson. Put this together for me, Major. And while you're at it, tell me what Anderson was doing standing in a field doing battle with these little bastards. He should have been long gone by the time they gained their senses. He should have had no less than a five hundred yard lead. Did you ask to see his body? Russian case? What? Am I supposed to think the Russians are in on this? Bullshit!" The Colonel finally took a breath from his disjointed monologue.

"Sir, your comments are well taken. I can't explain them. It just seems absurdly coincidental that someone else, someone not even involved, made a hit so close to the date we marked."

The Major didn't like the heat. "The new spokesman seems sincere about giving us our prisoners this time. I couldn't reason with the guy until I met his demands. But what the hell, Colonel, at least this will put an end to it."

"By god, it better, McCauley, or somebody's balls are going to fry and it's likely to be ours. Now get on with it."

Major McCauley steamed out of the Colonel's office. He was annoyed. He didn't like the hot seat. Mainly, he didn't like it because he knew he was smarter than the Colonel but couldn't show it. Politics was the only reason the Colonel always remained one rank ahead of him, and he resented it. Always the second, the tail wagging puppy, the buffoon. He was fed up, but his day was coming.

"Johnson, I want some answers and I want them now!"

"I told you, sir. We spotted Anderson at the end of a long clearin' in the jungle. He had been bringin' us in for about five minutes. We closed and then fired. Just like you said, we stayed back a good ways and used the door's sixty. We couldn't tell whether we got a hit or not; he never stopped runnin'. When he went in the jungle, we pulled out and tried to figure where he might go. We decided he only had one choice, west. We tried it hoping to connect with him somewhere and finish the job.

"We started a zig zag course workin' west. Out of the blue we came on this chopper. We checked the log and weren't no such traffic. We figured he had to have a pickup; it seemed only logical that this was it. We closed and tried to bring it down. Whoever had hold of that stick was some kinda crazy. There were two personnel in the chopper. One kept stickin' his head out the starboard door to make us, but he was dressed in civvies. I don't think they had guns. We finally put 'em down over the river. The bird crashed and burned, sir."

"Could you recognize Anderson in the door?"

"Not exactly, sir."

"Damn. Who was the pilot? Could you make *him* out?"

"No, sir. No idea. But he was some kinda good."

"Tell me about the hit."

"Well, sir, they went round this bend in the river where I showed you. We saw them as soon as we cleared the trees. They banked hard left. They were out about three hundred. It was an easy hit."

"Wait a minute. You lost sight of the chopper a few seconds before the hit? Were both men in the chopper when you sighted it?"

"I don't rightly know, sir. It happen' real fast. They were away from us when we first picked 'em up again. Then they made a hard left. The missile blew the damn thing to smithereens at that moment. I saw the pilot just as the round hit."

"I'll be a son-of-a-bitch. What you're telling me is that you don't know for sure whether it ever was Anderson. You're also telling me that you didn't really confirm the kill. You're telling me that at the instant of the hit you did not see the passenger. Is that right, Sergeant?"

"One thing I do know, sir. That wasn't a Russian pulling us into the LZ!"

Then Anderson could be alive, McCauley reasoned. If that were true, where in the hell was he? The whole organization better be finding out or the roof might blow right off the mansion he was yet to occupy. Worse yet, it might be his own head. How could they screw up such a simple operation? What should he do? He had no choice.

Anderson was on the loose and no telling where he might turn up. He was a time bomb waiting to go off in their faces. The Major was worried, money worried.

"Hello, is that you?" Major McCauley's voice was emotionless.

"For crying out loud, Major, of course it's me. What is it?" Coman seemed angry without yet knowing what the call was about.

"Our pigeon just flew the nest."

"Are you telling me that you let some no count grunt get away?"

"I can't confirm it. But the probability is high," McCauley admitted.

"Listen, you shit for brains. We can't have some leaky bastard wandering around. These people have got my asshole sewed shut. You better give me something to go on here, quick."

"The truth is, I can't even confirm that he is a leak. I mean, I'm not sure he has any idea what's going on. But he's got to be asking himself some hard questions about now. Like, why was he fired on by his pick-up."

"My guess is that he will show State side. If he does, it's your ass. Shit, Major, no wonder you assholes are losing the war against a bunch of pajama clad runts with Russian antiques for weapons." Coman was threatening.

"I'll admit it hasn't gone quite as well as I had hoped," the Major said, "but if you have half a brain, you'll keep that smart ass tongue of yours to your damn self."

The phone went dead. The Major could only stand there. He hated the Ivy League, draft dodging prick who had hung up on him. But a smile began to play over his lips. If irony was worth his own demise, it was in the fact that that asshole back home with his pool and his mint juleps hadn't met Anderson yet.

The Major finished chuckling and headed for records. No one except himself and a few noncoms knew what Anderson looked like. The states would need a picture and a profile. And it occurred to him that he had forgotten to ask Coman if the package had arrived.

CHAPTER TWENTY SEVEN

Takano waited patiently for Shimano to show the man in. The oriental was a slight but strong man with a huge, infectious smile. The long, clean, wispy hair shone black, accented by broad, auburn highlights in the afternoon sun. His eyes gleamed with the contrast of his excitement for life, which, in general, he took with a grain of salt. But business was a different matter; this he took very seriously for many depended on him, from the orient to the eastern shores of the U.S.

He worried about his front man. The big Caucasian was growing more paranoid by the day. It was dangerous to Takano's responsibilities.

Coman waited patiently for Takano's man to show him in. He nervously paced the small anteroom. An old injury had caused an arthritic condition in his neck, and it bothered him constantly, though more so when he was stressed. He rolled his head to the left and pulled his right shoulder down in an almost spastic attempt to stretch and ease the taught muscles in his neck. His once strong, athletic body had succumbed to the humbling changes of age: a few more hairs gone, a bit more gray, and the tire around his middle seemed destined to remain. Mornings were longer, and the stiffness in his joints less forgiving after rising from bed.

"Mr. Takano." The sound of his own voice reverberated in his head after the silence of the long wait.

"Ah yes. How are you? Join me won't you. How is your family?"

"They're fine. Thank you. I don't mean to be rude, but we think a problem may have developed. I wanted you to know. Apparently my men in the South have made an error. We will take care of it, of course."

"Please, go on."

Coman threw a file on the table in front of the oriental. Takano opened it. Without expression the little man studied the file: martial arts, light weapons, demolitions, medicine, nationally ranked marksman, survivalist, nurtured in mountainous back country. The list went on. Name: Anderson; decent: Scandinavian. And a picture.

"An interesting young man, quite accomplished, average appearance and size, but why the mystery? Why do you show this to me?"

"A leak, sir. He's Special Forces, untouchable. This kid was sent in to hit a bad apple. His pick-up was assigned to clean up. But now it appears that the cleaner missed. The kid seems indestructible, slippery. Bottom line: he's a lucky little bastard. Worse yet, he'd have to be real stupid to not know that something went down out there. He may know more. We don't want to alarm you but we think you should be aware that there might be a loose cannon. Just a precaution."

Takano's expression changed. He didn't like or trust this man. "You have disturbed me at my residence. You have jeopardized my anonymity for this boy. Let me explain to you your position. You are alone in this. You came to us because of a failing business, because you were frightened at losing face among your friends at the country club. You came like the greedy man to the devil, for promises of success.

"Don't let this trifle ripple our organization. Remember your place. You are nothing, a conduit, a diversion to serve the oriental influence in Los Angeles. You are entirely dispensable. Your survival depends on success and your continued business dealings in the South. Don't come to me again with trinkets.

"Now go and take care of your business. Don't make me have to do it for you. Shimano, see Mr. Coman out."

Coman was clearly shaken. He turned on his heel and left the gardens. As he drove through and out of Chinatown, he thought about his options and about how he had gotten into the business. Takano was right of course. He had tried to save his business and his standing in the L.A. social infrastructure. He had become an integral part of the city's business scene. But things had begun to sour. Manufacturing costs had begun to approach a flat market. Even though he was able to sell all that he could make, the cost to do so had finally crossed into his margin. Cash flow and his ability to sustain the life style that he and his family had become accustomed to began to be a burden he could no longer bear.

His dealings in the Orient had brought him in contact with men that had offered him a way out. He had been introduced to an Army officer in Bangkok at what appeared to be an innocent enough encounter at first. He realized only later that they had known and had played on his weaknesses. The scheme to use his many distribution channels to the States to cover the import of drugs appeared fool proof. It seemed likely that even if discovered, there could be no physical link to him personally. He didn't have to touch the stuff or even see it. For the most part, he didn't have to know when a shipment was made.

But things had changed as time went on. The profits were saving his business, and he was paying his bills. He began to take a more active role in the rates at which the unprocessed opium was coming to the California coast. The latitude that Takano gave him was unknown to those in Southeast Asia. They began to think of him as the number one man. The power that he began to command was exciting and profitable.

Albeit a self-made, strong, and confident survivalist in this world, he realized he was in over his head. He knew this was not his game. Basically, he was an honest, hard charging, college football hero, an all American type who had made it in the business world through hard dealings, obnoxious salesmanship, and an over bearing charm that shouted money. He had let himself be dragged into a world of international, underground crime of the worst kind.

Now this. How was he going to manage this? He was no killer. He had hoped that the Orientals would take care of it. Or maybe no one would have to. He had no idea how to accomplish it even if he could bring himself to do it or have it done. The real question was: How in the hell could he get out of it? He had to find a way to divorce himself from the whole thing.

Angela was seated by the fire in the den when her father came in. She barely acknowledged his presence.

"Angela, are you still moping about that boy? I'm sorry, but nothing can be done now. Besides, you only knew him for a few days. You'll forget him in time. I don't understand what this obsession with a damn foot soldier is anyway. Try to cheer up; there's thousands of fish in the sea. You'll find one of them sooner or later."

"Daddy, how can you be so insensitive. That boy, as you call him, was fighting for our country, or at least he thought he was. He was a decent person and warm and gentle. Damn, you make me mad sometimes. The truth of it is, I can't stand your club friends or their sons. Anderson died for his country. Don't you take any responsibility or pride in that, that he gave up his life twelve thousand miles away from home so that we could continue to lead the easy and safe life that we do?"

"Listen sweetheart," Coman said, "I'm not putting that down. But you deserve better. You are upper crust. That boy could not have taken care of you. He couldn't have had a penny to his name and probably never would have. And don't take it all out on me. After all, I didn't kill him." Angela's father finally gave up the argument and left for another room, removing his suit coat and tie as he went. He had to make a phone call. It hit him just as he was dialing the numbers. He placed the receiver back in the cradle and walked back into the room where he had left his daughter. He simply stared at her.

"What?" she asked.

"What did you say his name was?"

The Major hated complications. It made for lengthy paperwork. But now he had one. Find Anderson, if he were still alive, and waste his ass, again. Coman had made it clear that he didn't have the stomach for it. His pleading had disgusted McCauley. He was sitting back, his feet on his finely polished teak desk, wondering how to close this ugly mess when the phone rang.

"Major, I need to see you right away."

"What's up, sir?"

"Not over the phone."

Shit, McCauley grumbled to himself. What the hell did the old man want now, another party? Oh well, he wouldn't have to shag ass for the pompous bastard for long. He already had more money than the Colonel would ever see in his life. One more week, just one more run, and he was out of here. He could finally get back to the world and start living like he should have been doing all along.

As he entered the CO's office, he could feel the tension in the air. He could read the Colonel's body language after years of working with him.

"What's up, Colonel?"

"I'm not quite sure, McCauley. I can't seem to locate the file. It has been in the drawer along with the maps. You didn't take it did you?"

"No sir. It was there the last time I was in the office. I added to it myself."

"Major, we've got to recover that file. The agency will have our asses in a barrel if it's not found. In the wrong hands they may court-martial us anyway."

"I'll get on it right away."

The Major knew he had a hell of a lot more to worry about than the Colonel realized. There was information there that some smart ass CIA dick could uncover. The file had to be found. Loose ends would have to be tied up.

Ten minutes later a swarthy, muscular man sat in the Major's office. His air of confidence was well deserved. He had several kills to his credit, and he was known for cleaning up messes the Major left in his wake.

"We've got a problem to resolve," the Major began.

CHAPTER TWENTY EIGHT

"Can you talk louder? I seem to have a bad connection on this end." Anderson was shouting.

"I said that I have part of the information for you. I also have the names on the manifest." Bill proceeded to give Anderson the names of the men who had been aboard the helicopter that day.

"Thank you, Bill."

"About the file. I've got it. My wife has a friend who cleans there. We convinced her that it would be profitable to do us this favor. We wrote big letters so she could match the text to that on the file. Man, I don't know how you always get me mixed up in this crap."

"Don't worry. It doesn't sound like there is any connection to you. I can't believe you pulled it off. What does it say?"

"It describes the military's and agency's involvement in the drug trade. It goes on to rationalize their position to the good of the cause. It talks about American prisoners and a scheme to free them. Mostly bullshit really."

"Does it name anyone?"

"No. It's all pretty straight forward except for a reference it keeps making to some SF type who apparently was sent in as a double agent. He was supposed to monitor the situation and free the prisoners if the drug plan did not work. Gutsy son-of-a-bitch! I don't really get the meaning of the name Deja Vu yet."

Anderson's heart skipped a beat and his skin suddenly seemed ice cold. He couldn't believe what he was hearing. Had he killed an American hero, foiled the plans for which a brave American had worked, a work and a life that would never be known, like this side of the war that could not be known? Had someone used him to sacrifice Brenner's life for nothing more than unmitigated greed?

Anderson was grateful for Bill's help. He and his people had taken some dangerous chances. "Bill, I want to thank you for your help in this. I'm sorry I can't tell you anything. I'm only making guesses myself. But it's probably better that way."

"Hey, Anderson, don't sweat the small stuff. One other thing. They have some code names here. One that stands out is called Leupold. There's another loose sheet that also makes reference to something they call Vu Deux. Sounds like there may be a second file. Anyway, maybe I'll see you when I get to the States someday. Until then, be careful."

Anderson hated to hang up. The disconnection would seem to end the relationship, as though the man on the other end of the phone, and the world, would just cease to exist for him.

It was dark in the room. Bill settled back into the easy chair and thought about the events that had taken place. Surreal? He could only make out the shape but not the man. The figure did not move.

"Bill Baedeker?" The figure spoke.

"Who's asking?"

The shape approached slowly. As it did so, Bill could see another man, taller, standing farther away in the shadows.

“I’ve come for some information.” The swarthy, muscular man continued. “I understand that you were a good friend of Sergeant Anderson?”

“What do you want? The bar’s not open. Come back in an hour.”

“Please, Mr. Baedeker, be civil. Like I said, I need some information. The grapevine says he was in your bar the other night.”

“First off, asshole, Anderson’s dead,” Bill said, standing up. “Second, if you don’t get the hell outta here, I’ll tear your nuts off and stuff ‘em in your damn mouth!”

The man whirled on the ball of his foot like a figure skater. The side of his combat boot caught Bill in the jaw. He went down like a lead weight. He started to struggle to his feet as the boot caught up with him again, this time across the bridge of his nose. Bill saw red-yellow patterns swirling in front of his eyes. Tiny, brilliant, round spots floated randomly like dead sperm in a petri dish under a microscope.

“You’re not a very polite host, Mr. Baedeker. Maybe I’m using the wrong approach. Let me put this another way. You have five seconds to change your attitude, or that pretty little cunt of yours won’t need that fat little dick anymore. Do you get my drift, Mr. Baedeker?”

“I’m beginning to,” Bill said, leaning over and letting the blood drain freely from his mouth and nose.

“That’s better. Now, let me ask you again. When did you last see Sergeant Anderson?”

“About three weeks ago. I haven’t seen him since. I don’t know what happened to the guy.”

Suddenly Bill felt a dull pressure in his gut. He looked down to find the handle of a knife protruding from his midsection. His face contorted with the realization of his demise.

“Don’t worry, Mr. Baedeker, the blade is short. It’s a little persuader I use to get people’s attention. You need to worry about where I place it next. Come now, you’re an intelligent man; think about what could happen here. It's a simple question. Let me restate it. When did you last see Sergeant Anderson?"

Bill reached down and took hold of the black handle. He pulled hard and fast at the dagger, extracting it easily. He looked at it briefly and then threw it clumsily at the unknown assailant.

"I told you once; I haven't seen him in weeks. Now go ahead and do what you've got to do but leave my wife out of it. She doesn't know him from any other GI that comes around here."

Bill watched in horror as the intruder pulled a silenced Hi Standard .22 caliber automatic pistol from behind him. Bill had seen Green Berets carrying these pip squeak little assassin guns before. They were used at short ranges and the bullet delivered to soft areas of the head. The discrete elimination of double agents among indigenous personnel often took specialized means.

But the man tossed the pistol through the doorway to his accomplice waiting outside.

"Here, don't be too messy with Bill's little Asian squeeze; women just hate to look unattractive when they're buried."

With that Bill charged. Like a dancer, the man's left knee rose in the air carrying his body off the hardwood floor with it. With lighting speed, his extended right leg came forward and up as the left knee was driven down like a piston. The man's right foot drove squarely into Bill's face.

Bill was lying on his back semiconscious when he felt the dagger thrust. It was expertly placed just below the zyphoid process near the tip of the sternum at a slight upward angle. The killer pushed the instrument in deeply while moving the blade from side to side. Bill knew the procedure: lacerate the heart. He felt himself drifting into unconsciousness.

Peanuts saw the men leaving from the back entrance to the bar as she returned from her daily foray to the outdoor market. There was something suspicious about their movements. They got into a car and sped away before she was able to cross the street. She hurried to the club with increasing apprehension that only women seem to experience as their intuition begins turning on high.

"Bill, you here?" She tried again, shouting louder this time. From the office at the back of the bar, Peanuts could hear muffled sounds. She did not want to look. She felt it, something terrible, something she didn't want was waiting beyond. She forced herself forward.

"Bill, Bill, what happen?" She dropped her packages and ran to him. She knew by his eyes that he was he was failing. She knelt beside him, picked up his head, and cradled it in her arms.

"Peanuts. But I thought you?" His voice was weak.

"I been market. What happen? I get doctor."

"No. Listen. Go to the Mexican, Javiel Mendera. Tell him they killed me. Tell him that I finally realized what Deja Vu refers to. He must get word to Anderson. Mendera is the only one I trust. Send the file now to Anderson's address." Bill's eyes closed. Blood found its way to the corners of his mouth and a gurgle from deep within him forced more of the red fluid up.

"Bill, no." Peanuts closed her eyes and felt the tears running down over her high cheekbones. Bill moved. She looked up and into his eyes again. She watched the life slowly disappearing from them.

"Deja Vu," he struggled, "the Cong took it from the French. Years ago it became the calling card for a big time drug lord named Ta..." Bill's eyes closed again.

Peanuts watched as his shoulders and neck relaxed. She could feel the weight of his head grow more difficult to hold. His breathing was loud through constricted vocal cords. And then he breathed no more. She threw her body over his; the lifeless body of this giant, the life of this hero of the war and father of the child she carried in her loins had ended in her arms. She had meant to tell him of it today.

CHAPTER TWENTY NINE

Anderson drove slowly along the dirt road that overlooked the quiet little town where he had spent his youth. He had come to think, to rejuvenate, and to wait. He pushed the car along the Grade Hill road to the last switchback only a hundred yards from the top. The vehicle seemed to breathe a sigh of relief when he cut the engine, parking so that his windshield faced the place of his birth. Through his binoculars he could see the house far below, the road to the old movie theater, the lane lined with cottonwoods, the fields. Brown-yellow pastures surrounded the main town, spreading out like a patchwork quilt dotted with Herefords and Holsteins. The mountains grew slowly from the valley floor at first, then they ascended steeply to a majestic, gray escarpment flecked with pink by the setting sun. Bastion like monoliths jutted forward from the stone face like dark claws protruding from a sleeping lion's paw.

Indians had tried in vain to hold onto the valley nearly a century earlier: small bands interdicting the settler's difficult and patient efforts to forge a life in an unfamiliar land, the Indians land. Anderson was reminded of the Special Forces teams that trudged through the wet, green world of Asia wondering in their private thoughts where in God's name they were in the scheme of things; what were they doing, and did the familiar valleys of home still exist, or would they ever see them again. His pioneer ancestors must have felt much the same way.

The wind blew through the aspens behind him, their white skins bending and quaking below the flutter and shimmer of leaves that were at once green and silver. The smell of sage, yampa, Indian potato, scrub oak, and Brigham tea floated skyward along the ridge, infesting his nostrils with the forgotten security of his youth. He remembered the red haired girl whose promises stole his heart, whose tender lips and kind eyes had displaced his soul.

He had gone to Monica and the kids. It was the hardest thing he had ever had to do, or to endure, in his life. His own selfishness had embedded everlasting, unforgiving, unrelenting pain in those he loved. He had rationalized and miscalculated. It had been too much to ask, taking advantage of a lifelong friend, a relative, a personality who he knew would not, in the end, refuse him. He should never have asked for David's help. It was too much, and now he was gone from them.

Monica had taken the news as only the very strong can, a catalyst to Anderson's resolve. And now he had come home to plan retribution. He would let blood until there was no more in him or in them, empty shells left to bake in the heat of contempt, greed, and hate.

He took count of the assets he had and that he would need. Anderson remembered the ten pounds of C4 plastic explosive he had buried in the woods outside Fort Bragg, North Carolina. He knew also that the area was the Mecca for fast, competitive cars. And he knew in his gut that they would come to Los Angeles first. He started the engine and retraced his way down the mountain and on to the city. He would return to the valley later, and try when he did to avoid their eyes, their questions, their looks of inquisition as they formulated opinions about themselves while sacrificing him.

He turned in the rental car and flew Delta Airlines into Charlotte. But before he did, he drove by her new house near the University like a stocker, a voyeur, hating himself for it. Yet, somehow, the demons had left him, and the snakes twisted no more. He found himself smiling with relief as he pressed the gas pedal and slowly accelerated away from his past life. He was moving on. Angela.

It didn't take long for him to locate what he needed. He had wanted a plain, unassuming car that had been modified to scream. He had thought the problem would be in finding one that he could afford. But he quickly located exactly what he was looking for. A ten year old Olds 88 with posi-traction, overhead cam, twin carbs, and all the racing modifications that could be had without needing to put it in the shop every other day. Good tires left geometric designs in the soft earth; the engine spoke to him like a heated woman. Most importantly, it retained its original, dirt poor look.

Anderson drove out beyond Bragg and Camp MacKall to the spot where he knew the explosive would be and quickly extracted part of it. It had been over a year now since he had cached it in the pine forest under the beds of rust brown needles and into the depths of the moist loam. He couldn't even remember why: a tithing maybe, or a shield against his own paranoia, or the snakes that twisted in his gut at times and writhed to escape and demonize the world.

In his mind, he surveyed his belongings like he had that night on the plane. The rifles had arrived without a hitch. The vehicle would make do in both the city and the mountains, non-conspicuous in the city, but not too unusual in and around the small towns nestled in the mountains either. He regarded the knives and pistols as toys, but useful enough on occasion to make them worth including. He guessed he was as ready as he would ever be.

Anderson turned the Olds west and headed for home. In the dark of night, he left the Southeast for what he hoped would be forever, making his way home without incident. He would once again have to tell his mother that it was time to go; he would once again have to feel his heart burn. He drove steadily westward, stopping only once to sleep on a park bench in East Texas for a few hours.

He awoke hazily, his mind trying to adjust to the reality of blue sky and green leaves overhead, the jungle, the sticky air invading his sinuses. He looked up blankly for a few moments, until becoming aware of noises to his right, near his car. He rolled his head in that direction and saw fuzzy, silhouetted bodies somehow out of kilter, horizontal, moving about his car. Then he realized what was going on: something that had disturbed his sleep, men trying to open the door to his car. He stood and walked slowly toward the Olds until not ten yards separated him from what he now recognized as young men.

"You boys having a problem?" He said.

They turned slowly, displaying that cocky attitude that the young use to intimidate their opponents: the rest of the human race.

"So what the hell does that have to do with you," answered a large, sandy haired youth. Without hesitation, the three of them started walking slowly toward Anderson. He watched them with amazement. Each had dirty, disheveled, long hair. It was well below their shoulders, filthy, tattered jeans, tattoos, and bare, dirty feet. They seemed cloned. Maybe they were.

"Nice car. I just bought it," he said.

"Well now, ain't that some shit," the larger one said. "How does it feel to be so unlucky. I mean, this being your last day on earth and all." With that, the youth reached behind him, quickly swinging a knife forward in his right hand. A smile crossed his face as the other two laughed nervously and moved to flank Anderson.

"You boys go on home now. I can't play today." Anderson put his thumbs in his pants above his belt buckle as he spoke. He wished he had the .45 automatic as he unbuckled his belt and began to withdraw it from the pant loops. The young men moved forward cautiously as Anderson wound the end of the belt around his right hand twice, grasping the buckle in his left.

The boy held the knife low and lunged at Anderson. Anderson brought the belt down on the assailant's wrist, looped it quickly in one smooth motion around the arm, then raised it at the same time he brought his right foot into the man's groin. In one fluid motion, he reversed the loop and swung the buckle at the other man's face on his right. It hit squarely with a solid thunk, cutting deeply across his cheek. The young man drew back with a scream, grabbing his face as it began to bleed profusely.

Perhaps three seconds had passed when Anderson turned his attention to the man on the right who stood, mouth gaping open, unable to believe what had just happened.

"That's some kind of cool shit," he muttered. "Where'd you learn that?"

"Why don't you take care of your buddies while I get on my way," Anderson proposed and started for the car. As he pulled away, he thought about what had happened to America during the past two years. Before he had left the States, he had been able to hitchhike around the country, people bending over backwards to help him, nearly threatening one another just to get the privilege of being the one to give him the ride, offering to feed him, and generally accepting military personnel, and, in particular, Green Berets, as men to be thanked and looked up to. But now, just the opposite. He was treated like a war monger, a baby killer, the worst kind of citizen, contemptible.

And the dress, the hair: disrespectful and unkempt. The actress in Hanoi, young men forsaking their country and leaving for Canada, Switzerland, and the demonstrations. So cowardly. So what? He didn't know anymore.

CHAPTER THIRTY

It had been a long drive. As he approached the small structure, his mother's home, he noticed a car that he didn't recognize parked in front. Anderson slipped the .45 automatic in his belt near the small of his back and walked into the house.

"There's my boy now." His mother's eyes sparkled and gleamed as she looked at her son. She loved him immensely and the joy of having him back exuded from every pore in her body.

Anderson looked to the couch, at the figure seated there. He couldn't believe it. Javiel watched him and smiled, knowing how surprised Anderson would be.

"Hey compadre, what's going on?"

"What in the hell are you doing here, you ole Mexican?"

"Can I get you boys some coffee," his mother asked.

"Sure mom. Thanks."

After she had left, Javiel spoke.

"Listen, I've got bad news and a message for you." He didn't hesitate. "Bill's dead. Some spooks did him pretty good, then knifed him. But he left a message with Peanuts for me to give to you."

"What happened?"

"I don't know all the details. Peanuts thinks she saw the guys leaving the bar, the ones that wasted him. All she knew was that one of the guys was all muscles. Body builder type maybe. The other appeared to be an officer, somebody she had seen in the club from time to time but didn't know his name. She said that Bill told her something as he was dying. She had a tough time telling me what it was, but I finally got it. Apparently Bill had figured out something about the term Deja Vu. Had something to do with the French and some drug lord in country. She only got the first part of the name, but phonetically, it sounded like T A, Ta to me.

"I guess it was important enough to make it the last thing he said, so I thought I better find you. It was Peanuts who told me you were alive. Did your mother know you were supposed to have been canceled?"

"No. Actually I got a call into her before the letter got here. I told her that it would probably be coming and that it was just another bureaucratic snafu. Can you stay?"

"I got to be on my way. The mesquite trees, specks, redfish, and whitetail deer are calling. Listen, I don't know what you're up to but if you need some help, I'm in."

"No. That's alright; I don't know what the hell I need right now except a lot of rest and some time to think. How's the rest of the team? It's been over a month now."

"They're hangin' in there. When they heard you were sta bieno, they split a case of Crown. Scarza's his old self: political beam blowing out his ass so far it lights up the whole jungle. Two Dogs said he knew it all along; said he did a sing for you and although he didn't know a damned thing about it, it must have worked. Guessed he would return home and become a singer. Navaho for witch doctor, I think.

"OK buddy, with that bullshit out of the way, I'm off to taco land. Can't wait to set my ass down on some ole cactus just so I know for sure I'm not in the jungle anymore. Wouldn't mind a good home brew either. Don't be a chingaso, come and see me. I'll make sure you get some good puntang."

He spent the night packing. He wasn't sure where he would start, where he would go, or how to do what he must do. But he knew there were scores to settle for Brenner, for David and his family, and for Bill. He counted the money, dwindled now to less than four thousand dollars.

"People are asking about you. Can't you stay? Please." His mother implored him.

But Anderson could not stay, and he could not tell her why.

As he drove out of town that night he wondered if it would be for the last time. He hoped he would return one day to the mountains. Soon the valley disappeared as the highway snaked into the canyon, just south of Butch Cassidy's birthplace. It struck him as incredible that Leroy Parker's sister was still alive.

Now he was free to think of the work ahead. He was heading for unfamiliar territory. The streets of Los Angeles were not his turf. Survival there was based on myriad human involvement, business acumen, and an acute knowledge of how things went down on the street. He didn't have a clue.

CHAPTER THIRTY ONE

"He'll come for your daughter."

"Look Major."

"McCauley. My name is McCauley. Sure he will. This home spun asshole exudes romance out of every pour. You have told me that your kid is nuts about him. Now you're gonna tell me Anderson can resist her? Bullshit."

"Damn it. I don't want my daughter to be any part of this."

"Look you dumb, Ivy League prick, Anderson's the only one who can and will put the screws to us. Don't you understand? You're implicated in the whole thing, from the killing of an American agent to the international smuggling of drugs. He's got to be cleaned or we'll spend the rest of our days in the Federal pen."

"So what are you going to do?"

"I've brought fourteen of my men with me. They're good at what they do. Not only that but they're in this just as deep as we are so they can be trusted to do this. We've got a few days. All we have to do is wait. Anderson will come to us. Don't worry big man; you'll be the governor before this is over." The Major smiled. "By the way, who is the governor of this state these days? I'd like to meet him. I think we could do some business.

"That reminds me. Do you have the package I sent along with your daughter?"

"Yes," sighed Coman, "the briefcase. I'll have it brought to your room."

As Anderson drove toward L.A., he studied the map. He had to know the city as well as he could, the ways in, and out, and all the major streets. He only knew one way to fight and to survive. He would just have to plan it as though he were back in the jungles or the mountains.

But ever present on his mind was trying to fit all the pieces together. How was it that the Colonel could be right in the middle of all of this and still be innocent? Or was he? In his gut he believed the Colonel was being duped like everyone else. The answered had to be the Major. He had to have made the Colonel believe that Brenner had turned, to believe that eliminating him was what he deserved and what must be done to preserve the mission. And the drugs? How did the logistics work? Surely the opium came from the hills of the Karens and was transported by Air America. The money must have come from the CIA. But there had to be more of it than even the CIA could afford. Nobody in his right mind would do all this for what the CIA had to offer. There had to be another suppler. Who was it?

And Deja Vu? What the hell was that supposed to mean? Military code or mission names were made for reasons, or at random, or even for personnel whims and luck charms. But this one was more intriguing. Bill's last dying words were that he had figured it out. Did that mean he had stumbled onto the truth, or did he just remember something that was pure coincidence? Javiel had said it had something to do with the French, with a drug lord. It fit. Didn't it?

Anderson hated to think that Angela even knew people like the Major. Angela, good God, what was she going to do when she found out that he was still alive? It was then that another thought began to slowly germinate in his mind. Her father was an industrialist on the west coast. He dealt in the Orient and in Southeast Asia. He had ties to every contact that was anybody on both continents. Lord, he hoped it was not true. There had to be a tie back to the United States. Was Angela's father it? She had mentioned that he knew the major, and that the Major had stayed at their home in the past.

He checked the map again as he pulled into the city. Now to find a poor, crowded section of town where he could settle in and disappear into the melting pot of the second largest city in America, home to eighty four separate languages. Anderson had driven steadily for fifteen hours. It was early afternoon by the time he found a section of town that appealed to him. A boarding house or, even better, a tired old house to rent would do. It was dusk when he spotted a rent sign in the window of an old, dilapidated, wooden house in the entrance to a small, wooded canyon. It didn't fit his original plan, but it would serve his purpose just as well, maybe better. He dialed the number the sign had advertised. Two hours later Anderson was wandering through the run down little house getting to know his way around. Tomorrow he would survey the grounds and the woods. As time went on he would make larger and larger circles, becoming intimately familiar with his lair.

But first things first. He had to locate Angela. He couldn't go by her house. If what he suspected were true, they would be waiting. No, he had to get in touch with her in some other way, in some other place. He went over in his mind their conversations at the Opera and in Bangkok. He remembered her talking about a place she frequented. She loved the place for the music and the excitement it generated. He remembered also that it was always crowded.

Anderson made his way along the LA streets. He drove past the Hilton hotel and headed south. He had driven nearly an hour to get here, following directions a gas station attendant had given him. As he approached the bar, his apprehension was near the breaking point. He was nervous about meeting her again. What if he had mistaken her intentions or his dreams had made him believe what he wanted most, or maybe she had found someone else? But his greatest worry was her reaction to seeing someone she professed to love and whom she thought was dead. It wasn't going to be pleasant, but there was just no easy way.

He parked the car but didn't get out. Instead, he sat watching the young people come and go. His heart, his head, and his gut told him he didn't fit. Maybe the whole thing was a pipe dream. How did these kids pay for all of this, the cars, the clothes? They were from a different world, a world of relaxed, confident affluence. Several of the men sported long hair. Remembering his encounter in the park, his first reaction was disgust, distrust, and anger. He felt they were his ideological enemy, or at least his opposite. And yet these were Angela's peers, her people, so distanced from his. He knew they would not understand him, or where he came from, or what he had been through, nor he them. Anderson was at odds with himself. If he had the choice, he would pick a firefight again over spending just five more minutes in LA doing what he was doing.

Nor could Angela fit in his world of simple mountain folks, the military, or a natural world of survival. No, survival here was something quite apart from what he knew. But Anderson also knew that he must try, for he didn't want to spend the rest of his life suffering the realization that he had not tried once more for that person on whom all his thoughts were centered.

He swung the car door open and stepped out. He walked slowly, methodically toward the open door of the bar. He remembered the jungle, the green, the sultry heat, the sticky wetness. Sweat poured down his brow and into his eyes. The enemy was just ahead. He was the best. He had the edge. He was invincible. Bullshit.

Inside was the jungle of the city, the heat of decadence, and the squalor of human pleasure played out in a fury of sounds and lights amid the smoke. The music was loud as the base guitar sounded a whop, whop, whop and the lead picked his way toward the landing zone of the small, hardwood dance floor. Bursts of rocket fire came from overhead where a beacon spun lazily on its axis. Strobe lights threw shadows on the walls of half-naked, dancing marionettes. There was no sound to be heard but sound itself. Lips moved without speaking. Only human soul existed, surrounded and punctuated by the slow motion of overstated activity. He had come far to find himself in a different kind of war zone. He wondered with amusement what Chi You might think about this. It was Plato's cave to which the light of day had come without the shadows breaking through the surface, the light having brought with it a filtered mania. Shadows danced on the walls of the cave, bodies undulating in a chaotic choreography demanding release from invisible tethers.

It was difficult to discern the enemy from the friendlies. His eyes adjusted and began to search. He scanned the interior trying to imagine what she must look like in the foreign environment. Near the podium where the band threw their bodies about and flung disheveled hair, Anderson thought he saw her. The pulsing light gave only fleeting glimpses of a person standing with her head down, listening intently to the screams of a friend. He waited.

Her head lifted slowly. Her eyes found him. At first they stared through him, blankly into the conversation she was trying desperately to hear. Slowly her eyes began to change; realization and disbelief were at once fighting for recognition and empowerment. The eyes faltered for a moment, the head shook, no, no, but then they locked once again on the apparition on the far side of the bar. He watched the eyes struggle, knew that she had lost the animated monologue of her friend. Suddenly emotion collided with recognition somewhere behind those eyes. She smiled, blinked, and then was in motion, at first slowly, without taking her eyes from him. She dared not look away for fear the space now occupied by him would somehow empty and shatter what the brain had finally embraced. She began to jog, then run, and finally fly as she threw her body against his.

They held on to one another for long moments. Finally she leaned back and looked once more, into his eyes, into the soul of the dead. Now she knew; it was Anderson. Her intuition had not failed her. It was OK; everything was OK. They said nothing as she led him from the bar to a side entrance and into a small garden area.

"Oh god, it's really you. They told me that you had been killed only a day or so after your return. Are you alright? You look alright. Oh god, hold me."

Anderson embraced Angela and knew that he could do it. If he lived, he could handle whatever might be ahead. Only this woman mattered in the jungle, in the city, in the menagerie of human platitude and locked social infrastructure. He could feel the warmth of this woman, a warmth that cut his soul in half and entered there. He was lost to this beautiful creature who clung to him with all her might. They both remembered, and they wanted to taste the loving richness of each other again. They wanted to feel not apart, but to be one in themselves. They wanted the impossible, to be the other.

"I came with friends. Do you have a car?"

"You might not see it exactly that way but it will get us where you want to go." Said Anderson.

"Then come," she said, taking his hand as she had in the Opera hotel.

At first she just watched him. At moments she would touch him as if testing his reality. But then she burst into an excited chatter.

"My god Anderson, what has happened? I came back and I heard nothing. I didn't know if I would ever see you again. And the phone call. Major McCauley called to talk to daddy. He was almost blasé about the whole thing. I couldn't, I wouldn't believe it. But what choice did I have? I didn't hear from you. I don't even know who your parents or family are. How could I call? I didn't know what to do but wait. I finally began to resign myself to it. What happened? Where did you go? How did you get out? What are you doing here? How come the

Major thought you were dead anyway? Now the Major's here. My god, listen to me. I must sound like I'm crazy, jabbering away."

Anderson laughed, remembering her first words to him in Thailand, stirred again by the haunting and beautiful timbre of her voice, telling himself that it must feel to his ears and his soul like warm oatmeal mush must feel in the mouth of a toothless old man. "Tell me where we're going, and I'll tell you all I can when we get there."

The Major's there. Good.

"Right here. I mean turn right! Yes, that's it. Now just down at the end of the road. I have a girl friend who lives there. She's out, but I know where the key is."

Anderson pulled into the driveway and cut the engine. He opened the door and quickly rounded the car to open Angela's as well.

"Where did you get this beast of a car? It sounds like it's about to take off or something. Never mind, don't answer that. I think it's great. Besides, I love beat up gray. It's a ... very solid color ... sort of." She laughed, happy to be in his arms as they made their way up the low porch and to the door. She pointed out the spot where she hoped the key would be. He reached up to a broken brick and extracted the silver object. They both smiled as he opened the door and gasped at what seemed a very luxurious home to Anderson.

"What do you want to drink?" She flicked on the light and hurried toward a small alcove.

Glass tables, chromed metal seats, paintings with no resemblance to reality, plush crème colored carpet, brass pots from which earth toned, fake plants adorned corners and table tops, vaulted ceilings from which ornate, motionless fans were suspended, jutting into empty space: a useless, human aviary into which entered the restless bird to gather strength before flying into the streets again to prey.

"Bourbon, neat," he said, trying to hide his amazement.

"Well, you're easy." She handed him the liquid, which he gulped, a bit of physical pain to help temper the uneasiness he felt from his emotional high.

"Angela, I don't want to seem like a drag but."

Angela took Anderson by the hand. She deftly balanced the glass, his ego, and their desire as she led him down the hall and into a darkened room. At first he could not make out a thing. But for the firm grip she had on him, even she had disappeared. As his eyes adjusted he heard the muffled sounds of bedding.

Grateful, Angela took Anderson in her arms tenderly, affectionately. He kissed the tops of her breasts as he felt her place him inside her. He wanted to remain there, crawl into her womb, return to the liquid and the darkness and the security offered by the warmth and the beating heart nearby, and to guard against entering the soul and the heart of any other being.

Angela was fixing breakfast for him when he awoke.

"Be thankful that it's breakfast time. It's the only thing I really know how to cook. Come on and sit down. It's done."

She served him the eggs, toast, and coffee. He noticed her throw a ten dollar bill in the fridge.

"How does it feel, not having a beret on your head?"

"I'll admit it's a bit unusual after four years, but I'll get used to it. There are a lot of things I'm going to have to learn to get used to."

"Listen, I've got to get something off my chest," she ventured. "I know I'm rushing things. I think what I'm going to say would have been different if I had not believed you might be dead. But it made me realize how I felt and what it would mean to not have you around. Bottom line, I need to know where we're going here. I need to know how you feel and what you want to do about it."

"Angela, I want to go wherever you're going. I can't imagine life without you. But I guess it's time to tell you something that I had hoped to delay for a few hours. Their believing that I was dead was due to a military mix-up that I need to resolve. When I returned to the States, I got my discharge papers in advance. It didn't take much to make them official. So now I'm a free man. Since I didn't need to check back in after my assignment was finished, I just came on back home. It didn't really occur to me that they would report me missing or dead. But I guess it makes sense.

"When you return, please tell the Major for me. I'm sure he will want to know so he can straighten the whole matter up. Anyway, I need to go away for a few days. I've got to let some other people know as well. They will be a bit shook up, and I've got to let them down easily. Tell the Major that I've rented a house in the canyon. I'll be there until tomorrow if he wants to see me about anything. By the way, what is the Major doing here? Did anyone come with him?"

"Oh, I don't know. It's pretty strange actually. There's a bunch of his men with him. I think they decided to take R & R at our house.

"Come with me. Daddy will want to meet you and you can tell the Major yourself."

"Not yet, unfortunately. I appreciate the offer, but I need to get on back and put some things together. Anyway, I want to be a bit more presentable when I meet your folks. Can you catch a cab from here?"

"Ok. I guess."

Anderson watched this lovely creature fussing here and there, cleaning up. Her auburn, maybe red, no chestnut hair flowed to her shoulders. Her skin there was soft and warm, inviting a soft bounce to hit them as she moved. The index fingers of her hands curved slightly inward toward the others, each padded softly at the tips. Her waist was tiny, blossoming into full hips and straight, strong, long legs. She took short steps, her back held straight as an arrow. Her eyes were kind and warm and bright. Her head tipped slightly to the right from time to time like someone posing for a picture. Her lips were full, and when she smiled, white teeth gleamed, the slightest of spaces invading the perfection of them on the left side. He wondered how many beauty contests she might have won over the years. Yes, she was an extraordinarily beautiful woman. How could this be happening?

CHAPTER THIRTY TWO

Anderson parked the car on the hill above the house. He opened the trunk and retrieved the black case. He leaned it against the car's bumper and reached for the transmitter. The detonators protruding from the C4 plastic explosive were sensitive to electrical current. He put the transmitter in his pocket and the case over his shoulder. Fifty yards down the hill he hid the case in a thicket near a clearing and then continued on to the house. Once inside, Anderson checked the C4 wired to the receiver, and then settled back to wait. He knew they would come after him now; he knew it didn't matter how far.

It didn't take long. He first picked up the car's engine running at low rpm's as it slowly plodded up the canyon. He grabbed the binoculars and opened the blinds. He knew it could be any one of the residents who lived farther up the winding road, but his gut told him it was them. Anderson rotated the dial on the new ten power, German made instrument. As soon as the vehicle cleared the wooded area near a curve approximately three hundred yards from the house, he could make out four occupants. He followed their progress for another fifty yards before he was able to recognize one of the men in the front seat. He had been in the helicopter that had fired on him in Laos.

"Shit damn. You worry about everything. This asshole ain't suspecting us to chase his narrow ass all the way from Bangkok."

"Hey bro, it fascinates me how you've stayed alive to such a ripe ole age. You ain't got the brains it takes to pour piss out of a boot. If youda hit the sumbitch the first time, wees wouldn't be screwin' aroun' like this. God, I loves talkin' like a brother."

"Hey, Johnson. I hate to break it to you like this, but you are a brother." Howard yelped.

The four men laughed as they rode toward the canyon, trying their best to cover their fear. How the Major had found Anderson's 20 was beyond them, but it didn't matter. Wasting this SF bastard was not something that bothered their sense of fair play, not with so much at stake. But they knew in their gut that they were no match for this man; they could only hope that by their collective effort success would leave them alive at the end.

Assault weapons bounced softly against the car seats between them, their dull, matte surfaces the color of powdered graphite. Their magazines filled with full metal-jacketed bullets protruded from bright brass cases. A box filled with grenades rode safely between the two men in the back seat.

The car pulled to a halt two hundred yards from the house.

"All right, break out the grenades," Johnson ordered. "Colin, I want you and Howard to circle roun' the house through the wood there," he said, pointing, "and catch him if he leaves. Me and Mike'l go in the front door. We'll give you five minutes to get in position. Blast his white ass if you get the chance."

The two men struggled out of the back seat of the car with their equipment. They lumbered heavily under the unfamiliar load through the thick brush for several minutes. Finally, they found a small vantage point and settled in to see the fireworks.

Anderson watched the two men as they cautiously proceeded. It was easy to see that they wished their chopper was nearby to take the burden of their weapons and their equipment and lift them from the brush. He smiled at their awkwardness, concentrating on their task like a right-hander trying desperately to sign his name with his left. They were out of their element.

The car waited and then began to move slowly toward the house. Anderson climbed quickly through the window on the offside of the house. Out of sight from both the car and the men on foot, he made the nearby woods and began to circle back towards the hill and his gray Olds, moving easily through now familiar territory. He reached the black case just as the car stopped in front of the small, aging structure he had called home for less than forty eight hours. He uncased the rifle, and supporting his elbows on his knees, pulled the precision instrument against his shoulder as he rested its forearm on his left hand. He shifted slightly, bunching his buttocks and body into a ball like a stalking cat readies itself to lunge. He watched through the rear window of the house for the two men to burst through the door. Then, as if on his command, they did, pointing their automatic rifles wildly in every direction expecting the worst. The worst was about to come.

Anderson reached with his right hand for the transmitter that lay near him. Without taking his vision from the powerful scope, he pressed the tiny red button marked, "open". The window, the frame, and the wood that surrounded it bulged perceptible through the microsecond that Anderson's brain stopped and framed the action of the explosion. And then the terrible sound as the structure separated into thousands of pieces that flew in every direction, pierced his ears.

Silence. Nothing moving.

Anderson rotated his position slightly to his left. His open left eye quickly picked up the men seated in the thick brush as his right eye followed through the scope. The cross hairs settled between the incredulous eyes of a man approximately thirty years of age with dark brown hair and an overweight, flaccid body. Anderson let the rifle's weight move the cross hairs to his throat just as the trigger broke.

I got stuck on a bar ...

The recoil severed his vision with his target for an instant. Just as quickly the rifle returned to point of aim. The remaining assailant had risen and turned to flee when the bullet caught him in the temple. Just as the scope climbed from the recoil, Anderson suddenly realized what he had seen. It was the young man he had hustled in the pool hall in San Bernardino four years ago. Howard's forward momentum brought him to the ground hard, breaking the bridge of his nose. Both men lay silent.

Damn, Anderson mused to himself, and I really tried to be a nice guy too.

Anderson cased the rifle and grabbed the transmitter. He was back at his car in less than thirty seconds. He drove carefully back into L.A. His instinct had been right. Angela had been tailed. The question was: why had the tail or others of the Major's men not taken him earlier? The only answer that made any sense was that Angela's father had prevented it. Anderson knew he had been lucky; he knew that the city was not his turf, that he didn't have a clue how to maneuver in this world of high-rises, congested highways, and unfamiliar sights and sounds.

The high performance engine emitted a low roar through the insulated firewall as Anderson made his way toward Chinatown. Busy men and women scurried here and there in a frantic effort to make the day's agenda. Already the bars were serving those who were without jobs or on their day off. Ethnic diversity could be seen everywhere. Scumbags roamed the streets aimlessly. It was the city.

Suddenly the scene began to change and within a few blocks it seemed as though he were back in Bangkok. The streets were alive with people and activity. Tiny shops lined the street on both sides. Strange and exotic foods, fresh fish, gold jewelry, watches, brass objects of every shape and size and for every occasion were displayed in shop windows and on the street. People fought for meager livings on the sidewalk next to exquisite, teak and marbled shops selling jade Buddhas and ancient Chinese porcelain from inside expensive velvet covered vaults.

Chinatown was a world onto its own, excised and lifted from the orient, then wedged into place in a city halfway round the world. Oddly, Anderson felt more comfortable here than in the rest of the city. He had come to understand these people a little and respect their differences, their ancient culture, and their capacity to work constantly. He drove on, not knowing what he was looking for. He only hoped he would know it when he saw it.

It was then that he noticed several men dressed in business suits enter a restaurant. One of them appeared to be flanked by the others in a geometric fashion. This seemed like as good a place to start as any other. There didn't seem to be much doubt that the one with long hair was accompanied by body guards. Anderson pulled the car over and parked in front of one of the shops. He noted the environment around him. It would be almost impossible to escape, and behind the facades was a world he knew nothing about. He glanced in the rearview mirror. His hair had grown out, leaving the unmistakable GI look behind him. His clothes were casual and unassuming. He hoped he looked clean cut and generic, unattached ethnically, politically or otherwise. He wanted his demeanor to be anything but threatening. He carried no weapon and hoped that this fact alone would provide his safety.

Inside, it took Anderson's eyes a moment to adjust. The lights were low and the sounds quiet and guarded. A slim, efficient looking young girl approached him and spoke softly in broken English.

"May I seat you, sir?"

"I'm looking for friends. May I go inside and see if they are here?"

She smiled and nodded.

Anderson bore to the left and started down a dimly lit corridor of rooms. He glanced only momentarily at each as he proceeded. Ahead he could see the shoulder of a man near the door to one of the rooms. As he grew nearer, Anderson recognized the man as one of those he had seen enter the building earlier.

Anderson approached and stood in the door in what he hoped was a non-threatening manner. The group all saw him at the same time. Their motion and speech stopped abruptly, and they seemed frozen for the instant it took Anderson to bow deeply. During Anderson's early months in Southeast Asia, he had retained a young Chinese girl as his interpreter. He had picked up a few words from her and searched for them now.

"Gentlemen, please forgive me. I am so sorry to disturb your meal. My intrusion shows the worst of manners, but I have business. My I please take just a moment of your time?"

Anderson felt the man that had been at the door move closer to him. The thought struck him again that there was no escape, that he was completely vulnerable to the wishes of these men. He stood silent as the group measured this encounter. The distinguished, long haired man seated directly opposite Anderson's position finally broke the terrible silence.

"Your Chinese is worse than your manners. Please speak English. Who are you and what do you want?" But the man knew before he asked; he remembered the picture that Cowan had delivered.

"I'm Anderson. I have come to inquire of someone. I do not know where to start. I hoped you might help me."

"What is his name? Maybe I can help you."

"I do not know his name. But I believe he is known as the Deja Vu. I believe his name may begin with the letters T A."

"Known as the Deja Vu? How strange. It sounds very mysterious and romantic. French, I believe. What is it you want with this man?"

"I wish to ask for his help and his blessing."

"Why would you need the help of such a man, if indeed such a man exists?"

"Permission. I hope to get his permission"

"If I meet such a man, I can relay your message if you wish. Tell us what you request permission for."

Anderson began slowly. "Sir, I believe the Deja Vu to be powerful, an entity over which I am helpless. I do not wish to disturb nor become his enemy. Please accept my words as sincere. I am a man alone, a man from the country. I came to ask permission to defend myself and to extract retribution from those who have struck out against me and mine. I have no other interests."

The room was silent, the air damp and pungent with a confused mixture of odors: curry, salty liquids, strong mustards, sweet and sour pastes, and warm garlic. Silent murals on the walls spoke of ancient beauty and an art unsurpassed by western skills. The reflection of ornate chairs danced in the glossy finish of the rosewood and teak table. The smell of raw fish filled his nostrils.

Anderson tried to measure the reaction to his request but could not. The expressions of these men were flat, emotionless, and cold. Finally the man responded.

"That is a strange and serious request," he began. "We are only businessmen here. But it may be possible to let your message be known to someone. I cannot say what will come of it."

"I apologize once again for this intrusion. I hope that I have not offended you. I am in your debt, sir. With your permission, I will go now."

"Yes, it is no bother. You are a brave young man and polite. I wish you good fortune in your troubles. Shimono, please show Mr. Anderson to his car."

The powerfully built man waited only a moment for some sign to come from the eyes of his boss. But no message played across the smiling face. He turned and followed Anderson.

When they were gone, Takano continued. "These men have gotten out of hand. Their greed has long since overcome their ability to focus on business rationally. Letting them fight among themselves without connection to us may put an end to what I fear will be an inevitable problem for us anyway. Maybe this young warrior can eliminate the larger portion of a troublesome situation without our intervention. Follow him and find out where he is staying. Tomorrow you may deliver the permission he requests."

The drug lord continued with his meal, pondering over the fact that the man named Anderson presented but one more connection to his organization from the outside. Just how had he learned of Deja Vu, and how had he drawn any connection with the Chinese community in Los Angeles? Maybe this young fellow was smarter than he gave most Caucasians credit for. After all, he had escaped death from overpowering odds in North Vietnam and Laos. It made him nervous. Takano didn't like being nervous; it was bad for business. He decided to wait and see what transpired.

Driving back toward town in the late afternoon, Anderson realized that if he didn't want to sleep in his car, he needed to find a place soon. He was happy with himself, sure that he had made the connection and, so far, come out of it unscathed. He also knew that he had to find out what the Chinese would do about him, and the only way to know quickly was to ask. The Chinese did not like to play their usual games with whites. They knew that Westerners didn't know the rules, nor did they respect them when they did. Orientals dealt with the white man swiftly in most cases. But they responded to those who made the effort to understand and respect the ways and responsibilities of their culture. Living with and sharing the dangers of war side by side with the Asians had taught Anderson about the most important social requirements of these ancient people. Quiet and respectful submission to power often got those with guts a return on their investment through the use of social propriety and knowing one's place.

The Oriental had dismissed him without knowing how to reach him with an answer. Did they expect him to return or would they follow him? Follow him until the answer came or follow him looking for the appropriate opportunity to drop him from the list of problems such people were always dealing with? He decided he'd better watch his six.

But it was still too soon to know the outcome of his encounter with the Chinese. Of one thing Anderson was certain, the Chinese knew what he was talking about. The decision and his fate would be known soon. But this was only one of Anderson's problems. What about the police? By now they would be investigating the bombing of the canyon house and the death of four men. Who had rented the house? What make and model was the old gray car? What did the man who rented it look like; what was his name; what was the license plate number? Without doubt his car would be a prominent picture in the minds of those who took the job of policing the streets seriously. Anderson had paid cash and purposely spent little time talking about the rental. It would take the police some time to unravel what had happened while they looked for their only lead, the old gray car. Anderson would have to change that.

CHAPTER THIRTY THREE

"Drake, Evans, get in here," the L.A. Police Chief yelled. The two detectives hot footed it to the boss's office. "What did you find out?"

Drake answered. "The place was pretty well broken up, but near as we can tell there were four male victims. Two of them took it inside the house from the explosion. The other two were shot one time in the head. They were all carrying military weapons. What I'm saying is that they were not civilian AR-15's but military M-16's. They also carried grenades and other military gear. One of them was wearing dog tags."

"Anything else?" The Chief asked.

"Yes sir. Even the ammo they were carrying was military issue. But they were not shot with military ammo."

"How did you come by that? There hasn't been an autopsy yet."

"Well, at this point it's only a guess, but in neither case did the bullet exit. The range from which we believe the victims were shot would significantly reduce the velocity of any normal round. For a full jacketed military round to not have exited, it would have to lose mass by breaking up. About the only round that will break up at such a distance is the .223 cartridge, or something similar. The velocity is so high for its size that it will often come apart when it strikes bone for example. The hole we found in each victim's head was small. I believe these men were killed with a small caliber bullet, most likely a thin jacketed hollow point, the type used for hunting varmints or target shooting, or maybe a soft pointed hunting bullet. Chances are, it will be so damaged we can't make it."

Evans piped up, "Chief, we believe we found the spot where the killer took the shots. We measured it at approximately two hundred and fifty yards. One of the victims took the hit sitting down and simply fell forward. He was still in that position when we found him. The other appeared to be moving at an angle to the shot. The killer is either one hell of a lucky sumbitch or a world-class shooter. The demo crew tells us the explosive was definitely C4, also of military issue. We don't know yet whether this is paramilitary, some cult, or military infighting. We're checking ID on the one set of dog tags we recovered.

"There's more. The house was recently rented to a guy named John Schmidt. The owner doesn't remember the guy much except to say that he looked to be late twenties or early thirties, average size, white, dark hair, and drove an old gray car. Doesn't know what kind. The guy paid cash, so the owner didn't ask too many questions and didn't give much of a shit because he needed to rent in a bad way. He said the guy wanted to know if he had insurance on the place.

"A new rental car was parked outside. It's clean, but we're tracing the agency to find out who rented it and when. The whole thing is bizarre. We're not dealing with the average neighborhood shoot out. These guys look to be pros of some sort."

"I assume you have the renter's description, as well as the car's, out on the street by now?"

"Yes sir."

"Do you have someone out there combing the area?"

"Yes sir, about thirty of them. So far we can't find any trace of the guy who rented the joint or of the guy who pulled off the fancy shooting. There doesn't seem to be any clue as to how he got into position or how he exited. But we think we know the location the shots were taken from. We noted the angle the shot must have come from and began looking. We found a small depression on the hillside. There doesn't seem to be any footprints leading anywhere; there's no cigarette butts, not much of anything." The two detectives looked at each other.

"We did find something of interest there where we believe the shots were taken from, though, sir."

Evans withdrew a clear, plastic bag from his pocket and held it in the air, a mixture of triumph and confusion on his face. The Captain held out his hand, urging Evans to release his treasure.

He rolled the cartridge case in his fingers without removing it from the bag. The brass case was small and fat with a sharp shoulder. He pressed the head of the case against the plastic, peering at it through his reading glasses in an effort to identify it.

"What the hell." He murmured softly.

The detectives looked at one another again. "That's what we thought." Drake said.

".220 Russian. You ever heard of it?" He asked his two lieutenants. They shook their heads, resisting the urge to tell the Captain the other strange thing about the case. They continued to watch, wondering.

Finally Drake spoke. "There's something else odd about the case, sir. I mean besides it being foreign, Russian, whatever. From the head stamp, it would indicate that the caliber, bullet diameter, would be a .22 or thereabouts.

"Go on. I'm not in the mood to play. Just spit it out." The Captain said angrily.

"Well, sir, the opening in the case neck is .243. 6 millimeter."

The Captain turned the case in the plastic bag until the end of the case was visible. Sure as hell, he thought.

"It's a wildcat, sir. It's a reload. Least that's what we figure."

"So, maybe the shooting wasn't luck." The Captain looked up at them, more troubled than ever.

"We think the four stiffs went after someone in the house and it backfired on them. Whoever it was must have been waiting for them. We don't know how the explosive was detonated yet, but they're working on it."

Captain Kevin Dermit listened in silence as he faced the window and looked down over the Los Angeles skyline. It's a strange place down there, he thought. What's going to happen next? He turned to the two detectives. "Keep me informed. This might be an isolated incident. Let's hope it is. We've got plenty of bizarre shit happening out there without some half assed military junta like this goin' down. The dog tags sound like the best lead we've got, so keep on it. The rental car might pan out, but I doubt it. These guys aren't stupid, but they sure as hell are obsessed. Question is, over what?

"Check the case through the gun stores, the agency, rifle clubs, whatever you can think of. Call the nearest military bases. See if any of them have had any weapons come up missing. Get on it."

"That bastard took out four of my men, Johnson being one of them." The Major paced the floor, gesticulated like a madman. He was worried and the others knew it. It was like playing eight ball on a bar table. Sometimes it doesn't matter who's the best, just who's the luckiest. But the Major didn't want any part of luck. He wasn't going to leave the retirement of his dreams to chance. Bullshit, he had to outsmart this self-righteous bastard and smash him like a bug. He went on.

"Listen you dim wits, no mistakes from now on. You got me? We ain't got a clue where he is right now, but I'm banking on his dick. He's gonna come chasin' Coman's daughter sooner or later. Since we don't have forever, it's got to be sooner. I want a tail on the girl. He might contact her anywhere, anytime. We've got to speed the process up.

"Kramer, Coman's in the house somewhere. Get his sorry ass down here. I want to talk to him. The rest of you get the hell out of here."

The Major waited, thinking of Coman and just what the hell he ought to do about him.

"Good evening, Major. What is it this time?"

"Look Coman, Anderson got lucky. He blew two of my men to smithereens and drilled the other two. We ain't got all year to screw with this guy. We know he's soft on your daughter. We need to use her to clean Anderson. Here's what I want you to do ..."

CHAPTER THIRTY FOUR

Anderson knocked on the door. As he did, he felt in his gut that it was a poor decision. Why be pegged down to a place, an address? Why not revert back to what he knew? The autonomy of the jungle made him feel safe. He was operating out of his car for the most part anyway. He was about to follow his better judgment when the door opened.

"Yes? Can I help you?"

Anderson found himself staring back at a beautiful woman, groomed in the tight professional attire of an attorney or an advertising executive. His hair began to stand up on the back of his neck. The scene, it was out of place; it didn't fit. He wanted to ask her the age old question: What the hell is a girl like you doing in a place like this?

"I'm sorry to disturb you. I saw the rental sign on the house around the corner. I wanted to ask the price."

"Six hundred a month, and yes, it is still for rent."

"I wonder if I could look at it?"

"Listen, I'm on my way out of here. I've got to be across town, and I'm running late now. Can you come back?"

"I'm sorry, but I need a place tonight. I need to move in right away."

"Well damn, wouldn't you know. Look, here's the key. If you like the place, go ahead and stay; you can bring the money by tomorrow. If you don't like it, just leave the key inside and lock up. I'll get the key later. I've got another." With that she locked the door and trotted toward her car, arms and high heels flying from side to side belying the graceful lines of a perfect body. She opened the door of a sleek Jaguar, turned sharply around one hundred and eighty degrees, and literally dropped her attractive posterior into the bucket seat. Anderson watched with fascination as she swiveled two finely muscled and nylon clad legs into position. She grabbed the wheel with both hands. He could almost see the knuckles turn white as the blood was pressed from them. She continued to strangle the wheel as she rotated her head over her right shoulder. What happened next seemed to do so in slow motion.

The Jag shot into the street. The woman had just brought her head back around to the left when the other car hit her, not hard but enough to jolt her, disheveling the woman completely. Anderson ran to her aid.

"Miss, are you alright?"

Before she could answer, a burly voice behind him shot out a string of obscenities.

"Hey dumb ass, don't you ever look where you're goin'? You gonna pay for this, bitch."

An arm shot past Anderson's shoulder and grabbed the lapel of the woman's jacket. Anderson's reactions were immediate. His right hand grabbed the man's crotch and with a fluid motion turned him over in the air. He let go and watched the intruder float toward the concrete where he lit first on the back of his head.

"Of course I'm OK. Get in the car."

It didn't take long to assess the situation. Cops would be rolling in. Apart from being fascinated by her, he didn't know this woman, or the man, or much of anything about where he was. But he sure as hell knew he wanted nothing to do with the police at this point.

"Take off. I'll follow you." Anderson yelled as he jumped into his car and made a U-turn in the small street. The Jag was already accelerating away from the scene. The Oldsmobile's racing engine responded, and the Jag couldn't pull away from him. Those Southern boys know their cars, he thought. But another thought was occupying his mind. What the hell was he doing following this strange woman?

The Jag sped through the streets of L.A., gliding over the asphalt like it was sucked down to the pavement. But Anderson's gray junker kept the pace, winding along palm lined boulevards. The ever changing financial stature of the neighborhoods was unmistakable until, finally, the expensive sedan pulled into a driveway and proceeded up to a Porte-cochere canopy that covered the entrance to a fashionable country club. He was still trying to decide from what part of his brain had come the order to follow her. Poor genetics maybe?

Once inside, Anderson thought how easy it was to understand why so many young, returning Vets suffered. To be torn from the jungle one day and then to be thrust within tasting distance of the opiate of opulent American society the next was a transition their young minds could not easily sort out and deal with. The drugs that wrung the fiber from them in the cities and the jungles of Vietnam laced the horror of the wounded, mutilated, dying children, women, feeble brown bodies, and their brothers with a self-protecting mental estrangement. But the return to the light from the depths of the cave was to reverse the anguish of those hidden from the rest of the world by the plush American lifestyle lived by the few and vicariously by millions of humming television sets.

America had taken advantage of these young men and then abandoned them. The return to the world was fraught with an incomprehensible punishment. The confusion of a reversal of American commitment and resolve coupled with scorn for what these youth perceived as ultimate sacrifice for their own was intolerable. Their minds blanked the soul, the self-life, the essence of themselves that was so important to the continued existence of what made them human.

Anderson thought of Hanoi Jane, the symbol of the enemy within the sanctuary. There was no home to return to, only the cave. And the cave was ugly in its own beauty. He thought of Angela and of grasping at the sanity and the normalcy of a past era. He thought of the beautiful woman whose tapered, muscular legs danced in front of him as he followed them through the corridors of affluence. From one jungle to another. But again, why in the hell was he following her?

When she stopped, he waited.

CHAPTER THIRTY FIVE

Angela paced the floor.

"Daddy, I told you. He wants to come meet you, but he has to take care of some things first. I really don't know where he is."

"Look baby, he must have told you something. I might have to go up the coast for a few days. I would like to meet him now. If you're this serious about this guy, I need to meet him. Please see to it, Angela."

Angela made her way back to her room. She pondered over her father's sudden interest in anything she did. She decided that the prospect of marriage must be particularly important to him over other aspects of her life. She noticed the Major come through the garden door as she left.

She was just opening the door to the room when the phone rang.

"Hello?"

"Angela, its Anderson."

"Sweetheart, my god where are you? You won't believe it. Father and I were just talking about you. He wants you to come to the house right away to meet the family. He has to go to San Francisco and then to Southeast Asia. He is anxious to meet you. He can't wait. When can you make it? Where are you?"

"I can't make it right now. I'll call again. When is he going to leave?"

"I'm not sure. He said a couple of days. Are you alright?"

"Oh yeah. Pretty dull actually. Maybe I can come over. I guess I could postpone my trip a little. But I'm not sure exactly when. I'll call again tomorrow. I should be able to make it by then. Is the Major still there?"

"Yes, but he's acting kind of strange. He's nice enough, but something. I don't know. He seems as anxious to see you as daddy."

"I wouldn't mind saying hi to him myself. How many of his men does he have with him? I'll bet I know most of them."

"I don't know, but quite a few, maybe ten. I really don't know what they're doing here. Most of them stay in the house we have in the back. They spend their time by the pool. It won't hurt my feelings when they leave. I don't get much swimming done anymore. They act like a bunch of horny old bulls. It's a bit more than I can take. There used to be a black man here. I think that he and two or three others must have gone back already. I haven't seen him around for a while.

"Sweetheart, make it as soon as you can. Father is going to be happy. Please call back soon. I love you," she said, a mournful inflection in her voice.

"I'll try my best. I'm looking forward to meeting him also. Bye, baby."

As soon as Anderson hung up, Angela was on her way to tell her Father. She burst into the room.

"Father, Anderson was just on the line. He's going to come over."

The Major spoke first. "That's good. I really want to see that boy again. He was a fine soldier. I have a tremendous amount of respect for those young men, so courageous and patriotic. It will certainly be a pleasure."

"Angela, did he say when?" Her father asked.

"No, but probably tomorrow. He said he would call."

CHAPTER THIRTY SIX

"Say good looking, where have you been?"

"Sorry, I had to make a call. No sweat."

"Come here, I want you to meet some folks."

Anderson felt conspicuous. He wasn't dressed to meet these people, and he had absolutely nothing in common with them to talk about. Small talk and prying interrogation was followed by back slapping comparisons of pocket books, cars, horses, and beach houses. Inevitably, the conversation turned to sex.

"Well, you all will just have to get your own. This white knight just rescued me from the jaws of a dog."

Anderson, suddenly aware that the conversation was once again centered on him, looked up.

"Say, do you think we could get out of here. I've got a few things to take care of, and the house, remember."

"OK, what the hell. Let's go look at the house then." She said as though giving in to an impatient child.

Anderson once again found himself following this woman through the city streets, but in a different direction. It was not long this time, however. She led him to a home that was like nothing Anderson had ever seen, palatial, in the old plantation style, but with very modern interior furnishings and decor.

Still in awe, Anderson reminded her of his need to settle into a place and get some sleep.

"Oh baby, I'm sorry. I'm not much of a host now am I?"

With that she led him into another wing of the house and opened the door to what was either her bedroom or one hell of a play pen. Once inside, she turned to him; her head tipped slightly forward, an eyebrow arched, and her eyes studied his. Her stare was unequivocal, leaving nothing to guess work. She let the black silk dress fall from her shoulders. Her bare breasts heaved slightly with her quickening breath as she moved forward. She stopped momentarily to allow Anderson to look at her, savor her body standing before him. The sight of her was transfixing. He felt her move closer.

The cat toyed with him, playing with the emotions she knew was being aroused. He could smell her perfume, heavy in the air as she removed his shirt and then his pants. She was delighted when she found that he wore nothing underneath. He remained silent and still as she slid down his chest and hinted at contact with him. Again she stood and moved closer. Anderson could feel her soft, pointed nipples touch and then press into his chest. The sensation was electrifying. His body shuddered involuntarily with excitement. He felt her hips move forward, rotate slightly, forcing her mound closely against him. Her silky hair pressed against him; her soft lips found his; her tongue glided warm, wet, and soft into his mouth, titillating his own. Her body was luxurious in Anderson's hands. He was lost in her womanhood. He thought of Angela, hated himself, and then fell into the abyss of passion. He was lost in the cave, fighting, shoving his way in and against a world he had never known, entering where he knew instinctively that he didn't belong. The predator had become the prey. Then suddenly Anderson reeled, trying to be polite, but backing off.

"Look," he said, "I appreciate your concern, but I can't do this. I've ... I don't even know your name. I ...

"Sheila," she said, "My name is Sheila. You can use the building out back for the time being. I can't get back to the rental for a few days. I'm sorry, but I think this will be comfortable for now. In case I forget, keep the key to the rental. You can go on over there whenever you get the urge or decide you don't like it here."

Anderson rose early to work on the car. A trip to the auto parts store and a couple hundred dollars later found him changing the face of the Oldsmobile. He buffed the old paint lightly with sand paper and quickly repaired the small scratches and rust spots. He dug at the larger rust spots with a screw driver until a hole appeared in the thin metal, then sanded the areas until sliver metal shone through. He pounded around the hole to make an indenture. He covered the hole over with aluminum tape and then brought it back flush with Bondo. He sanded them smooth and flat to match the contour of the car. After taping the chrome, Anderson applied a quick dry primer. This took the better part of the day, and by nightfall he was ready to paint. It was nearly midnight when Anderson finished transforming the old gray racer.

He left the garage in the early hours of the morning. The dark blue car pulled from the posh driveway and turned left. He needed new license plates. The car would have to be left behind soon, and he knew it. It wouldn't take long for them to realize he had either painted the old car or picked up a new one. He also knew that Sheila was a risk, a big risk. He guessed her friends would know he was living on her estate within forty eight hours. She would also be asking about the face job he had given the Olds. But now he needed sleep.

And then he heard them. It would not have given him a second thought until he heard more than two car doors shutting quietly. He moved slowly, not wanting to disturb Sheila. From the front window he could see the cars near the front of the house. He caught sight of two men just as they passed the corner of the house, out of sight. It didn't take a military genius to know they were Army. Even dressed in civvies, they stood out like warts on a nose.

Anderson climbed quickly into his jeans. Everything was in the car. He couldn't afford to let them see it now; he had too many things to do in the next couple of days. He made his way to the garage, slipped silently into the vehicle, and let the door come softly to its latch, closing it with a barely audible click. He remembered the slope behind the guesthouse not thirty yards away. As he slid the key in the ignition and turned it, he felt his heart beat quicken. The roar of the huge engine in the small garage charged his body with renewed surges of adrenaline and animal fright. The powerful car lurched, and he was on the far side of the slope and out of sight before the Major's men could react. He navigated around a few trees, bored a hole through the hedge, and was on his way along the city streets within five seconds.

He was sure it had to be one of Sheila's friends that had compromised his position: country club types that knew someone who knew someone who knew Coman. "Oh my, you can't believe what came into the club the other day on Sheila's arm, looking for sugar that she was obviously providing. A rather rough looking character," and on, and on, until Coman had put two and two together, Anderson found himself imagining. Oh well, it was for the best. He had to get away from her soon anyway. At least they didn't know yet that he had painted the car and neither did she. He was reasonably safe until he could figure out his next move.

He might as well meet the bastards head on. They certainly wouldn't expect such a bold move. It might net him another three or four of the major's men if the hit was hard and fast. But how to do it? He had to make sure Angela was gone from the house.

CHAPTER THIRTY SEVEN

Anderson's first stop was a plumbing supply house. He bought short lengths of small pipe and a few couplings. The store had a spray can of flat black paint, which he took as well. A hack saw, a roll of friction and one of duct tape, and flat and round files completed the list. At a saddle shop, he found a square foot of thick leather.

He headed for the canyon and the safety of the woods. Finding a lonely spot hidden within the trees and brush, he laid the supplies in front of him and began working. He looked at the M-16 CAR. He was not particularly fond of the Colt Automatic Rifle, but it was a hell of a lot better than the Danish 9mm. The CAR fired a .223 round weighing only fifty five grains, but in the shorty rifle with a barrel only eleven inches long, the velocity was a sorry 2600 feet per second. With its telescoping stock, it was, however, concealable as rifles went as well as light and easy to pack, though the accuracy was poor at any range, and the knock down power was even poorer. But it did have a use to which he intended to put it in the next few hours.

He first removed the flash suppresser from the muzzle; then he cut one threaded end from a six inch length of pipe using the hack-saw. He smoothed the rough edges of the cut with the files. Anderson slid the pipe over the barrel and tried the fit. He kept at this process until the pipe fit perfectly. To the remaining threaded end of the pipe he screwed the first coupling. When it was tight, he cut a small, round piece of the thick leather, pierced the center of it in the shape of an "X" with his knife, and forced it into the coupling until it rested against the smaller, inner pipe. He screwed another small length of pipe into the coupling until it held the leather piece tightly against the first. Anderson continued to connect the pipe and couplings in this way until three pieces of leather were held tightly in place approximately one inch apart.

He slipped the assembly over the barrel and secured it in place with the duct tape over which he tightly wound black friction tape. When it was firmly in place, he rubbed dirt on it to rid the tape of its sticky surface and then sprayed the contraption with the flat, black paint to match the rest of the rifle.

He inserted a twenty round magazine in the CAR, took hold of the cocking peace with his first and second fingers, pulled sharply to the rear, and let go. The bolt slammed home, carrying with it a .223 round into the chamber. Thirty yards in front of him stood a giant alder. He took aim over the short barrel and squeezed the trigger. Phiiiit! Clank! It was not perfect, but the shot was silenced enough for his purposes. The bolt made an unfamiliar sound, but at least it was not so loud that it would wake up the neighborhood. He tied a second 20 round magazine to the first with the cartridges turned down. With a quick motion he could release the magazine, turn it, and insert a second 20 round magazine into the receiver.

It was nearly dark when he phoned Angela.

"Hi," he said.

"Anderson, it's you!"

"I was wondering if I could come over now?"

"Sure, just let me tell daddy."

"No. Look Angela, my car's on the fritz. Could you come get me. Don't tell your dad just yet. We can call him later. Is that OK?"

"Sure. Where are you?"

"Well, I'm afraid it's quite a ways. Do you know where the steak house is just south of the Anaheim Hilton near Disney Land?"

"I can be there in an hour. I'm on my way."

Angela hung up abruptly. Anderson was only three blocks from the house when he made the call. He pulled away from the phone booth and wheeled down the street. He had to see Angela leave the house. He had to be sure she was safe.

He sat back in the old car's seat, slumping into the worn fabric until he was just high enough to watch the driveway between the dash and the steering wheel. What to do with his hands? He rubbed them together, noting with mild astonishment that they were dry. They should be moist with perspiration forced from his body by fear and excitement. Then it occurred to him that he was not particularly nervous. Something was wrong, out of kilter. It was not a good sign. Fear produced awareness, heightened his edge, kept him alert and alive. Maybe he was getting used to this shit, or maybe he was losing it. He touched the M-16 rifle, ran his fingers along the cold surface, traced the lines of it, almost invisible in the darkness of the vehicle. Picking the weapon up, he pushed the magazine release and felt the electrical taped magazines jump into his hands. He inspected them, pushed them back into place in the rifle until they purchased, and he heard an audible click. He pulled the bolt to the rear and let it slide home, the heavy spring driving it sharply into place with a loud clang. He pushed the safety into position and then tugged forcefully on the magazines. They held. He was ready.

"Alright, Daddy Warbucks, we just intercepted our long lost snake eater. He's out near the Hilton in Anaheim. I've sent three men to stay on your daughter's heels. We'll have the son-of-a-bitch inside two hours. I can't wait to get this business over with."

While the Major paced the expensive floor, Angela's father sat, stoic, not wanting to think about his part in all of this. As much as he allowed it to happen, he just as much rationalized away his part in it. He had nothing to do with these killers; he was simply a businessman who had found himself in a bad spot. He couldn't let his family down. It was simply a means to an end, to ensure that a business survived, to ensure that people kept their jobs. None of the rest of it had anything to do with him.

The major continued his vigil, waiting for word from his men. He hoped it would be his last night in Coman's house, or in Los Angeles. Time was running out.

It was dark when Anderson slipped through the garden wall and headed for the house. Coman didn't keep any regular security, believing it would only draw suspicion from both the community and his family. He was making it easy. Several of the GI's loafed near the pool, waiting for the Major to come out and give them the happy news. They were living in the opulence they hoped to assume when the war was far behind them.

Anderson had been keeping count of the Major's men. If his information were correct, there couldn't be more than six left and another three in the car that followed Angela. There were four by the pool. Two could be in the house or elsewhere with the Major. When the men's attention turned to themselves, Anderson stepped from the vegetation that punctuated the manicured yard. Now a bead of sweat raced down his forehead, and he felt distinctly better as familiar sensations returned to him. He walked silently alongside the pool, watching intently the group at the far end. None appeared to be carrying a weapon, but he could make out two automatics lying on the table beside a bottle of Crown Royal.

Anderson approached the group in a slow, upright walk, the CAR held low in his right hand. He was not more than twenty yards from them when the man he recognized as a helicopter pilot looked up at him.

"What the f ..."

There I was all alone . . .

Phiiiit, clank. The .223 bullet hit its mark. The warrant officer's eyes rolled up in their sockets as if to look at the hole in his forehead in astonishment. With his eyes still open, he began to slump, the life quickly draining from him.

The other three were momentarily perplexed by the action of the scene they watched. In the seconds it took their minds to register the reality of the event, another of Anderson's bullets made its way into the neck of a man seated near the table, killing him instantly.

Wishing I were home ...

As a third soldier reached for one of the weapons, the fourth ran for the house. The barrel of the automatic began to turn in Anderson's direction. A third bullet stopped the rifle's movement as the man holding it took a round at the point of his chin.

Anderson felt an explosive blow to his right shoulder. He was flying toward the water before he realized what was happening. He didn't know where this one had come from, but the guy had a firm grip around his shoulders. They were at the deep end of the pool and sinking slowly. His assailant managed to get a hold around Anderson's throat, his chin resting on the man's elbow. Anderson tried to think what the hell to do. He drove his elbows into the man's ribs, but the water cushioned the blows. He tried to work his hand around to the man's groin, but this wouldn't work either.

He thought about waiting the guy out. Maybe he could hold his breath longer. But he knew better. Although the man didn't have the best hold on Anderson's neck, he was denying oxygen to his brain, a problem the other guy didn't have at the moment.

His lungs were on fire, red spots raced across his vision, and the world began to grow dark. Fear walked through his body, creeping up through his thighs and stomach like the angel of death marching steadily through the mist without pausing, sure of its victim.

He remembered the pocketknife and struggled to get it out. Black dots enveloped by white shrouds began to appear in a formless black and red void in front of his eyes. A tingling sensation slowly grew somewhere in his body, maybe everywhere. He tried to think. It was like a nightmare from which he could not escape, though he knew it was not a dream. It was terrifying. He knew he was beginning to black out; it would not be long now. In his haze he plunged the knife alongside his own face and into the assailant's. The man let go immediately. Anderson struggled for consciousness, watching the black before his eyes turn to a blood red, growing brighter as though a strong light shone through the veil. He opened his eyes and seemed to look through pale, vermillion fabric as the pool's edge, the tables, and the trees began to force reality back. He swam as hard as he could, instinctively, pulling at the water fiercely until he touched the side of the pool and catapulted himself onto the side. His lungs exploded as he fought for air.

The M-16 still lay there, cold, uncaring in its ominous blackness. He grabbed it quickly, stood, and faced the pool. The man was holding his face, the knife protruding from his eye socket as his lips contorted in agony, calling for help with a soundless voice.

The ship it got wrecked with the captain and crew ...

Anderson pulled the trigger and watched the instantaneous spray of tiny, ruby spheres dot the water's surface.

He turned and sprinted back along the route by which he had entered. He was in the blue car and on his way in seconds. The whole affair had taken less than six minutes.

As Anderson raced along the streets toward the Anaheim Hilton, he began to go over the past few days in his mind. He had to leave. He was known now, his chances of detection increasing by the hour.

He felt pangs of self-hatred at that moment, knowing that he had used and betrayed Angela. He had spent most of his life, and particularly the past four years, cultivating honor, going to any lengths to solidify an image of loyalty among those around him, to be no less than a man bound by his word. How could he explain his actions now? Had he strived to ensure Angela's safety, or had he used her to set up the Major? He had not been true to the woman he loved; he had nearly bent to his lust in spite of her. He felt the fabric of his character unraveling. He was fighting himself. The Gabriel Center, the words of Kennedy, the oaths, all writhing in the dust.

He saw the face of David's wife, his two young children, too young to understand. No. The bastards had to pay.

CHAPTER THIRTY EIGHT

"That son-of-a-bitch! He's done it again." The Major's stomach churned. Deep within him lurked panic and doubt, but it was masked at that moment by anger and confusion as he yelled into the night.

"What the hell do you mean, he just walked in and started shooting? What kind of damned soldiers are you? You guys just sit around the pool with your head up your ass? Didn't you post a watch? I guess I should have brought a battalion. He's just one lousy green beanie asshole.

"Alright, get rid of the bodies. Tell the guys tailing Angela to waste the bastard at any opportunity. I don't give diddly squat what it takes."

Anderson stopped the car across the street from the restaurant. He laid the compact binoculars over the steering wheel to steady them. His index finger rotated the center wheel. He closed his right eye, turned the center dial, and watched as the left lenses cleared. He closed his left eye and rotated the diopter of the right lens. When it too was sharply focused, he opened both eyes and rotated the center wheel until the cars in the parking lot were focused sharply. Lights hung over the black asphalt like satin moons shimmering in the sky. He searched the cars, looking for Angela, but thinking as he did so that she would probably be inside the steak house waiting for him. He moved the glasses slightly and began studying the tables inside. It didn't take him long to locate her. She had a window booth and sat sipping a dark liquid. He watched her delicate lips caressing the glass, her eyes looking at the wall beyond, unaware of his presence, his probing, secret eyes, his using her.

Where the hell were the Major's men? He finally spotted them. The three men sat smoking and talking, waiting for their prey to show himself. They would find him soon enough.

Squelch blasted from the short-wave inside the four door Jeep Wagoneer.

"Jerry, are you there, ... over?"

"Yes sir, we're in position ... over."

"Listen, your good friend took four more of you out right after you left the house. I'm sure he's on his way there. Keep your eyes open. Waste that chicken shit bastard the minute you see him. You got that, ... over?"

"Yes sir!"

"Did you hear that? We've got to get that asshole soon, or we got to drag our butts the hell out of here, one. We're fightin' a losing battle. I ain't no damned commando. This guy's some kinda animal."

"Shut the hell up," Jerry hissed. "You're an opium runner, you dumb sumbitch. We got to get this dickhead or we're finished anyway. Now you keep your mouth shut and do your job, or I'll waste your yellow ass myself."

The fear in the SUV could be touched. Each of them in their own mind knew they were no match for the experienced commando. They wanted to take their money and run. They couldn't decide who to fear most, the Major or Anderson. At the moment, Anderson seemed to be the odds on favorite.

Anderson crossed the street on the dark side behind the men's vehicle and walked casually toward them. There were three cars between the soldier's jeep and his position. He waited until a couple leaving the cafe got into their car before he inched forward. Anderson bent down and waited for their heads to turn toward the interior of the steak house. He hurried forward and then hit the asphalt silently. It was not difficult getting under the rear of the vehicle, but he wanted to get to the front. He inched forward a little at a time; he couldn't afford to get caught under the damn thing.

He finally reached the passenger's side front wheel. Anderson kneaded a small ball of C4 into shape and planted it against the side of the wheel housing, inserted the detonator, and then pulled the pin from the tie rod nut. He loosened the nut until it just hung on the threads. When the C4 was secure, he began pushing himself back toward the rear of the four-wheeler. Anderson was back across the street and walking toward the Oldsmobile in less than a minute.

He started the vehicle, put the transmission in low gear, and moved slowly forward toward the restaurant. The roadway passed between the building and the jeep's location. He idled in front of them, making sure they recognized him, and when they did, Anderson tried to look surprised and floored the racer. The jeep pulled out of its space and squealed as it made a ninety-degree turn. As much as they regretted it, the three men were in pursuit of their enemy.

The noise caught Angela's attention, and she turned just in time to see Anderson sprinting by in a blue car. She recognized the Major's men and the jeep as it sped after him. Her mind drew a blank when she saw them pulling full automatic weapons to the windows. The look on their faces shocked her. She realized they were after Anderson. Her pounding heart found its way to her throat, seeming to clog it, obstructing her breathing, and she reached toward her throat in a reflective and protective gesture.

Anderson headed for open country. He didn't want anyone else getting hurt because of his internal war. The Olds was running smoothly and handling well as he sped toward the canyon, the only place with which he was familiar enough to execute what he planned to do. The jeep stayed with him, and he made sure it did, holding the Olds back. He looked through the rear view mirror and saw the rifles being pointed at him. He could hear rifle fire. He felt a hot pressure bite his shoulder. It didn't hurt, and he was too engrossed in what he was doing to take much notice. He floored the pedal and accelerated. If he made them concentrate on their driving, maybe they would be too busy to fire.

"Major, come in ... over."

"Jerry, go ahead ... over."

"We're on his tail. We got him on the run!"

"What's your twenty, soldier ... over?"

"I'm not sure, sir. I think we're headed out of town ... over"

"Don't lose him, or I'll have Kramer so far up your ass you'll wish that bastard in front of you had gotten you first! Stay on the air. I want to know what's happening ... over."

"Yes sir ... over."

When Anderson finally reached the canyon, he waited for the road to be clear and for a hard left turn. He remembered there was one ahead. His right hand reached again for the radio device. He held tightly to the wheel with his left hand and started into the turn. It was clear ahead, and dark. He noted a tree on the right side of the road at mid turn. Anderson pulled on through, slowed down, and turned. He stopped, facing the turn.

"Jerry, what the hell is going on? ... over."

"We're still on him, sir. He's pulled into a canyon. It looks good. The road's getting narrower. Maybe he'll get boxed in ... over"

"Damn. He's pulling you into something. Keep your eyes open. I don't know where he's goin', but I'm betting he does."

It was only seconds before Anderson saw the jeep pulling into the turn at full speed. He waited for the instant the tree would disappear in their headlights. His back felt wet and sticky, and his left shoulder was getting stiff. He changed the transmitter to his right hand.

"Sir, he's sitting right in front of us. He's pointed toward us like he's waiting ..."

"Oh shit ..."

So there was only one thing left to do ...

Anderson pressed the "open" button on the small device. He watched as the front passenger's side of the vehicle raised in the air. The jeep became a huge phantom moving in slow motion from the darkness into the light of its own high beam. The wheel shot from it into the night. When the jeep landed, the forward momentum and the missing wheel forced the rear of the automobile up and over its own front end. The Wagoneer made three end over end rolls before exploding into a ball of flames, the heat touching Anderson's face, lighting it with a warm, orange glow.

Anderson rode slowly back into Los Angeles. There were no more than four or five of them left, including the Major. The only thing he knew about any of them was that they were scum. But the Major would have a personal bodyguard. Angela had spoken about a man the Major called Kramer. She was scared of him. Although he was very polite, there was a look in his eyes that she said sent chills up her spine. She had told him that this man stayed to himself, often working out in the backyard, calisthenics, judo, that sort of thing, not joining in the lazy antics of the others. He didn't leave the house unless the Major did. The thought of this pair struck fear in him. He smiled, remembering that fear was good. Like pain, it heightened his senses, sharpened his edge, and made life ... more.

But right now he was worried about Angela. He knew she would not hang around the restaurant this long. He stopped at the first telephone he saw.

"Can you page a young woman for me please? It's very urgent. Her name is Angela Coman. Thank you."

He was very surprised when he heard her voice.

"Anderson?"

"It's me."

"What happened? Where are you? I saw you pulling out of the parking lot. Some of Major McCauley's men were following you. They had guns with them. They didn't look too happy. God, I've been on pins and needles sitting here wondering what to do. I hurried to call the police, but decided to call daddy and tell him first. He told me he'd call them and to just sit tight until he got back to me."

"Listen Angela, don't worry. I'm sorry about all this. I can't explain just yet. I've got some slight problems. You've just got to trust me. I'll get back in touch as soon as I can."

The conversation fell silent.

"... Angela?" Anderson said softly.

"Yes, I'm listening. What can I say? How much longer is this mysterious stuff of yours going to take?"

"Not much longer. It'll be OK. Do you have a friend your family doesn't know that you can stay with tonight?" Anderson asked.

Angela thought a moment. "Well, where we were I guess."

"Go straight there. Don't call anyone. Wait until tomorrow to call your father. The Major will be leaving by then, and when he has, you can return home. Please trust me," he said.

"When will you call?"

"I'm not sure. A few days."

"How do you know the Major will be leaving?"

Anderson didn't answer.

"It's all bullshit. You know that too don't you." She hung up, furious with worry.

Angela slumped back in the booth. She was perplexed by her actions. A man she had just met, spent only a short time with, barely knew him, his home, his family and yet, she was doing what he asked. She trusted him completely and couldn't begin to explain why. She had decided the Major was not only strange but becoming a bit too familiar as a guest, often acting like he owned the house and not the other way around. And Kramer, just looking at him had begun to make her skin crawl. Now this. It was so far-fetched she couldn't draw any realism from it. It seemed out touch, out of place, so unbelievable that conclusions escaped her. She waited for her father to call.

Of course, neither of them knew how long it would take to bury four bodies in their back yard. The Major watched the TV intently as the police Chief briefed the press.

"We're not sure what happened here. Apparently there were three victims in the vehicle when it turned over. Apart from that we don't know much about how it happened. We're looking for witnesses now."

"Chief, what do you make of the weapons found at the scene? Someone said they're full automatic military issue. Can you tell us anything about that?" a reporter asked.

"No."

"The recent bombings up the canyon? Any connection? Similar military equipment was found at the scene there also wasn't it?"

"We're still investigating that one as well. We'll let you know as soon as anything breaks."

With that the captain turned and walked back to the burned jeep. Drake and Evans were once again expounding theories. They knew damned well there was a connection, as did he.

"Look sir, it's the same MO. Plastic explosives. Military types. You can spot them a mile away. Whoever wasted those dudes up the canyon put the shit on these poor bastards as well. The bomb was detonated remotely, expertly."

"All right, what have we got? We haven't found a shred of evidence that it has to do with drugs or money. It's not a cult. They're amateurs; this is a pro. I don't think it's the mob. They're not that good either. With bombs maybe, but not with a rifle. It's got to be government, but none of the agencies work this way. Seems to me we've got some kind of elite military in-fighting. The shooting, the bombing, they're tactical. Those dog tags we found on one of the victims appear to be military issue. But why just the blood type? Why not a name? Shit, I don't even know where to start. Marines, SEAL's, sniper units, Rangers, what?"

The Major knew who it was. Seven of his men had been taken down that night. With the three in the canyon, he'd lost eleven men. Only Kramer and two others left. He had to do something quick. The Colonel would soon find out that he and his men were not returning. It wouldn't take long for them to put two and two together. He could hold Angela and bring Anderson to him that way. The problem was that he couldn't get in contact with Anderson. He'd have to wait him out. No, that might not work. He was desperate. He'd have to go to Takano. It was the only way now.

CHAPTER THIRTY NINE

Anderson phoned his mother. Yes, an envelope had arrived from Thailand. Yes, she had sent it along. It should have been at the Post Office in L.A. already. Anderson looked at his watch, 4:30 PM. The office would be closed in half an hour. As he drove, he thought about the file he had seen in the hotel that night lying on the floor amid all the other planning paraphernalia as the Colonel issued his last orders. He thought about Bill's last words: Déjà vu, the drug lord, Takano. There must be something in the file he could use.

"Yes, yes, I have the envelope. Here you go."

Anderson smiled at the postal clerk and turned to the door. As he walked to his car, he gripped the file tightly. At last he had it. He had to find a place to go through it, and he needed coffee.

Anderson opened the envelope. Inside was the file he had seen, or at least it was the file cover. He turned the cover over and began to read. For the most part it was full of military jargon and acronyms, but one section stood out:

"Colonel Langlinais is given the authority and the means to establish an intelligence network within the Thailand-Laos-Cambodia triangle. Among his primary objectives shall be the establishment of rapport with the native tribesmen and nomads in the area. This will be most easily accomplished by providing those indigenous personnel with the means of a constant source of income and the protection of traditional means of sustenance and social mores. Three immediate candidates shall be developed.

"The Karen is a nomadic tribe residing along the forested border between Burma and Thailand. These tribesman claim independence from both countries. Both, however, claim them as their own, consider the nomads pariah, and seek to exploit their natural resource: opium. The Meo grow poppy in the hills along the border and often use Karen labor. Transportation, via Air America, of their resource is authorized. In return they will provide clandestine Karen territories within which Laotian commandos can be trained. Further, American officials promise temporary immunity from intervention by either Thailand or Burma.

"The Colonel shall employ Special Forces personnel to accomplish this assignment. Special Forces personnel are trained as teachers, in counterinsurgency warfare, in establishment of intelligence networks, and in commando tactics. The agency shall provide the Colonel with the funds necessary to transact Operation Deja Vu within his requirements.

"Laotian commando units, acting in tandem with these advisers, shall harass, interdict, and strike at the morale of the enemy along its major supply route, the Ho Chi Minh Trail, at any point deemed necessary and/or productive. More importantly, these units shall be used for reconnaissance, locating expanded units and other abnormal movements along the trail, providing strike coordinates for tactical air units based in Udorn, Thailand.

> "Colonel Langlinais shall have at his disposal, and by use of his authority, all necessary means to accomplish this operation."

The file continued with Colonel Langlinais' notes:

> "Three in-country Special Forces teams have been employed to date. These comprise twenty men ranging from Staff Sergeant to Captain garnered from the 46th. Use of covert military equipment has been supplemented with currency and incentive to accomplish operation milestones.
>
> "Karen and Meo tribes have been neutralized. Cooperation excellent. Shipments of indigenous crops have been successful in bringing these tribesmen along. Air America appears dependable enough.
>
> "Sergeant Brenner deployed inside North Regular's camp near the Laotian border. Convinced the enemy of his disgust of America's actions and egotistical, tyrannical involvement. Offer made to help train Regulars in American tactics. Inside information on movements and American prisoners exchanged through opium trade. Information very valuable. Assignment is extremely dangerous for Brenner. Wish him the best of luck. Must pull him out soon. Major McCauley has been working with Vietnamese to release prisoners through drug profits."

There it was! Brenner was a plant, not a traitor. The Major ran the drug operation. It was he who had convinced the Colonel that Brenner had turned and needed to be eliminated. He was surely siphoning the drug money. That greedy piece of shit tried to put him out of the picture as well. David had taken the hit from a bunch of scum! And this document: it wasn't Army; it was CIA.

Anderson read on.

"The official results report is the responsibility of Major McCauley, my assistant. His document has been labeled Vu Deux."

There was no question what the motive was now. The kills were greed. The Major had to go. It was only a matter of time and the amount of insulation he had put between himself and Anderson. There were only a couple of the Major's cronies left. Then it was Kramer and the Major. Kramer, the brawn and the Major, the brain. Their element was the street. He had to get them out of their element.

Anderson had rented a room for the day near Disney Land. The small cinderblock motel was set back from, and ran perpendicular to, the street, but it had a wing at the back that ran back to the north. It sheltered his car from sight. The rooms were clean and quiet. Not many people came and went like they did at the larger hotels to the south. He nursed the wound near his left, upper shoulder. It was a flesh wound only and looked clean enough. A full jacketed, military round had entered the muscle just above the shoulder blade and exited just above the collar bone. Not to worry, he thought, and turned his attention elsewhere.

Thinking that he intended this to be his last sojourn in the city, any city, he picked up the document and finished reading it. Then he picked up the telephone and called the Coman residence.

"Yes."

"Hello, is this Angela's father?"

"Who is this?"

"Let me speak to the Major, sir."

Without a word, Coman handed the phone to the major. From the look on Coman's face, the Major let his intuition decide who was on the other end "Hello, boy. What you got on your mind?"

"Well, sir, you seem to enjoy having your men follow me around. I thought I'd give you some inside information. Make it easier on you.

Suppose I tell you where I'm going. That way you can follow me without having to play detective."

"Follow you my ass. You're coming to me this time. I've got that sweet little girl of yours. If you don't show up inside the next two hours, she's dead. Do you read me, Sergeant?"

"That's bullshit, Major, and we both know it. Now listen closely. I'm headed east as soon as I hang this phone up, and you're coming after me. Your task is to waste my ass. You're scared shitless I'll turn your little drug operation in. I'm sure by now you know the Asian isn't going to help you. He sent a couple of his thugs to tell me so several days ago. In fact, unless I miss my guess, he's hoping I'll clean you and save him the trouble. You're the liability to him now, not me. We're taking this little gig to the end. I've got the File. You've got only one chance to save your ass and that's to get it. Now listen up you worthless, murdering piece of dog shit. You drive west to Vegas, find highway 89 and follow it north until you get to Junction, Utah. Ask someone there how to get to Mount Delano. You can take the road out of Junction through City Creek. Follow the signs to Big Flat. Head Northeast toward Marysvale from the meadow. My guess is that there's only four of you left. Let's see how good you and your soldiers are. Personally, I think you're all a bunch of soft ass pussies, full of beer and big talk. You've been sitting on your ass so long, Major, I don't think you can earn all that blood money you stole or those phony gold leaves on your lapel. You're not a soldier. You're a greedy coward, full of beer and self-importance. Bill, Brenner, and my cousin David want your ass."

"Listen, you shithead."

Anderson had already hung up the phone.

CHAPTER FORTY

Evans brought a communiqué to the Chief. As they sipped their morning coffee, the L.A. Police Chief opened the envelope

"Evans, this is it! The whole story. Listen to this." The Captain nearly dropped the coffee mug in his haste to put it down and grasp the document with both hands.

A note was attached to the file. It read:

"I guess I've caused a little more than my share of havoc in your city lately. I must apologize for that. I know you are probably up against it trying to solve the problem. Let me try to explain. Mr. Coman is a substantial resident of your community. He is at the moment host to several Army personnel. The officer in charge is Major McCauley. He and his men have been running a drug operation out of Thailand. They are here to dispose of me for knowing about it. I have not included the entire file, but I think you have enough to understand the situation. Colonel Langlinais, Major McCauley's superior officer, is not aware of the Major's activities yet, but he soon will be I suspect, because the Major and his men will not be returning to their post.

"Sir, my actions have been in self-defense. The Major and his men have already killed several people including my cousin, a man named Bill Baedeker, and a Sergeant Brenner. They are after me now, having concluded that I'm the last link that could stand between them and the good life.

"I will have moved on by the time you read this, and I'll be taking the Major and his men with me, or what's left of them. I felt I should tell you this so you would know that the past incidences are at an end in your city. Oh, there is one more thing, but it's the last. Suggest you make a thorough search of Coman's back yard. With a bit of luck, you will find four of McCauley's men there, recently deceased.

"I would have enlisted your help from the beginning, but I'm afraid you might have lost some good men in the process of doing your duty. The way I see it, by the time you went through your bureaucratic procedures, the end result would have been the same anyway."

De Oppresso Liber

The Captain jumped up from his chair.

"Can you believe this! Get the District Attorney on the phone. What the hell are we going to do with this?" he mumbled to himself.

The Captain, Evans, and Clark were standing in the Assistant District Attorney's office within the hour.

The DA, Devlin by name, shook his head.

"I don't really know what the hell to do with this. First, get hold of the local military and see if you can verify that this document is authentic. Next, see what you can find out about this Coman. Get some men at the bus depots, airports, and alert everyone assigned to major highways leading out of the city. Also call the Police Chiefs in each of the nearest cities on those highways to keep a sharp eye. Then visit Coman."

Evans and Clark headed in opposite directions. Evans had prior military MP experience and figured he could quickly find the person in L.A. that wrote most of the orders. If that person couldn't verify that the document was legit, he could probably tell Evans who could. At the same time, Clark got busy arranging bulletins to various agencies and cities, the airport, and bus depots.

It was early afternoon when all four headed for Coman's. On the way Evans informed the Captain that the document had been verified. Clark hadn't heard any word yet.

They were not surprised by Coman's home. L.A. was full of them, opulent to the point of vulgarity, statues to success, or white elephants goring and crushing the owner into the reality of the situation he had allowed his fantasies and indulgence to take him.

Coman himself answered the door.

"Can I help you? Is something wrong?"

"Mr. Coman, I'm with the District Attorney's office, and these gentlemen are with the Los Angeles Police Department. May we come in? We need to ask you a few questions if you don't mind."

"Yes, yes, by all means."

Coman led them through a short corridor, past the gaming room, and into the library.

"Can I get you gentlemen something to drink?"

"No thank you, sir. My name is Devlin. This is Captain Dermit and these are detectives Evans and Clark. Let me get to the point. We understand a Major McCauley is staying with you as well as some men under his command. We would like to talk to him."

Coman's face turned ashen. Shit, he thought, this is it. He didn't know how to answer. How much did they know? Could he get away with denying it?

"Mr. Coman?"

"That is true, yes. But I'm afraid they have already left."

“Can you tell us how to get in touch with the Major or any of his men?”

“I don’t know. I just assumed they were on their way back to their base. They were here on R&R, I believe is the term.”

“And where is that, Mr. Coman?”

“Thailand.”

“How long ago did they leave?”

“Early this morning. Why? Is something wrong?”

“Mr. Coman, do you have any idea what the term Deja Vu might pertain to, a file, a code name?”

“No sir.”

“Mr. Coman, I understand you’re an independent businessman.

What might that business be?”

“I own and operate an industrial plant. I refine precious metals from the waste products of other plants.”

“Do you have any business connections in Southeast Asia?”

“Yes, I do business with several foreign countries. Why? What is this all about? Maybe I should refer you to my lawyer.”

Just as the Captain was about to speak, Angela entered the library having heard part of the conversation from outside the room.

“Hello officer. Is this about Anderson? Is he in some kind of trouble?”

“Who is Anderson?”

“Oh, thank goodness. I suppose it can’t be about him then if you don’t even know him. He’s my fiancé. *At least I think he is.* He just got out of the Army. He was a Green Beret. I haven’t heard from him in a couple of days, and I was a little wor ...”

She caught herself suddenly. Get hold of yourself Angela, she thought, don’t be so damned naive. Keep your mouth shut. Pull yourself together and stop babbling.

The officers looked at each other. Their expressions shone like light bulbs turning on. Green Beret. They realized they had just found the link, and the name.

"Miss Coman, was your fiancé stationed in Thailand by any chance?" The Captain looked at the girl and was beginning to know Anderson more by the minute. Born into wealth and upper social status, this young woman was poised, elegant, and beautiful, with long silky legs that didn't support spoiled, aristocratic snobbery, but a genuine, warm human being.

"Why yes, how did you kn...."

She was cut off by her father.

"That's enough. Any more information will have to come through my lawyers. I would appreciate it if you would leave."

"Just one last question. Miss Coman, Angela is it, can you tell us when the Major and his men left here?"

"Well, they kind of left in shifts. I mean a few would leave and then some more. The Major and the remaining three men left late last night." She hoped that with that news the police would leave their house and rush after them.

"I have to caution you, detective. Do you have a search warrant?" Mr. Coman asked.

"Yes, sir, we do. May we?"

"On what grounds would you be issued such a thing?"

"You, sir, are suspected of drug trafficking, harboring drug traffickers, and murder. I hope you will cooperate and not make us drag you in just yet."

"This is preposterous. What do you think you'll find?"

"Evans, get the dog."

Angela stood, dazed.

Evans re-entered the house a moment later with a golden retriever. It didn't take long to find the four bodies the Major had had buried in the acres of landscaping Coman owned.

Anderson was well out of town. He didn't have time to nurse the wound in his shoulder; he would have to tend to it later. He was pulling into a little town near the eastern California border. He decided he should stop and have something to eat. Got to eat or sleep. Can't go without both, he thought.

Anderson ordered his favorite: sirloin, lemon pie, and coffee.

"Sheriff, we've got a guy in here." Mary Ann, the waitress spoke in nervous, whispered phrases. "I think he's been shot; I can see blood on his shoulder under his jacket and a bullet hole in his shirt. He's got intense eyes. You better get down here just in case." She hung up the phone, not waiting for an answer, and hurried back into the cafe.

When the officer entered the small building, Anderson was just starting on his lemon pie.

"Mary Ann, cuppa joe if ya don't mind, and suma at err lemon pie. Looks perty good taday." He didn't look at Anderson, but sat down beside him at the bar.

"Hello, young feller. How's yer hammer hangin'?"

"Hasn't been a problem, sir." Anderson answered, looking down with a smile.

"Looks like a right nasty cut on yer shoulder."

"Just a scratch."

"Mmmmm, man, that's some kinda lemon pie. That yer Olds sittin' out front? Bet it lays some rubber down ... magine?"

Anderson didn't answer. He was beginning to realize he had made a mistake coming here; this redneck was about to shit in his mess kit. He turned and looked at the officer.

"Where ya from, boy? Where ya headed?"

"What's the matter, officer, you run out of things to do?" Anderson knew he'd just made his second error. He guessed it was all he had.

"Well now, why don't you just stand up real calm like an' put yer hands onna bar. Let's be a good ole boy, now." Anderson heard the cop unload a wad of phlegm infested tobacco behind him onto the concrete floor of the seedy diner.

Anderson felt the cuffs dig into his wrists as the cop pushed him along holding on to the chain. Once inside the small community's single, filthy, jail cell the officer continued his interrogation.

"What we gonna find inna car, boy? Gawd, I luv this job. You punks all alike: drugs, guns, loose women; wouldn't get a damn job if yer live's depended on it. You one of those stinkin' hippies, flower child ... magine? Don't know why you assholes don't join the Army or somethin'... chickenshit drifters. Gawddamn."

The cop was still carrying on as he exited the door. "You gonna wish you'da never drove inama town, boy."

Anderson couldn't believe it. A thousand ways to get his ass in it, and it has to be some redneck cop in California.

It didn't take long for the officer to return.

"Quite an arsenal ya got 'ere, dipshit. What is this thing anyway?" The officer turned the custom rifle in his hand. "Guess I had ya figgered wrong. What? Banks, donut shops, the Treasury ... magine? Well, guess I'll just let ya cool yer sorry ass here while I find out. Back inna mornin', sweet cheeks."

He laid Anderson's black case down on the desk and wandered out again. Anderson looked at the cell. Shit, he didn't have time for this. He took the shroud line he carried rolled up in his hip pocket and tied it firmly to his boot. He poured everything he could find into it and looped the line around it. He got the boot swinging at the end of the line and then watched as it arched through the air. The boot landed on the desk. As he pulled the line in, the boot began dragging everything on the desk with it. He winced when the case hit the floor. The case was too heavy for the boot to drag it along the concrete floor. After several attempts, he managed to bring the desk lamp within reach.

Anderson bent the lamp into a hook and pounded the end flat. He tied the line to the other end and tried again. This time he snagged the cloth case. When he had it in the cell with him, he opened a small side pocket and extracted a portion of the C4 plastic explosive from inside. He had one cap and timer device left. He placed it directly below the window.

He retreated to the far end of the cell, put the bed mattress over him, cupped his hands tightly over his ears, and waited for the deafening report. I've seen this in the movies, he thought, hope to hell it works.

"Yer tellin' me he's a what? Shiiiit. I had him pegged for some beatnik drifter."

The Chief tried to calm the officer on the phone. "Listen, officer Carlson, you did just fine. Can you tell me which way he might have gone?"

"Don't reckon I can tell ya much of anything except the size of the hole that sorry bastard left in ma jail. Bleve he' hurtin' though."

"Why is that, officer?"

"Well, he was shot when he come in 'ere, but whatever blew the hell outta my jail must have added to it, cause there's blood everwhere. Weren't bleedin' like that when I left him, no sir ... not like that."

CHAPTER FORTY ONE

Anderson drove west, toward his beloved mountains. He was planning his fight, and he welcomed his return home. But his decision to do so was bothering him. In his enthusiasm to return to the familiar and comfortable environment of his youth, he had not considered what might happen. He didn't intend to tell or disturb anyone by his return, but things had a habit of going sour. In any case, there was better than an even chance that the outcome of what was about to happen would be found out. The trauma of finding the bodies would alone be stressful to his people. But his being found to be connected with it would be much worse. The pain it would cause his mother would be significant. Yet he had no other way to stop what had been set in motion. He would just have to hope for the best. And he wanted it on his turf, in the mountains.

Anderson had cached supplies on previous trips, sensing that he would find use for them in the ensuing weeks. He still had a few hours to go to reach them. He chose the most remote entrance into the area, turning onto the Cove Fort road leading to the mouth of Marysvale Canyon on Highway 89. This side of the range was uninhabited and had been since stone carving, Fremont Indians divined petroglyphs of an ancient people in the canyon walls. About half way along this highway, Anderson turned south onto a dirt road leading into the mountains, the mountains of home.

The elevation of the canyon floor averaged six thousand feet. Anderson was heading toward the peak of Mount Delano that towered above the twelve thousand feet mark. The west side of the peaks of Delano and Baldy were covered with thick brush and forest. He could discern the elevation simply by noting the vegetation around him. In the river bottoms, cottonwoods and birch grew, making the waterway look like beaded strings snaking through the earth's tapestry. Yellow in the early fall sun, they were often mistaken by the neophyte as the quaking aspen that normally grew much higher around the eight to nine thousand feet elevation. Between them were thickets of scrub oak, willow mahogany, and juniper, giving way to ponderosa pine and spruce until trees suddenly disappeared above what is commonly referred to as "above timberline." Here the snows often lay peacefully in the perpetual shadows of the north faces. Rock chucks, manzanita, and lichen shared the sparse, rock-strewn slopes with stunted junipers that hugged the ground as though afraid to rise above themselves in the airless, pale blue skies. Cliffs, plummeting thousands of feet along the east faces, stood like gargantuan stone guardians of the mineral rich peaks. The land was harsh. It was here that Anderson and David had grown, and hunted, and nurtured their alliance with nature. It was here that David's murderers would meet David again in combat, here on Anderson's turf, no logistics, no backup, no gun ships, just the silence of the mountain.

Anderson drove confidently along the dirt road, climbing steadily. The car jolted and bounced on the rocks and ruts. The flesh wound in his shoulder ached, but it was the punctures over the rest of his body that hurt the worst, extracting the heaviest toll. He guessed whoever had written the movie scripts hadn't ever tried using a mattress when C4 blew a cinderblock wall all to hell. He decided to wait and wash the blood off himself in one of the streams higher up. He knew the wounds weren't serious, but each had bled a small amount, and together, had drained precious bits of his strength.

He remembered his days training the Special Forces Guard units in the mountains just to the north. Young men who were in shape had succumb to the elevation as hyperventilation often overcame these seasoned professionals not accustom to the altitude. Anderson, distracted, stopped momentarily to watch a couple of mule deer bucks, their tawny profiles bathed in the gold of early morning sun.

He could imagine the aroma of them on his hands and clothes, could remember the long hours in the mountains hunting them, and then the arduous task of dragging their dead, limp bodies for miles to his home, the beauty and grace of them reduced to venison on his family's plate. It was a smell, a touch, a task he loved, and the sight of them took him back to pleasant times. He never tired of watching them, but now pushed on toward his goal. He would be in position before nightfall.

This entrance to the range did not go to the top, or at least didn't allow an Oldsmobile to do so. Anderson abandoned the hotrod, and after shouldering the rifles and a few other sundry items, struck out for the top on foot.

Keeping a steady pace, he would crest the summit by late afternoon. Anderson had never been in better shape, and his young legs carried him effortlessly up the steep slopes in spite of his wounds. But he knew he would be stiff and sore in a few more hours. The afternoon sun shone golden on the peaks, and the weather was crisp, dry, and beautiful. Blue skies shrouded the twin mounds in surrealistic beauty as white and yellow quakies fluttered an orchestral winter herald just below. Heaven could not be far in Anderson's opinion.

"That little prick is about to piss me off."

The Major and his men had driven through the night in the four-wheeler. It made him nervous that he didn't know what he was heading into, but he judged Anderson too much of a macho fruitcake to enlist any more help. The way he saw it, the "Green Beanie" wanted to hunt. No bullshit, the Major hadn't fallen off an onion truck that morning. They had him out numbered four to one. Mr. Macho, or rather, the fool, was finally going down.

"Pull over, Kramer. Let's ask these small town hicks where the hell City Creek is."

The Major walked inside the small country store and gas station with the usual chip on his shoulder.

"Hey there. Say, could you tell me how to get up City Creek? We're vacationing here from out of state. We heard the Big Flat area was nice."

"Right across the street, fella. Just head west on that dirt road. Turn left up along the mountain just past the old log house. You can't miss it." Stu Brinkman pointed to the west.

"You don't happen to have some brandy do you?"

"I'm afraid not. You'll have to go fifteen miles north to Marysvale to the liquor store for that."

"Well, we're kind of in a hurry. Haven't you got anything else?" The Major sounded desperate.

"We've got Coors, but you'll have to wait till tomorrow. Can't sell ya none on Sunday. Sorry. We got vanilla though. Some folks drink that when they're hard up."

The Major turned on his heel and bolted out of the store.

"Come on, Peters, get that heap movin' before I stick a quarter pound of C4 on the shitter wall and blow this dump off the face of the earth ... vanilla, shiiiit!"

"We got Aqua Velva." He heard the man say as he let the door slam.

The dirt road turned Northwest across open sagebrush flats. Dust boiled oppressively, seeping through the seemingly sealed doors as the small party drove toward the mountain. The back was loaded with gear that grew white with powder as the miles rolled by. It was night before they reached the turnoff, and they found themselves winding up the switchbacks that Anderson had traveled so many times before. They watched the lights of the town to the south grow dimmer, melting away into the night as at last they navigated Grade Hill, crested the summit, and were swallowed by the blackness of the forest.

They were alone in the night, watching the headlights bounce from the endless trees that created images like the undaunted shadows of Plato's cave as they passed in a monotonous and mesmerizing rhythm. They each had the same thought: how in the hell had they ended up half way round the world on this unfamiliar, god-forsaken mountain chasing a no-account hick?

Presently, the four men came on a second sign pointing the way to Big Flat. They turned the car north and continued on. Only a half hour had passed when the winding mountain road finally gave way to an expansive meadow. They were at their destination. Rather than roll out their gear, they elected to sleep in the car until morning. It was cool in the thin air, but comfortable. They felt well hidden in the trees.

The Major did not worry. He knew Anderson would not take them at such a logical site, not by ambush at this spot. He had invited them to the mountain to hunt them. The stupid Green Beret was too caught up in the arms of mother integrity for such a pragmatic action. He knew Anderson would only be satisfied by fair chase on his home turf. He slept soundly.

When morning came, the party was up early, busy putting their gear in order. The Major counseled his men on the psychology of Anderson. He explained again that Anderson would not take them on the flat or in the camp. Their best chance would be to stalk him on his own hunting ground. They had him out numbered four to one. If they kept their eyes open and their radios on, they could flank him. There would be no room for his escape.

But the truth was that the Major only hoped to cover his ass long enough to have Anderson wasted by any one of his men. His own job would be to stay out of the line of fire. After all, it's hard to spend good money six feet under. Major McCauley told his men that they would walk to the edge of the flat to where the mountain's eastern slope began. From there they could get the lay of the land by sight to augment their studies of the topo maps they were carrying. From there they would also finalize their strategy.

The Major turned to a tall, young soldier wearing a baseball cap and told him to take point. Kramer followed, then the Major. Peters, another chopper pilot, brought up the rear. They had only gone a short distance when Peters spoke sternly.

"I'm not going. This is the end of the line for me."

The group stopped suddenly.

"Excuse me? Say that again, soldier." McCauley was surprised by the outburst.

"Look Major, there is no way in hell that we can take this guy on his own turf. The truth is we couldn't take this guy on any turf. Admit it, we're no match for this dude. That drug money ain't worth dying over. I'm doing all this, and I haven't even seen the money let alone spent any of it."

The Major turned on his heel and lashed out.

"Look, you sniveling little asshole, there's a cool million in the brief case I just locked in the vehicle. You're running out of choices, boy. You have exactly five seconds to make the right decision here."

"Sir, don't you get it yet? He's going to kill every one of us. Get the hell out of here and take your chances. What's he going to do about it? He doesn't have the resources to follow us or hunt us down. I don't care what you think. This guy lives this stuff, thrives on it. This is his game. He doesn't know anything else. Right now he doesn't need to. Ten men couldn't take this guy. Give it up while you still can."

From behind the Major a shot rang out, punctuating the silent, calm mountain air with an explosive, echoing roar. The Major watched indifferently as Peters sank to his knees. The wound in his neck was not immediately apparent, but it was lethal just the same, having severed his spine, spewing bits of bone and blood on the meadow grass behind him. Kramer leveled the rifle on the other man.

"Hey sir, I didn't say a damn word. That was all his idea. Let's go." The tall, muscular man backpedaled for all he was worth.

"That's good. You men drag that crybaby into the woods. We don't want the whole county up here looking around just yet."

Anderson couldn't make out the conversation, but he heard the shot and watched the man fall. He lowered the binoculars and smiled. One down, three to go. His work was getting easier by the minute. He cut through the trees, quartering the little band's progress and dropped into Ten Mile Creek Canyon. The soreness slowed him some, but he was intent. The forested slopes engulfed him in the familiar, dark green world that was home to wary mule deer and elk; his people knew it as "Black Timber", an apt description of its essence.

They had taken the challenge. The next few hours would bring some release to Anderson's tormented soul. He had gunned down an American from the depths of deceit, without warning. The young man had had no chance; had had no realization of the danger in the jungle, lurking, waiting to end his dreams and aspirations to be back in the world again.

David, who had counted on him, had trusted Anderson's judgment in that land of which he knew nothing, cried out in his mind. His cousin had staked his life on him and gotten burned for it.

And Bill. The gentle giant had died trying to help him in his hour of need, doing whatever was asked of him, knowing that the danger of detection was high. Yes, it would be sweet, this revenge in the mountains of home.

CHAPTER FORTY TWO

"OK, I think we've got something here. At least some of our guesses were right: this guy Anderson is from Utah, was in Special Forces, but just recently mustered out; he is some kind of sharpshooter, although not assigned as such in the military, and he was stationed in Thailand under the command of a Colonel Langlinais who is somehow attached to the CIA. The link is the Major. Apparently he was second in command to Langlinais. Seems that he made most of the deals in setting up some kind of teams over there. It doesn't look like it's going to be possible to find out what the hell they were all doing, however."

Evans paced the floor as he continued the monologue.

"There's more. Anderson was trained for three years at the Special Forces Headquarters in Fort Bragg, North Carolina, better known as the Special Warfare Center. He was trained in medicine - his primary MOS - demolitions, light weapons, counter insurgency warfare, etc., etc. Jump school at Benning, Rangers in Florida, Pathfinders in Panama. Shit there's no end to it. This guy's got a Ph.D. in doing what he's been doing. Our own government trained this guy at the cost of god only knows how many of our tax dollars, to, in effect, run around our city wasting men at his discretion. He's almost too good to be caught."

The Chief stood silent, chewing on the information.

"No. That's all hype. They might be highly trained, but it's for sure they are driven by loyalty for their country. Most of them are college educated. The spook shit is a bit over stated. Usually they are sent in to help indigenous people with better methods of agriculture, medical treatment, and the like. Most of them are deployed to establish rapport with third world, backward peoples and to set up intelligence networks. This guy was wronged. What he says only makes sense. He's doing what he figures we and the US Government won't do, and he's right."

The Captain paused.

"Sometimes I hate this job. OK, put a call into this Colonel Langlinais in Thailand. Maybe he'll know where Anderson is off to. Also we ought to alert him about the Major's sting, the drugs, and this fellow Brenner before he's caught in the middle of something he won't know how to get out of. I don't know where we'll get any other leads. Coman isn't talking. We don't have a clue where the Major got off to. We don't know a damned thing about their mode of transportation. I'm sure Anderson has done something about the car. Coman's daughter doesn't know anything either, and I don't think we'd get anything out of her if she did. I guess we better call the FBI."

Anderson watched the elk in front of him. The rut was just starting and the bull was nervous. He waited, watched, and hoped the animal would bugle his challenge to the world around him. He could smell the musky odor of the animal carried on the breeze. Its antlers were those of a royal majestic bull, dark and thick, giving way to ivory tips. The herd bull brought his head up and back, and Anderson could see the ends of the beams touch lightly near his hindquarters. Then just as suddenly, the animal tipped its walnut brown head back down, stretched his neck forward, lowered his mandible slightly and gave forth the shrieking bugle that signaled he owned the area. Guttural, breathy grunts followed, blending with the echo of the shrill whistle that bounced off the rock and pine strewn ridges.

He tried once again to capture the essence of the past few years. The meaning of the strife tended to elude him. At times he felt the greatest patriotism for his and his comrade's actions, but at other times he was greatly disturbed by the absence of any real understanding of what it had all been about. What was important?

In the beginning it had all seemed OK and reasonable. Superiors told you what to do and you reacted. It could be no other way. He remembered the duty he had when he was first assigned to a team in southern Thailand. It all seemed innocent enough upon arriving. The duties at the camp were fairly slow. Nestled in the jungle, the American Green Berets had gained quite a reputation for taking care of the locals. The team was assigned to train the border patrol against marauding Communist terrorists, or CT's as they were called. When one night they raided the American's camp, officials from the American Consulate in Malaysia immediately invaded the camp. When the diplomats left, they had given a document to the camp's commanding officer. The officer, in turn, had let each of his team members read it. He even offered to let any team member have a copy if he so desired.

Each read it, but each walked away, considering the act of having the document in their position an act of treason. Politely, but without question, the document was a declaration of American intent. It left each team member confused and shocked, depressed about the state of his own role as the antenna of that American intent. It was less than flattering to the integrity of these men, and without question a catalyst for significant change in the way they viewed themselves and their country.

The men spoke little about it. In fact, they spoke nothing at all about it. The document read in a cold, political, pragmatic, business style, far removed from the rhetoric that drove these men. There was little about the domino theory, nothing about national security, nothing about trying to help and to free an oppressed people, nothing about defending a people's right to rule themselves, to be free, to be independent. The document was a matter of fact, pointed declaration of misdirection. Project Omega troops, used by the CIA instigated the Gulf of Tonkin Incident, which to many marks the date of the Vietnam war for the USA. But America had been involved in Vietnam affairs for years. Colonel Aaron Bank, the father of Special Forces, parachuted into Vietnam for the OSS back in the 40's and met with Ho Chi Minh. He recommended that the USA support Ho Chi Minh because he was primarily a nationalist who was forced to rely on the communists for support. Had we heeded Colonel Bank's advice, we could have avoided the most costly war in our history.

The men had been too busy extracting the information from their memories to let the depression take hold of them for long.

Anderson looked back in retrospect at the events of the past four years. He was shaken in his disappointment. And now these money hungry scum, once honorable warriors, had let the same base desires be their own lighthouse in a sea of obsessed avarice. But he could trust David and Bill and himself. What more could it matter?

Anderson waited. The sun rose in the sky, diluting the strong forest shadows with rays of yellow heat. The thin mountain air amplified the midday solar energy pounding on his back. He had worked his way between the Bear Hole and Mill Canyon. They would be but a few hundred yards from him now. Surely they would try to locate his position and flank him. He wondered if they were getting a taste of hyperventilation. The slightest smile crossed his face.

And what of Angela? How could she be happy with his sort? He knew she was willing to take him as is. But it would be unrealistic, even unfair, to think that it would last long for her. A different religious bent, a different social level, a different understanding of what was important in life. But could he live without her? Even through the mire of this heated battle to which he had committed himself, he had difficulty thinking of anything or anyone else. Would the distraction of her get him killed? Maybe. Probably? What the hell difference did it make. He thought of the highlights in her auburn hair, the softness of her touch, the kindness in her eyes.

Anderson noted movement on the north slope of the ridge that ran to the valley floor thousands of feet below. The figure was standing near the top in a small clearing he knew was a pack trail. He figured him for approximately one thousand yards. It was a tactical error. Anderson quickly cut northeast. The figure was undoubtedly the east flank.

Anderson disappeared over the ridge to the north and flew through the pines. It would only take fifteen minutes to cover the ground between him and the figure. The soldier was standing on the northwest face of the ridge, the side covered with black timber. The opposite face would be sparser, with groves of quaking aspen. This sudden change in vegetation would take place at the ridge's apex.

He followed the ridge he was on, staying near the top on a well-used elk trail. The ridge slowly lost elevation until he bottomed out and would have to begin the climb up again to where the man stood. But he must do it without being seen. Twelve minutes had gone by when Anderson reached the top. He quickly dropped to the more open side and followed a gully to the bottom. He worked his way to where both ridges met to form a saddle. Anderson picked a rocky outcrop that was well concealed in the trees.

From his hatband, Anderson extracted a long leather throwing sling that his father had made him many years previous. He had used it often to frighten bucks out of thickets, presenting him with a shot in the open areas of the south face.

He knelt and found a suitable stone. He placed it in the leather pouch and then held the pouch attached to the leather thongs out at arm's length. He let the pouch drop and swing past his right leg. When the pouch was a foot or so past his leg, he brought his forearm up and over his head. His arm picked up speed slowly at first and then accelerated as he brought his arm down like a baseball pitcher. He let his thumb go, releasing one of the leather thongs from his grip. David was after Goliath.

The stone described a high, silent arc in the sky. It struck the south face of the ridge the man was on with a thunderous noise in the trees, sending hollow, echoing sounds through the mountains. Anderson quickly repeated the action and then sat down on the rock upon which he had stood. He shouldered the little rifle, got in position, and waited.

It hadn't been thirty seconds when he saw the Major's man come to the top of the ridge to investigate. The slim, muscular man moved smoothly, a bit of arrogance in his stride. He couldn't see as well as he would have liked, and, with caution, advanced down the side of the ridge searching for a better vantage point.

Anderson watched, a strange familiarity, he thought. His finger pulled evenly on the trigger as he found the aiming point.

So I drank that old green river dry ...

The crack of the rifle sounded far away to Kramer and the Major. It reverberated through the canyons as the soldier fell. Anderson watched through the binoculars for five minutes for any movement. There wasn't much doubt that the man was dead. Major McCauley and Kramer stood transfixed, bathed in their own fear, each on their own part of the lonely mountain. They couldn't possibly know what had happened. Was it Anderson? Which? Yet in their gut they knew. They didn't want to admit it, but they knew the pilot had been right: the chances were too damned good that they would die on this mountain, Anderson's mountain. Delano.

It suddenly occurred to them both what was going on: Anderson was saving the Major for last. They were two ridges apart when they each began to plan his way out of an obviously ill-conceived plan.

Kramer knew the Major would never let him go. He wasn't about to go anyway. Maybe he and Anderson could deal. Screw it, he didn't deal with anybody unless it was at the end a knife or his automatic, but at this point he didn't mind using the Major for bait. He hated the self-righteous prick anyway. Maybe Anderson would call this off if the Major were down. Hell, that's all Anderson wanted.

Major McCauley had other thoughts. His best chance now was to have Kramer take Anderson out. If anyone of his men could, it was this one. Kramer was a street fighter who had been trained by the best. He was cold as steel and didn't give a damn about anything. This seemed to make him invincible. Kramer was mean, born with a natural killer instinct. He thought about leaving, going back to the vehicle and just taking off with the money, a nice sum to add to his already ill-gotten fortune. But Anderson remained the only person who knew everything. Or was he? Kramer.

The Major decided to remain hidden, not move, and see what happened. If Kramer got him, it was over. He could breathe easily again. Kramer could be dealt with later. If it were the other way round, he would get his ass out and let the chips fall where they may.

Anderson remained in the timber. It was dark, cooler, and slightly dank. It gave him a sense of contentment and pleasure. It always had. He felt alive yet at ease on the mountain. His legs and lungs had adapted almost immediately, and he had no problem moving fast if he had to. His mind faltered momentarily as he thought about the body count he had left behind here in the States. But he shook himself and forced his mind to another subject.

He thought about Angela and the police. By now they would have read and tried to analyze all that he had said in the note. And the document. He knew they must be working at how to deal with the information. Where would they go first? The only place they could, Angela's.

Their days together had been nourishment to his lost soul. He wanted to re-establish this link to normalcy. But again he knew it was not time to wallow in desire. He had a couple more things to do before he could begin to let the edge dull. They were out there on the mountain.

CHAPTER FORTY THREE

"What are they doing here daddy? Are you in some kind of trouble?" Angela was perplexed.

The Captain cut her off.

"Mr. Coman, the dogs have already found three dead bodies in the yard. We need some answers. Where is Anderson, and where the hell is the Major? He isn't on his way back to Thailand is he.

"Daddy?"

"Look, I don't even know this kid, and I don't know how the bodies got there. They must be some of the Major's men. I'm just a businessman for crying out loud. The Major is simply an old friend. He and his men were on R&R like I've already told you. They mostly lounged around the pool all day. They drank and played poker in the evening. They went to movies. They went to bars and dinner. I'm a busy man. How am I supposed to know what they did all day?"

Coman's lawyer interjected. "That's enough John. Captain, are you charging him?

"Not yet. I'm just trying to do my job. It would be considered co-operative if you would let me do it. But since you don't seem to want to do that, I think three dead bodies in his back yard is enough to take Mr. Coman down town. Sir, if you will."

Angela was beside herself. What was going on? What did Anderson have to do with it? The thought of three dead men buried in the yard she had played in and partied in made her shudder. She wished Anderson would call, so she could make him tell her. This was getting past secrets, and stalls, and mysterious things he seemed never able to tell her. This involved her father, her family, herself. She wanted answers.

Angela watched as her father was driven away in the squad car.

Anderson had purposely left pages out of the file that mentioned Takano. The Chinese had let him be, and he owed them. He had also not left anything to incriminate Coman. Coman had made some stupid involvements, but he wasn't blaming him for Brenner, or Bill, or David. Maybe his subconscious was just looking for a way to let him off the hook with Angela. So far as it went, the note to the LAPD was sincere.

Anderson looked at his watch. It was nearly four in the afternoon and the mountain began to cast long shadows down the sides of the ridges, cooling the temperature quickly. Darkness would be upon them soon and turn the beautiful countryside into a lonely prison where spirits could only be lifted with the dancing flames of a campfire. There would be no such luxury tonight.

He turned his attention to Kramer. He had not made his location. He did not fear the Major nearly as much as he did this man. The officer had seen his better day, and Anderson knew he would be relying on Kramer to take care of shutting him up forever. The Major would push; Kramer would get the job done.

Kramer was an intimidating personage. His carriage, his eyes, his physique left an impression of confidence, power, and resolve. Yet he had the undertones of danger and cold indifference. Anderson knew that Kramer had given his life to the service. He had been trained for many years. Kramer would be tough, and to play by his rules would be suicide.

Anderson approached the fallen soldier cautiously. He looked at the body to ensure the kill. The torso was wrapped in a bullet proof vest. He moved closer. "Oh, my God ..."

Anderson moved on up the hill, over the top of the ridge and sat down at the edge of the clearing. From this position he could survey the area where he knew the two remaining men must be. His camo blended in perfectly with the surroundings. He made no movement, but waited for the other side to tip their hand. They were hunting him now and had to move to do so. It was only a matter of time.

It didn't take him long to spot the fleeting glimpse of an object slightly out of place. He raised the binoculars and studied the area. It was Kramer, about six hundred yards out and moving at an oblique angle to Anderson along a well-trodden mule deer trail near an area called Prospect. But he would never expose himself to the opposing ridges. Anderson knew the trail would follow the elevation contour to the saddle and then angle up over the top. He quickly made the top of the ridge and went over to the other side. Now, unexposed to Kramer, Anderson moved fast toward the same saddle.

Kramer took cautious steps. The timber was silent except for the sound of the wind on the upper branches of the trees. A squirrel barked at the intrusion. The annoyance was a vague lump in his subconscious. The air had a slight chill. A Stellar Jay dipped in its flight from tree to tree. Kramer studied the terrain in front of him, what he could see of it. His ears listened intently for any sound outside the ordinary.

Anderson picked up Kramer's trail and fell in behind him. He watched the muscular man, his camo fatigues moving among the shadows of the black timber where Anderson had hunted deer so many times. He was struck by the odd similarity of it. He slid the safety off. The short M-16 felt cold and harsh in his hands as he tried to close the gap between himself and Kramer.

A cold shiver ran through Kramer's body prompted by an uneasy feeling that something was wrong. He stopped and listened. Suddenly his hair stood on end, his skin tightened, and his stomach cramped. He turned slowly around, dreading what he knew he would find there. His eyes widened perceptibly as Anderson spoke.

"Here ya go pardner, a little something from Bill."

A three round burst hit Kramer directly in the chest. He stepped back. An exposed tree root caught his heel and he fell backward. The rifle flew in the air as he tried to regain his balance. He no sooner recovered than a knife appeared in his hand. Without a sound, he charged Anderson. Like a rhino, Kramer came, closing the gap rapidly. Anderson was awe struck by the man's ability to take such punishment, and by his speed. He remembered the bulletproof vest on the dead soldier. He pulled the trigger. Nothing.

Army crap!

Kramer jumped, throwing his left foot forward toward Anderson's head. Anderson ducked the blow and felt the M-16 CAR knocked from his hand. He watched helplessly as the rifle slid down a small embankment. Anderson looked back around at Kramer's smiling face.

"My, my, what are you going to do now, Green Beret?

Anderson slipped his belt through the loops of his pants and curled the end around his right hand.

"Kick your murdering ass, most likely."

Kramer advanced, turned to his left, and jabbed. Anderson sidestepped, letting the knife travel by him. He wrapped the belt around Kramer's wrist, pulled upward, and kicked hard with his right foot.

The blow caught Kramer in the groin. Kramer's eyes opened wide, and he gulped for air without success.

Anderson jumped and rolled down the hill. He caught the CAR on his way over. When he landed, he was holding the rifle pointed at Kramer. He pulled the cocking handle and let it slam home.

"My, my, what are you going to do now, dickhead?"

Kramer wasn't five feet from Anderson when the rifle barked again sending another three round burst of full metal jacketed .223 bullets into Kramer's face. The first bullet hit the man's right jawbone, the second found the apex of his nose, while the third bullet entered the top of his forehead on the left side. He hit the ground in a lifeless heap. Anderson looked down at the back of Kramer's head. Each bullet had exited. Kramer was still holding the knife.

Anderson looked up at the skies and shouted into the silence of the forest.

"Hey, Major, you're next."

He knew the Major would leave the way he came. He wouldn't risk getting lost by breaking new territory. The officer's trip to the Grade Hill would take at least forty minutes under the best of conditions. That was all the time Anderson needed.

Anderson headed north from a knoll that swelled to a naked outcrop of rock at its top called Mary's Nipple to the crest of the mountain. Once he made high ground, he cut south on a trail that ran along the mountain's edge above the cliffs. After about three miles, he changed directions to southeast, then east, and began a slow decline along the finger ridges that angled away from the crest. Anderson settled into position east of Grindstone Flat and waited.

One switchback on the dirt road that the Major had to navigate was particularly aggressive. A straight, steep decline approached the one hundred and fifty degree turn. The turn itself couldn't be taken at more than five miles per hour without a vehicle sliding off the edge.

The switchback was only one hundred fifty yards from where Anderson now waited. His breathing was regular, and he was quite calm when he saw the four-wheeler come into view. The rifle was shouldered and the cross hairs placed on the front windshield in seconds. Anderson could still see the man in the driver's seat clearly even though the hour was late and only minutes of daylight remained. The vehicle was moving toward the turn and straight at Anderson. A finger touched the trigger softly and began to squeeze. The AP was engaged.

Just to get back home to you ...

Again the silence of the mountain air was shattered by the report of the little rifle. The four-wheeler never faltered on its path toward the curve, but it didn't make the turn. Instead, it flew off the edge of the road in a spectacular display of metal and rubber suspended in the air.

The four-wheeler hit a large tree as it navigated the hill. The metal box seemed to break in half. Anderson watched as it came to a halt, high centered on a boulder, its wheels still turning helplessly.

He made his way down the hill. As he approached the wreck, he could see the Major, a neat round hole stuck ominously in his forehead. Except for the location in his white skin, the tiny 6mm bullet hole looked like a mole. The round had not exited, rather it had pierced the skull and then, breaking into pieces, churned the brain into a dark red, clotted soup.

It was over. There was no more he could do. He turned and started to move away. In his path lay a partially opened, brown leather briefcase. From it protruded the corner of a manila file folder with the letter X exposed. Anderson knelt and pulled slowly on the paper object. As he did so, the remaining letters came into view: V U D E U. VU DEUX. It was the missing file. Anderson quickly threw open the case, looking for more. But only green bills met his eyes. "Damn" he muttered, "look at this." He fumbled through the packets of bills, noting that they occupied the rest of the expandable case.

It was dark now. He sat, smoking a cigarette, looking at the lights of his hometown. His mother's home was near one of the bright street lamps at the east edge of the little community. To the north along highway 89 were Marysvale and his brother's house, the lights of which were presently blocked by the ridge upon which he sat. Anderson could easily walk off the mountain and be home in little more than two hours. Why not? It was over.

It was a beautiful night. Stars hung in the sky, shining through the crisp night air like pinholes opening his world to some new and mysterious dimension. He sat watching the flickering lights in the valley below and remembering his childhood: the nights in his bed idly looking at the strings of venison strips his father had made dry into delicious jerky as they hung from the pipes that carried heat to the radiators, the nights waiting for his father to come to his room and "scrunch" raw potatoes with him that he prepared by peeling, quartering, and salting the huge, raw, home grown tubers, and waiting until the morning when they would run the thoroughbreds together, his father teaching him songs as they rode from race to race.

He waited now, next to the wreck and the dead Major McCauley and sang his father's song softly to himself. He waited for resolution.

I was floating down that old green river
On the good ship rock and rye

But I floated too far
I got stuck on a bar
There I was all alone
Wishing I were home

The ship it got wrecked
With the captain and crew
So there was only one thing left to do

So I drank that old green river dry
Just to get back home to you ...

Anderson rose and shouldered his gear. He looked again into the valley of his birth. Then he picked up the briefcase, turned sharply, and headed for the Oldsmobile.

CHAPTER FORTY FOUR

John Coman's arraignment hearing had already begun when Anderson entered the elegant room. Only one person connected with any of what was going on knew or had ever met him. Certainly no gasps or even significance were given to his presence. He remained standing near the entry door waiting to get the gist of what was happening. He listened as Coman's attorney stood and began his oratory.

"Your honor, we strongly urge you to consider the evidence. It is without doubt no more than circumstantial. My client stands accused of importing illegal substances into the United States and using his business and business contacts to do so. There is not one shred of hard evidence to prove such an allegation. There are no witnesses, no documentation, no links of any sort to support the State's claim."

Anderson wrote three words on a piece of paper and handed it to the bailiff with instructions to deliver it to the District Attorney.

The DA opened the note. It read:

De Oppresso Liber

The DA turned and looked at Anderson, studying him intently. The interruption turned other heads as well, one of whom was Angela's. On seeing Anderson she jumped to her feet and hurried up the aisle, hugging him, unabashed by the circumstances.

The judge barked at the commotion with his gavel. The DA asked for a short recess and was granted thirty minutes. In an ante room, Devlin interrogated the ex-Green Beret.

"It is our understanding that you may know a great deal about what has transpired here in Los Angeles over the past few weeks? In fact, did you not send a note to the Chief of Police stating as much?"

"I have some evidence that I believe you should have. You will want to work with the Federal Government on it," Anderson said.

"Where are Major McCauley and his troops?" The DA didn't seem to be listening.

"On a hillside in Utah," Anderson replied.

"What do you mean, on a hillside?"

"They're dead, sir."

"Somebody get the Judge in here, asap. We need to see him."

"Listen kid," the Captain spoke softly, "do you suppose you could just start at the beginning and tell us what the hell has been going on?"

"I have a document in my possession that I believe will put this matter in a much more understandable light. But I am not willing to part with it unless both the Agency and the US Provost Marshall are called into the case. I will call you at 9 AM tomorrow morning."

The DA was furious. "Who the hell do you think you're talking to? We could throw your ass in jail for the duration and subpoena whatever documents you have. We've got enough on you to anchor your ass permanently."

"Bullshit, sir."

Devlin's eyes raged; his face grew red, veins bulging.

The Captain interjected, trying to calm the situation down. "Look, kid, what guarantee do we have you'll show? Why not just produce the information now?"

Anderson was calm. "Sir, if I were going to skip, why the hell would I be here now? I have just recently gotten hold of a document that belongs to the military, specifically to Colonel Langlinais. Since he's in Thailand, I'm not willing to give it to any other military authority outside your presence. I want the Agency here so you can watch their face when you all read it; I think you might be interested in the military's reaction also."

The few people allowed into the small room to hear Anderson stood dumbfounded. He was a murder suspect. Certainly they couldn't just let him walk out of here. But they also knew there was nothing to be gained by keeping him or locking him up. The truth was, it didn't matter to most of them beyond a huge dose of curiosity one way or the other. Why not let him walk? It was interesting if nothing else. But Devlin wouldn't deal.

"Captain, I want this man bound over, now. Take his ass to jail. My office will begin an investigation immediately."

"Devlin, come here a minute." The Chief ushered him to a corner of the room. "Look, you can't intimidate this guy. He's already been through more shit than you or I will experience in our lifetime. What good will it do to lock him up? Do that, and we'll never get to the bottom of this thing. Let him bring the documents in, and then we can do whatever. Put him in the can and we'll never know how deep this thing cuts."

Angela was waiting with her father when Anderson walked out.

"Please, can you come to the house? You need a place to stay anyway. I don't want to let you out of my sight again. Oh, excuse my manners. This is my father. Dad, this is Anderson; the one I've been telling you about."

"How do you do son? I've heard a lot about you. You're welcome to stay at our place if you'd like."

"Thank you, sir. I think I'll take you up on the offer. The truth is I could use a regular bed for a change. I'd like to talk to you while I'm there if I can.

"Angela, I'm afraid I'm going to have to leave for a couple of hours. I've got something I must get done before I come over."

"Well OK, but if you don't show, you might as well face an end to life as you know it."

Anderson waited until Angela and her father were gone and then walked north. He had left the Oldsmobile several blocks away in a protected garage. There was too much evidence to be caught with it. He hadn't known how his appearance at the arraignment would go, but he was reasonably sure that if they took his deal, he would be followed. He reasoned that the Agency wouldn't know as yet what his involvement was. Coman had not been in any position to call anyone. That left the Captain.

Anderson looked for a plainclothes policeman. What the hell does a plainclothes cop look like anyway? He made a few left turns and could see no one that seemed to be tailing him. He hailed a taxi and after several turns directed the driver to the garage where the Oldsmobile waited.

Anderson made his way to the small hotel he had used before. Once inside he opened the briefcase and grabbed several packets of bills and placed them in a box. On it he wrote the address of Monica. Anderson dug in the case a second time and after securing several packets in another box, addressed it to Bill Baedeker's Cellar Bar in care of Peanuts.

He was about to close the case when he noticed a large zippered pocket. The briefcase appeared to be empty otherwise. He pulled on the zipper's handle and could see an envelope inside even before the pocket was completely open. The envelope was unmarked and closed. Anderson opened a blade on his pocketknife, made a neat incision along the top, and dumped the contents on the bed. Before they made a landing, he recognized airline tickets. They were a one-way flight to Rio. He spread the rest out across the bed. Most were funds deposits and account balance sheets from more than ten banks in the US, one in Rio, and three in Swiss accounts. Anderson didn't stop to add it all up, but he realized the total had to be staggering.

One sheet of paper remained. He picked it up and studied it under the lamp. It contained the names of the men the Major had brought with him, along with five others. Surprisingly, Anderson's name had been included at the bottom. Beside each of the first fourteen names were dollar amounts - payoffs. Each line had been crossed out. Kramer's name was among them, as was Brenner's. Anderson's name had been repeatedly circled. Anderson could feel the anger of the man. Of the remaining five, Takano and Coman were included. Anderson didn't recognize the other three.

Anderson paid the clerk for the week and left for the Post Office. The briefcase was in the trunk. He had no idea how much had been in the case, or how much remained. He didn't really care. He had other worries. Certainly, by now, the DA and the Captain were talking to the military and the Agency, and it would only be hours before Takano and Leupold knew. They would want his ass. What the hell. He headed for Chinatown.

"Sir, I am sorry to disturb you a second time."

"What is it my young warrior, more information for imaginary men?" Takano smiled broadly.

"I wish to thank you for listening to me in the past, but I would not come here and intrude just for that. I have news."

"Yes, I am listening?" Takano was intent.

"Military documents have reached the authorities. I have read these documents, and they incriminate the Deja Vu. I came to tell you that they make no statement as to who the Deja Vu is or where he resides, but they do talk about a man called Leupold. This man is apparently a high ranking American official. The documents make it clear that it is he who has betrayed the American people, he and certain American military personnel. It is also quite clear who these men are," Anderson bluffed. "The documents mention businessmen as well, but here again they do not say who these businessmen are.

"I am indebted to the Deja Vu. He granted his permission. He saved my life. I came here to pay a small fraction of my indebtedness." Takano's stare measured the young man's character.

"Where are these documents now?"

"The LAPD has had one of them for several days. The other was recently mailed to them, the local Provost Marshall, and other agencies."

"I see. And where are you going from here." Takano smiled.

"Well, sir, with your permission, I hope to get married."

Anderson drove the Oldsmobile toward Coman's, his last stop. He had already made up his mind how he would approach the man. Coman would not have a choice. Anderson wondered about Takano. He knew the man wouldn't let his business be compromised. Had he played out enough line to catch the big fish?

"Anderson, come in." Angela was her usual brilliant self. "Come, dad's in the library."

Anderson marveled at the rooms as they moved through the house. Basically Victorian, they had been adulterated with fine oriental art objects. He wondered about Angela's mother. Never mentioned, had she allowed such a mixture of distinctly different styles? In any case, Anderson was impressed with the obvious wealth that surrounded him. This portion of the house was dark and a bit foreboding. Buddhas sat in stoic repose, yet menacing in the dim light. The library was austere and intimidating.

"Daddy, Anderson's here."

The large man rose from his chair and approached the ex- soldier.

"Hello, young man. I'm glad you made it. Angela, could you leave us for a few minutes? We won't be long."

Disappointed at the brush-off, Angela still couldn't hide her obvious delight at the two of them finally meeting.

Coman eyed the young man and tried as Takano had to estimate what he was made of. Anderson beat him to the punch.

"Look, sir, let's get straight to the point. I've got enough on you to hang your ass out to dry. I also know that, although you don't mind making a bundle pushing drugs, you haven't got what it takes to waste me. The way I see it, it's my ball game and you've got no choice but to play it by my rules. What's it going to be?"

"Lay your cards out, kid."

"I don't give a shit about you or Takano. I can't rid the world of scum like you. After all, you're just businessmen, amoral dickheads maybe, but businessmen just the same. No, what I want are the assholes that take the oaths to serve and then use their power to grow rich off of other men's lives, all while drawing a salary from the taxpayer.

"The Major and his men were what I wanted. But there's one left. I can get you out of the fix you're in and save Takano's ass in the bargain. I want the man."

"What are you talking about?"

"Leupold. I want his identity. If you want to hang on to this nice lifestyle of yours, you'll give it to me. And don't try to convince me you give a shit about him, I know better."

Coman was stunned. He couldn't believe this upstart had such a set of balls.

"Let's sit down. What are you drinking?"

"Just get on with it." Anderson was getting hot, knowing the man was about to start on a snow job.

"What's the deal you're offering me?" Coman took a long drag on a scotch.

"Not that it makes any damn difference to the conversation, but I can put the link in the prosecution's case. McCauley has hanged himself with his own documents. He admits he shipped the opium stateside and where he got the money. A large part of it came from inside the government, but without the government's knowledge or authorization. McCauley had very few conceivable contacts with whom this trade could have been made. Without proof, it could be any one of them. They don't have the key they need to open this case, but I do. I am offering you a chance to take the heat off yourself. If you supply Leupold's identity, that heat will shift. It will be the scoop of the century. Who will give a damn about taking the time and effort to bag your ass? Now who the hell is he, and how does his scam work?"

Coman sat transfixed. He knew he had to take this punk kid's deal, but it pissed him off to no end.

"Leupold is Chairman of the Military Funding Committee. Because of the critical nature of that body during wartime, he has access to unlimited funds. Response time is often critical. It's easy to get away with not accounting for every expenditure. No time, etc. He knew what the Agency was doing to establish rapport with thousands of tribesmen scattered throughout Southeast Asia. It was easy to subvert funds to officers stationed there under the guise of funding requirements. He used his influence with the FBI and other agencies to ferret out drug lords. Once he had that information, it was a piece of cake to set up networks that would net him and others a growing income for as long as the war lasted.

"The drugs were bought with those funds along with those purchased with the CIA's effort. The tribesmen were paid five dollars a pound. The dope always showed up in designated cites like Bangkok and then burned. The additional never arrived and was never accounted for. Insiders picked the stuff up at remote drop points. These men were paid ten dollars. In the states, this same pound netted one hundred dollars, god only knows what the street value is. We knew that certain military types were skimming, but they were difficult to deal with where they were. Besides, the take was so large, nobody really gave a damn."

And now Anderson knew. He had half guessed some of it, but he didn't know enough about the upper level machine to piece it together. It didn't help much. It made him sick.

He looked up at Coman who sipped his scotch, intent but beaten, his head bobbing as he tried to loosen the tight muscles in his neck.

Anderson started for the door, but before exiting he turned back to Coman.

"Oh, by the way, I'll be running off with your daughter."

CHAPTER FORTY FIVE

"So where is this second document of yours?"

Anderson handed the Chief the folder labeled VU DEUX.

He looked at the men seated around the huge mahogany desk, a monolith in the center of the otherwise austere room. Glasses accompanied by a water decanter as well as cups and a carafe of coffee sat in the middle of the polished wood like ships adrift at sea.

A very stiff looking, older gentlemen sat at the far end of the table puffing on a Cuban cigar. His military garb looked all the more crisp with his tight little mustache and colonel's insignia. Anderson figured him for the Provost. The DA, the Captain, and his two sidekicks were seated to his left. On his right sat the judge and another individual unknown to Anderson. This one had to be spook. A short distance from the group a court recorder sat poised and obsequious as though trying to be oblivious, a nonentity whose demeanor seemed quite apropos for the surroundings.

Devlin called a clerk for more coffee and copies of the file to be made. Anderson waited silently while several of the men in the room chatted idly. When the documents were passed around, the officials began to pour over them. Eyebrows peaked above muffled profanity. Anderson could see the looks of utter amazement and incredulity in their expressions.

The Deja Vu file laid out the CIA's efforts to build rapport with the tribesmen, set up intelligence networks, and peruse the southern Chinese border as it had since the early fifties. Though precarious to a Boy Scout version of American character, the plans worked; though shady, they technically broke no laws. The plan made exchanges: payoffs for prisoners, purchase and destruction of dope for loyalty. The spook tried to project indifference when the file detailed raids into North Vietnam, but the flush in his cheeks was unmistakable.

It was McCauley's insurance policy, VU DEUX, that brought blaring indignation and disgust from the audience.

"Deal made today. Can purchase all that Meo can produce. Air America pilots to drop half the load at camp near the Laotian border. Remainder will ship as scheduled.

Priced at $5 from Meo. $10 from Regulars. This for return of American prisoners. Total cash = $15 per kilo for raw material.

Leupold supplying funds for any quantity Meo can produce. Los Angeles pickup originate Singapore. Distribution connection Los Angeles."

Anderson interjected. "I believe it is possible to compromise Leupold's identity. Mr. Coman may know who this person is."

"And you, Mr. Anderson, do you know who this person is?" The judge peered over the top of his reading glasses and waited for an answer.

"No sir."

"Then what leads you to believe that Mr. Coman knows?"

"Sir, this is the Major's file. He spent several days as Coman's guest. I understand they were close friends. The Major may have mentioned something; Coman may be able to deduce."

"Son, you are in a great deal of trouble here. You would do well for yourself if you told us what you know." The Captain's voice was firm, professional.

"Yes sir."

"Yesterday, you told us that Major McCauley and others were dead. How do you know that?" the Chief asked.

"I was there. I found the file lying on the ground next to him."

"Mr. Anderson, you are testifying to the authenticity of the document. You are not answering the question." Devlin was impatient.

"Because I killed them," Anderson said flatly.

The room fell silent, as cold and hard as the mahogany furniture. Faces stared at Anderson in confusion and amazement.

The Chief spoke first. "Are you confessing to murder?"

"No sir."

"What then?"

"I killed them in self-defense?"

"All fourteen of them?" Evans broke in.

Anderson didn't answer.

The spook squirmed in his chair. "Gentlemen, this is a fascinating subject, but could we get back to the issue at hand? I have a busy schedule. In fact, I only came by because I have business in the city. The documents you see here are pure hogwash. The CIA doesn't get involved in buying prisoners or using drugs to pay for it. If there were payoffs, you can rest assured that the Agency had nothing to do with it. Colonel Langlinais would have acted on his own. Unless you have other business for me, Your Honor, I'll be going."

"Just hold your horses, young man," the judge cautioned. "Go on, Mr. Anderson."

"Yes sir. Major McCauley convinced the Colonel to have Alex Brenner hit. Brenner was working inside. The Major realized Brenner had caught onto his drug scam. Colonel Langlinais was pressuring Major McCauley to pull Brenner out. He wasn't really needed anymore, and the Colonel knew that the longer he stayed, the more chance there was that the Viets would catch on to him. The Major couldn't let that happen. He convinced the Colonel that Brenner had turned, and that he had begun feeding the enemy information."

"How do you know this?" The stiff military type had decided to chime in.

"Because I was the one ordered by Colonel Langlinais to make the hit."

"Boy, are you telling us that your Colonel ordered you to kill another American soldier whom he had ordered into the camp in the first place? That can't be."

"And did you?" the Chief asked.

"Yes sir."

"But how did you know what was going on prior to locating the VU DEUX file?"

"On Delano, sir. One of them told me just before he died. He tied up the loose ends that I had been struggling with. I watched the Major's right hand man waste one of his own. Turns out he was best friends with the other one that told me. Guess it was his way of getting even.

"There's something else." Anderson handed the judge the envelope.

The judge opened it. He read down the list of names that Anderson had placed on top of the pack. Suddenly his eyes grew larger. Then.

"Oh my God!" He paused and looked at the table in front of him.

Anderson guessed what the judge had seen: Leupold's name. Although Anderson didn't know which of the three it was, he was betting it was one of them. The judge was putting two and two together, adding it up for Anderson. But then what the hell, one phone call to Washington would tell him who chaired the finance committee he was interested in.

Anderson looked at the official. "Notice there's a plane ticket to Rio along with several bank statements. They are in Major McCauley's name. Unless I'm way off in guessing what Army officers make these days, I would say they further substantiate what I'm saying."

"Your honor, we have a very delicate situation here," the Provost said through a mist of pale gray smoke. "I believe it would be best if you turned it over to the Army. A thorough investigation will be initiated. The entire story sounds preposterous. It would be a travesty to allow this to become public at this crucial period in the war effort. After all, we are having enough trouble with the SDS and other groups. We will talk to the FBI about Mr. Coman ourselves. We will also take up the matter with the subcommittee charged with overseeing international trade.

"The fact is," the Provost continued, "you don't have a strong evidential case on anyone. There isn't much to gain by spending the people's money. It would take forever and tie up considerable resources to convict Mr. Coman. You don't have much on Mr. Anderson here either that's worth spending the taxpayer's money on. We can't touch him; he's a civilian anyway. In the end an empathetic jury would let him off the hook on self-defense. These documents belong to the government, the Army in particular. I suggest you turn them over to us and forget the whole matter."

Devlin was furious. "Are you serious? Just what in the hell do you suggest we tell the press about a whole cast of dead bodies spread around the county over the past couple of weeks, just a rash of military suicides? Your Honor ..."

"Let it go, Devlin," the Judge admonished.

The Captain stared at the note pad in front of him. They were right. He felt more like shaking Anderson's hand than arresting him. He looked up at the man in the pressed green uniform. His hand reached for the files. Slowly, deliberately, he pushed the folders containing the originals toward him, then stood up.

"If you don't mind ..." He turned and left the room.

Devlin's mouth hung open in disbelief. "Jeez ..."

"Sergeant, I would expect a call from the FBI and the Army very soon. Leave me an address." The Colonel knew he was in charge now. "Your Honor, if you agree, would you please hand along the other information the Sergeant gave you."

It was nightfall when Anderson got back to the hotel. He tossed the briefcase on the bed and lay down beside it, exhausted from the entire fray. He fell asleep thinking about David. He saw the explosion, pieces falling in slow motion to the water. He drifted off into a labored sleep.

He had seen the separate chapter.

The next morning Anderson made a call to the Coman residence. Angela answered.

"How would you like to take a little trip, meet my mother, well, you know?"

"When?"

"How soon can you be ready?"

"Give me two hours."

The Oldsmobile cruised out of town and into the desert. The hot sun danced on the earth's floor, prepared to show no mercy. Mirage made distant objects appear to stand above the ground, plunging their bottoms into shimmering lakes of quicksilver. The heat waves played across the road in front of him, telltale signs of the wind's direction and intensity.

They were each buried in their own imaginings. Angela finally broke the silence.

"I didn't know you were a businessman." She said, smiling at her own humor.

Anderson felt the rifle recoil to his shoulder. The man's expression changed to surprised disbelief as the tiny hollow point bullet entered the brain cavity, began to mushroom, and then break into pieces. He raised his hands toward his head as though to grab the offending stimuli. His knees buckled and he fell suddenly and hard to the ground; his body convulsed, legs pumped an imaginary bicycle, and arms grabbed at empty space. The scene was vivid, bathed in gold on the windshield of the Oldsmobile.

Anderson thought back to the mountain. He had walked up the ridge and found the soldier laying in a stand of manzanita. He had recognized him immediately.

"Oh my God," he had murmured.

"Hey pard. Surprise. Not exactly what you expected am I." Alex labored with each breath. He had obviously been hit in the upper spine and couldn't move.

Anderson stared at him, not comprehending. His ears felt hot; his brain hazed and hummed with confusion. He had not considered the possibility. Then,

"It was a good hit, Alex. Who the hell was he?"

"I had this feeling, drove me crazy. A prisoner. Gave him my baseball cap, shirt, black pajamas, and told him to get his ass out there, a little R & R from the cage. He was a spitting image. Didn't have my class, but what the hell."

"How did you get here?"

"You shot the bar on the prisoner's hut." Alex was having more difficulty talking now. "They escaped in the confusion. I had to stay. Major came back for the big payoff, but no prisoners to exchange, settled on me." Alex smiled through the shock and the increasing distress his body was in.

"The Major figured he'd take me along and then waste me later. Greedy bastard. But I convinced him to let me help get you.

"No hard feelings, eh, sport?" Alex' eyes glossed over, his complexion turned ashen. "Listen, Anderson, I'm a city type. Pretty day. Great here, but I don't want to die in these mountains. I don't want to die alone. Stay and talk some. Tell me how they scammed you into it." He closed his eyes.

"Sure, Alex." Anderson knelt to his side and took his hand. Alex gripped hard, but just as soon, the life and the strength left him.

"Alex, what was the prisoner's name? Alex ..."

But he was gone.

Anderson remembered the list: Alex's name had been there, not as a hero, not as a traitor, but as a taker, just another scam. Anderson looked down at their hands and, for the first time, noticed that Alex was holding something. Then it hit him. A hot blade seemed to pierce his stomach, twisting its bright hardness inside him. That's what had been missing, what had given Anderson that odd feeling that something wasn't right when he engaged the target in the clearing. No tan dog. No plastic strip between his fingers. Alex had not carried the exchange with the prisoner all the way. Why hadn't he realized?

"Sweetheart, are you listening to me?"

"Sorry, what was that?" Anderson was pulled back from his reverie.

"The briefcase lying on the back seat, silly, what's in it?"

Anderson watched the moon rise above the eastern horizon. The Oldsmobile purred as it ate up the miles, sloshing fuel in its steel belly. A slight smile formed on his lips. He wondered if Takano had taken care of Leupold for him yet. He knew the damned political machine wouldn't.

He reached in his shirt pocket and withdrew a small piece of plastic film. He held it in his left hand for a moment and then began to flick it.

"Our future." He finally answered.

His eyes surveyed the horizon as the light of day gave way to the sinking sun, and the shimmering heat waves were pulled back into the earth's crust. The last mirage.

He had moved through the bush and through the city and survived. Both were jungles to navigate and to overcome. His life seemed just a complex series of steps as though in a dance. What would the future hold for them?

Made in the USA
Columbia, SC
13 June 2017